BUSH CAMP

GUY ALLEN

ISBN: 978-0-9938107-6-3

Publisher: Talisman Publications
New Westminster, British Columbia, Canada
Publication Date: March, 2016

DEDICATION

Bush Camp is dedicated to all the prospectors, geologists, claim stakers, line cutters and other adventurers who have tramped the bush in Canada hoping to find Mother Earth's secretive hiding places of the ever-elusive deposits of valuable minerals. The wet, cold and snowy days are endured for the sake of stumbling on the next show of glitter or the view from a mountaintop that few have experienced. Some have struck it rich, but many have had their lives enriched by the search.

CONTENTS

DUSTY

Dusty settled into one of the soft plushy chairs in the waiting room and closed his eyes. He could hardly stay awake and just wanted to end his mental turmoil by getting up and walking away.

Financially, he needed a job. He just didn't particularly want this job, but it had been a tough winter. After recovering from the gunshot wounds in the spring, he was physically exhausted from all the turmoil of his prospecting and drilling contract in the Foster Lakes country and the nearby gold-salting scam at Jenny Lake in the fall. Then there was nothing all winter until two short-hole drill jobs near Carlyle in southeast Saskatchewan. After that was spring breakup, and everything ground to a halt. Instead of beating the bush for more work, he had spent a couple of months unofficially helping RCMP Corporal Lucie Hansen with a murder investigation in the old tunnels under the city of Moose Jaw.

He knew he had to be alert for this morning's meeting, but too many cigarettes, too much coffee and twenty-five hours on the road had taken its toll. Hopefully, this was the only time he would need to meet with Archie Campbell, and he had vowed that the deal would either fly or die based on what happened today. The man was notorious on Howe Street, and all the stories Dusty had heard about the older man warned him to stay in control or stay away. But it looked like Campbell had scored the first point. Yesterday, Dusty had gotten the call on his mobile phone just as he was leaving Moose Jaw on his way home to Calgary. Without any preamble, Campbell had launched into his spiel, quickly describing the job, setting up the meeting and was insistent that it start on time. Dusty had made every effort to be there at the appointed hour, driving straight through to reach Vancouver, and now Campbell was late, leaving him to cool his heels in the outer office. As he settled in and relaxed, he became more aware of his surroundings. The reception area was a modern blend of glass and stainless steel, all straight lines and crisp angles. Dusty mused about its intended effect. Either it was an attempt to intimidate, or it was an effort to suggest a level of integrity that was far from real. Steel doors, desks, bookcases and fixtures were scattered about the room. The steel wall panels had a sickly green wood-grained pattern that did nothing to ease the queasiness in his stomach. Everything else was covered with glass. Only the rug, which buried his shoe tops, and the blond receptionist seemed out of place. "Certainly not designed to create warmth," he thought. He liked the rug. It was a soft gentle contrast to the rest of the décor. He wasn't so sure about the receptionist. His third attempt to learn her name finally met with success, when she announced with a chill in her voice that she was Suzanne, Mr. Campbell's personal secretary and that Mr. Campbell was expected at any moment. Dusty also received the unspoken message that she didn't wish him to bother her any further and that she probably wished he would just go away. Dusty gave up pursuing a conversation. She had obviously not been hired for her intellectual capacity or charming personality, but the reason for her presence in this workplace was visually obvious. Her beauty was difficult to ignore. Most noticeable was the deep golden tan that covered all the exposed areas of her body, of which there were many, leading Dusty's imagination into a side trip of speculation about the extent of the tan on some of the unexposed parts. Suddenly, an explosion of activity in the outside corridor broke his reverie. The door burst open and a large man in a rumpled suit charged into the room. He stopped suddenly and looked around, almost as if he was a stranger in his own world. His gaze fell on Dusty, and he thrust out a meaty hand in greeting. "You must be Sherant," he boomed. "Sorry to keep you waiting. Still having trouble getting used to the traffic in this damn town. Got into another snarl on the bridge this morning. Some damn fool's car broke down. Makes me mad. If they can't afford to keep their cars tuned up, they ought to be kicked off the road and forced to take the bus. But enough, come on into my office and we'll have our talk," he continued, as he put his arm around Dusty's shoulder and led him through the steel-paneled door.

"Suzanne! Bring us a pot of coffee and hold my calls." Dusty followed Archie Campbell from one room of steel and glass into another. The only differences were: the chairs were softer, the rug deeper, the desk wooden and Campbell was considerably less attractive than his secretary. The two men settled in facing each other as Suzanne minced in and poured two steaming cups of coffee. The diversion gave Dusty a few moments to size up his man. Campbell was large, six one or six two and at least 270 pounds. On the turning edge of sixty, what had obviously once been a trim powerful body now showed the ravages of too many liquid lunches and sedentary habits. His baldness was trimmed with white and his bulbous red nose was skewed to the right, probably a remnant of a bar fight in his younger days. Although his reputation indicated all the wiles of a Vancouver promoter, Campbell still looked out of place in the business setting. It was like he had his D7 parked at the curb and had just dropped in for a cup of coffee and a chat.

Dusty was feeling less at ease, and fatigue was setting in as the morning progressed. He had rehearsed his role for this first encounter on the drive last night, anticipating some of the problems that seemed inevitable. But now, he sensed his confidence dropping. Campbell's size and hearty outgoing manner was intimidating, and Dusty felt any control of the meeting that he might have had slipping away. He knew he had to slow things down and try to deal with this man on an equal basis. Settling into the deep easy chair, he forced himself to relax.

"I'm sure you can't wait to get up north and get this job going for us," Campbell announced. "Merv gave you a good recommendation. He said you're well respected in the industry and would be the man to get the job done at the best price. That's what decided us to accept your bid."

Dusty winced at the mention of Mervin Chipman. It was another sore point about this deal that he had tried to forget. He did not feel good about being recommended by Chipman and had agonized over taking on a Chipman generated program, but a job was a job, and right now he needed the money and wasn't in a position to be that fussy.

"This is as good a time to get started as any," he replied. "Most of the snow is gone from the area we'll be working, and reports indicate they have had good weather for about three weeks now. I can start moving men and supplies into the first camp as soon as I receive the deposit we agreed upon."

Dusty knew his initial fears were justified when he saw Campbell's face darken at the mention of the deposit money. He had hit the nerve.

"Well," the older man replied slowly, "there may be a bit of a problem there. It looks like the funds are going to be delayed a few days, but I'm sure all the money will be in hand by the end of the week. The Securities Commission seems to be dragging their feet on a final approval. Unfortunately, I just can't reach into my pocket now and put it all on the table. I suggest you go ahead with the startup plans and get the program under way. I'll forward the cheque as soon as things are straightened out around here."

"I'm afraid I can't do that," Dusty replied. "That's not the way I work, or what we agreed on. I thought it was understood that the initial money was to be paid before I commenced the program. Perhaps Merv Chipman neglected to make that clear."

"Of course! Of course!" Campbell blustered. "But we're just looking at a few days. I don't see how that can affect your plans to any extent."

"No, I'm afraid it does," Dusty replied. "I'm sorry, but that deposit payment has to come first. I've had some unfortunate experiences in the past with promoters in this town, and I'm a bit gun shy when it comes to the money end of the deal. I can wait. I'll just suspend things until I receive payment."

"Look, Sherant. You can't back out on this job. You've signed a contract." Archie Campbell punctuated the last remark with a thick finger jabbing across the big oak desk. "And besides, from what I've heard, you're all geared up to go with a bunch of men hired and supplies bought."

Dusty was getting more and more fed up as the discussion continued. He decided to call Campbell's bluff.

"That's right, and I can get ungeared just as fast if I don't see some money," he replied. "As for the contract, I suggest you read it more closely." Dusty pulled the agreement from his briefcase and continued, "It says, here in Paragraph Four, 'that a payment of fifty percent of the accepted bid shall be made to the Contractor at least ten days prior to said Contractor commencing field operations.' My bid for this job, which incidentally you accepted in writing, was $190,000, so accordingly, I need to see a certified cheque for $85,000 before I turn another wheel. In fact, the way this thing has been going so far, I'd just as soon you didn't pay me, and I could pack the whole thing in right now."

Dusty leaned back in the chair. He felt better. He hadn't won, but now he had nothing to lose. He looked relaxed, and this puzzled Campbell. He had checked Dusty out thoroughly and had learned, to his pleasure, that due to an extended period of recuperation from gunshot wounds the previous year, some bad investments and a recent period of unemployment the past few months, this man was broke, owed money and had no other work presently lined up. He had been sure that he could whittle Sherant's price down and delay payments long enough to make a few extra bucks on the interest.

"Alright," Campbell replied. "Let's cool down and forget all that fancy lawyer talk. I'm sure we can work out something. I told you we're a little strapped for money right now, but I can probably dig up a few bucks to tide you over, and I guarantee we'll have the rest in a week or ten days at the most. As I told you, the problem is that the money raised from selling this new stock issue is still tied up. These kinds of delays don't do our market any good. The shareholders are getting uneasy. They've been calling all week asking when we're going to start exploring those claims. What the hell am I supposed to tell them? We need some news to get the people interested in our stock and start trading it again. It would help to tell them that the field program has begun."

"Okay," Dusty replied. "I can appreciate that, but like I said, I've been through a couple of these deals that went sour before. The company keeps promising payment and then when the job's over, and I'm in hock up to my neck, I find out the principals have taken off with the money, and the company has gone bankrupt and been delisted. I'm not saying that's going to happen here, but I'm not taking any chances of going through that scenario again."

"Well, we're far from bankrupt," Campbell replied with annoyance." You can check that out."

"I already have," Dusty replied. "I also found out that your last issue was completely subscribed and that the Securities Commission has instructed the trust company to release the funds. So, don't bullshit me that you can't get your money."

"Yes, that's true," Campbell replied uneasily,"but we haven't got the cheque yet, and quite a bit of that money is required to pay off Company debts. You know," he added, "I haven't received any salary for six months."

Dusty could see the whole pattern playing out again. That last remark dispelled any remaining concern that he might be taking too tough a position. It was obvious they would look after themselves first and then, if there was anything left, he might get paid. It was beginning to look like he was going to be out the money he had already spent to set things up, but there was a certain amount of relief in the prospect that he might not have to deal any more with Campbell, his partners or Mervin Chipman over the next few months.

"You should know by now that if you start shuffling those approved funds into places other than that for which they were designated, you're going to have trouble with the Commission," Dusty went on. "I read your prospectus. Chipman recommended a $212,000 program to evaluate those claims. I contracted to do the complete job for $190,000, saving you a total of twenty-two grand right off the bat, and you are still going to try and chisel me. Well, to hell with you. Have the money by five o'clock tonight, or find yourself someone else. I'll be here in town if you want me, but if I don't see the money, I'm out of here tomorrow."

Dusty scribbled the motel address and phone number on the back of his business card and threw it on Campbell's desk.

"I think you're taking a damn poor attitude about this, Sherant. You talk like we're a bunch of crooks. Maybe we should find someone else for the project, someone who has a little more understanding for our problems."

"Suit yourself," Dusty replied as he walked out of the office.

The morning sun had surrendered to the heavy gray bank of clouds that were spitting rain when Dusty emerged from the building. The early lunch crowds were starting to scurry along Pender Street as he walked to his truck.

"It is going to be a rough year if things continue at this pace," he thought as he slipped a parking ticket from under the windshield wiper.

The phone in Dusty's motel room rang at three-thirty. It was Archie Campbell.

"We've decided to go with you, Sherant. You are fortunate that it is too late to dig up someone else. Your cheque is here. You can pick it up in the morning."

"That's more like it," Dusty replied, "but better still, you have it certified, and I'll be there in a few minutes to get it."

KITCH

The sunlight flickered through the freshly uncurled leaves and kept the shadows dancing ahead of their footsteps, as the young man and the little girl walked slowly down the tree-lined path. Occasionally a passerby would turn and pause for a second look at the pair. He was slim, of medium height and well built, with long black hair lapping unevenly on his shoulders. He walked with the steady even grace of an athlete. His fair complexion contrasted with the darkness of his eyes. His whole visage projected an image paradox of confidence and sadness.

She was small and very tiny-boned with fine features, and her short blond hair hung in ringlets. The resemblance between the two was, however, unmistakable. In all appearances, it was a father and his daughter out for an afternoon stroll. Her dress was fresh and spotless and was a perfect pink match for the rest of her outfit. Today was a special day for Julie.

The park and picnic areas around the zoo were surprisingly quiet for a warm spring day. Mothers pushed baby buggies along the walkways or gathered in small groups to supervise their toddlers in the play areas, as the father and daughter walked slowly, hand in hand, toward the animal pens. For a few minutes they joined a group at the penguin enclosure and watched as a young bird played with a fish, trying to instill some movement in the lifeless body.

"Would you like some ice cream, Julie?"

"No thank you, Daddy."

"How about some popcorn or peanuts?"

"No, I'm full."

They strolled over to the bear pens and sat down.

"We walked a long way today. I'll bet those little legs of yours are just about worn out."

"I guess I am kind of tired."

"I'd better get you back home pretty soon. We've been here quite a while. Your Mom will worry about you if we're gone too long."

They watched quietly as one bear began cuffing another smaller bear with a huge paw. The animals, however, held little interest for the girl.

"Daddy, why didn't you visit me for such a long time? I missed you very much."

"I had to go away and couldn't get back until now. I wanted to come and see you, but I couldn't."

"Mommy went to visit you. Why couldn't she take me with her? I asked her every time she went, but she always said, "no.""

"I know, but that's the way it had to be. The people that own the house where I was staying don't want little kids to come there."

"Maybe you could have called me on the phone."

"No, I couldn't even do that. They wouldn't let me use the phone very often, but I wrote you letters."

"That must have been a bad place with mean people that wouldn't let me come to see you or call me on the phone."

"It was."

"Are you going to stay at home with Mommy and me now?"
"No. You remember what Mommy told you. Daddy can't live at home any more."
"Oh yes, that! I know what Mommy said, but aren't you ever going to visit us?"
"I will for a few days, but then I have to go away again, probably for most of the summer."
"Are you going back to that mean place that doesn't like little kids?"
"No, honey. I hope I never have to go back there. This time I've got a job up north. It'll be too far for me to come back and see you very often. I'm going to miss you, but Daddy has to make some money."
"Why can't you work down here near us and come and see me?"
"I wish I could, but this kind of work is out in the forest a long way from here. It's the only good job I could find. I'll try to come back and see you as much as I can."
The young man stretched and looked at his watch.
"I think we had better go. It's getting late and we've got that long walk back to the bus stop."

Glennda's basement suite was one room consisting of a combined living area with a fold-out bed and a kitchen nook. There was a community bathroom down the hall that was shared with two other tenants. To Kitch, the dreariness of the place was overwhelming, but it was still a lot better than his prison cell. At least, for the eight years they had lived together, they had been able to afford something better than this. She had tried to brighten the place up with fresh paint, floral curtains and some pictures she had picked up at a second-hand store, but it had minimal effect in dispelling the gloomy atmosphere of a rundown house in a neighborhood that had seen better days.
The kitchen table, normally folded up against the wall, had

been lowered for tonight's dinner to sit three. During the meal the conversation centered on Julie and her day at the zoo. As Glennda cleared away the dishes, the little girl crawled up in her Dad's lap, hugged him and tried to stay awake, but soon her eyelids were permanently closed and she was carried off to bed.

"Julie was so glad to see you today. I didn't realize she missed you to such an extent. It surprises me since you weren't around that much when she was younger, and when you were home you didn't pay much attention to her."

Kitch winced at the words but said nothing. He knew they were true, and he had made up his mind not to react to her bitterness this time.

"Father didn't want me to let you come over today. He feels you are a bad influence, both on me and on Julie," Glennda continued as she poured their coffee.

"That doesn't surprise me. He never was one of my big fans right from the moment we met. He made that very clear even before we were married. I suspected he encouraged you to break up with me back then. Was it his idea to start the divorce?"

"No, I made that decision on my own. Dad did help me sort out how to do it. I know he never really accepted you, but you didn't make much effort to get along with him either. I wanted the divorce and still do. I've reached the point where I can't live your kind of life any more."

"Do you think this place you have here is any better?" Kitch asked, looking around the room.

"It is for me. Sure, this is a dumpy little suite, and the neighborhood stinks, but at least there aren't twenty people lying around stoned out of their heads all the time. The friends I have now are true friends, not a bunch of strangers hanging around because you scored some dope. They're living life, not trying to escape from it. I will not go back to the old ways, and I'll never expose Julie to them."

"I hear what you're telling me," Kitch replied. They had

been over this so many times that Kitch knew the futility of trying to change her mind.

"If we could get back together, I would go for counseling and try to get my head straightened out. I could live the kind of life you want."

"I know you would try," Glennda answered. "It would work for a while, but for how long? A month, maybe three or four and then something would go wrong at your job, or someone would say something to get you mad, and the whole thing would start all over again. I can't live with the possibility of that anymore."

"I think you're wrong this time," Kitch replied slowly. "Things have changed. I've changed. The days when I was locked up were long, and I had a lot of time to think. I'm really out of that old space now."

"Are you off the stuff?"

"Most of the time. I just do a little pot now and then to calm my nerves."

"That's something. Did they put you through some sort of cure in prison?"

"Are you kidding? It's easier to get drugs in there than on the street, but I don't need to do the heavy stuff any more. I just want to get on with my life now and preferably with you and Julie."

"I hope you can sort it out, Aaron. I really do, but you are going to have to do it by yourself. I can't help you any more. It has been too long, and too much bad stuff has happened. Maybe, out on this job, away from the city and your friends, things will come together."

"Will you at least leave it until the end of the summer before you make up your mind about us?"

"I don't know," Glennda answered as she refilled their cups. "I will have to think about that. Right now all I want to do is get on with my new life."

Kitch could see the futility of trying to change her mind as he looked about the small room. At least he would like to provide her with a better place to raise their daughter. This was too dreary. The small windows, set high on the wall, looked out at ground level over a patch of grassless yard. Dirt and debris mounded up in little piles against the glass as if trying to escape to the clean warm room inside. The furniture was old and cheap, and most of it was familiar to Kitch. He recognized an easy chair they had purchased secondhand when they were first married. He had seen most of the other stuff scattered around the room during his infrequent visits to her parents home.

"I know how I want to live," Glennda said as she curled up on the sofa. "It would be so much easier to make the adjustment if you weren't in our lives. If it was just you and me there would be no problem, but Julie loves you and wants to see you."

"I guess I understand, even if I don't want to. The prospect of losing you two hurts. Whether you believe it or not, I did miss you both very much. If you want me to stay away until the end of the summer, it shouldn't take too long for Julie's memories of me to fade. I truly would like to try and make it together again, but I guess you won't believe any more of my promises."

"I can't, Aaron. Do you blame me? I've been hurt too many times."

"I know. I haven't given you much reason to believe in me." Kitch's hands were shaking as he lit another cigarette. "Are you going to get married again?"

"I hope to someday. I still want Julie to grow up in a normal home with two parents."

"I wondered, because one of my friends saw you having dinner with some old guy in a restaurant a couple of weeks ago. I thought it was your father until he described him. Is this something serious?"

"I don't know," Glennda replied slowly. "Fred is good to me and Julie likes him. He adores her, and I think he would make a good father. His wife died a couple of years ago,

and they never had any children."
"That's all great, but do you love him?"
"I think I'm past the point where that really matters. I like him, and I feel secure with him. He's predictable and stable, and I need some of that in my life. Whether it will go any farther, I don't know."
"I guess that kind of spells it out for me. Maybe we are more different than I thought. Whatever way it works out, I would like to see you and Julie again. I have a break from this job sometime in the middle of the summer and would like to come down then. Would that be okay with you?"
"I don't know. Please write me first, Aaron, before you come."

ARNOLD

"Arnold! Have you finished packing yet?"

"Sure Mom. I'm just about done."

Clothes and equipment lay scattered about the room: on dressers, chairs and the floor, everywhere but in the suitcases. All of it was new, having been purchased over the past two weeks on recommendations by his Uncle Mervin. Arnold Chipman sat stretched out in the big easy chair beside his bed and surveyed his disarrayed kingdom. "If they had just given me the cash they laid out for all this stuff," he thought, "I wouldn't have to bother taking this damn job."

"You haven't even started. Why did you tell me you were packed? I expected you would be all ready to go. I'm surprised and a bit disappointed you are not more enthusiastic about this position your uncle has obtained for you."

Arnold met his mother's stern gaze as she entered the room. "Here we go again," he thought. "I wish I could just figure a way to get out of this crummy job without getting everyone on my back."

"Just a figure of speech, Mom. You know I've got it all sorted out in my head. I'll be ready in time. Don't worry."

"Well, see that you get it done right away. Your Uncle Mervin is coming over in a little while to see how you are doing. I assured him that you were excited about this opportunity and anxious to get started. I want you to thank him for arranging this position for you. I'm sure you know how difficult a time your friends are having getting summer work, and here you are starting such a fine job."

Arnold knew exactly how much trouble his friends were having convincing their folks that they were desperately looking for work, while they were avoiding any potential offers. "Mother dear," he thought. "I know exactly how much difficulty they are having. I have been one of the unfortunate. By the end of June, when all the high school kids are out, my friends will have fulfilled their roles as job hunters and will be spending the rest of the summer at the beach. But no, I have to be slogging around in some God-forsaken forest nightmare."

"I forgot to tell you that your new boots arrived," continued his mother. "Uncle Mervin suggested that you wear them around the rest of the day to get used to them and see if they need any adjustments before you leave."

She unwrapped the boots, set them in his lap and walked out.

Arnold slowly ran his finger over the hard toe of one of the boots and contemplated how far he could propel his uncle with a well-aimed kick. Stuck in the laces was a white business card. Arnold slipped it out and read aloud, "Compliments of Dr. Mervin H. Chipman, Professional Engineer."

"Don't tell me the stingy old fart actually paid for them himself," Arnold thought. "I wonder how many of his boring talks I'll have to sit through for this."

Deftly, he took his pen and stroked out the word 'Engineer' and printed 'Pain in the Ass' in its place. Then he struggled into the boots, lacing them firmly to the top. Fortunately, they did fit.

"Hell, I might as well give him the full treatment," he thought as he slipped into a new pair of khaki pants.

"Let's see, a brand new khaki shirt to match the pants, a sheathed Swiss Army knife on the belt on the left side, a Brunton compass on the belt on the right side and a rock hammer stuck through my belt at the back. If this belt ever breaks I'm in trouble. Now, what else? Oh, yes, a rock glass on a leather cord around my neck, waterproofed notebook and two freshly sharpened pencils in the breast pocket, shatterproof sunglasses, a backpack, metal clipboard and finally a pith helmet placed on my head at the proper angle. There, that should do it. As long as I stay in the house I'm okay. If I go outside looking like this, they're liable to pack me away."

"Boy, do you ever look weird."

"Young man," Arnold replied to his brother, "I would like you to show proper respect to an important member of the Wildwood Exploration Limited official team."

"Maybe it will impress Uncle Mervin. He's down in the living room waiting to give you a few words of advice and encouragement."

Arnold had received his 'few words of advice and encouragement' four times already. He could almost recite the routine word for word. However, in a few minutes he was downstairs, comfortably seated, prepared for Uncle Mervin to drone on through the fifth session.

"Dusty Sherant is a good geologist and respected in our mining community," Mervin Chipman began, "and you will be in a position to gain valuable practical experience through this association. I had a long talk with him and explained that you had just completed your first year of Geology and were eagerly looking forward to applying your newfound knowledge in the field. He was more than happy to offer you a position with his crew. I expect you to pay close attention to how he performs his work and carefully and enthusiastically carry out all instructions. You will, of course, be the junior man, but that in no way should lessen your respect for the job. "

"You couldn't lessen it any more than it is right now," Arnold thought.

"Have you completed your preparations and check-listed everything twice as I suggested? You cannot be too careful."

Arnold nodded, silently controlling his temper.

"Excellent! I see you are wearing your boots. Remember, your boots can be your best friend or your worst enemy in the bush."

"Oh No," Arnold thought. "Not the 'Eulogy to the Boots' routine again."

"Every night your boots should be rubbed with a good waterproof leather preservative. Dry your boots slowly, when they get wet and keep them firmly laced at all times. Now, are there any questions that have come up since we last met?"

Arnold, knowing that the only question he had would not be appreciated, shook his head.

"Good," Uncle Mervin replied, getting up. "I anticipate a very profitable summer for you and will be looking forward to a full report when you return."

Arnold smiled. He had finally discovered something good about the job. For four months he was not going to have to put up with Uncle Mervin and his big mouth.

It was his last evening in a civilized part of the Country, and he didn't want to waste it. After dinner he politely said goodbye to Uncle Mervin. He grabbed his guitar and headed for Rudy's. It saddened him that this would be the last chance they would have to jam together for a while.

"What a shame," Arnold thought, as he strolled down the

street. "All this crap had to come down just as we were getting our act together."

Rudy was working his way through some riffs on the piano when Arnold entered the garage. His friend was a year older and a head taller, but Arnold was the recognized leader by virtue of his superior musical ability.

"Great to see you could make it. The way you talked this afternoon, I had my doubts. I've got some exciting news. It looks like we're finally being noticed."

"Why? What happened?" Arnold asked.

"You remember that gig we played at that old age home in Richmond last Spring?"

"I do. That was a blast. The folks really got off on those sixties songs."

"One of the old guys that lives there called me. It took him this long to track us down. Anyway, his son is in the recording business, and he wants us to go down and audition for him. I told him you wouldn't be available for a few months. He figured it would be better if we could do it right away, but he could hold off for a while."

"How long?"

"Probably a month or so, but any longer and it sounded like the opportunity would be gone."

"This damn job is really becoming a pain," Arnold observed. "I have to figure some way of cutting my time up there short. We're supposed to get a break in the middle of the job, but according to good old Uncle Mervin, that will only happen if we don't get rained out a lot. I'll probably need some kind of injury or sickness to get out early without everyone being pissed off at me."

"Can't you just level with your folks. Tell them you have no interest in this work and that this great opportunity to pursue your music has come along. I know my folks would understand."

"You know that is not going to work. My old man does everything his brother tells him. I wouldn't be taking these useless courses if it hadn't been for Mervin Chipman. Some day I will get an appropriate kind of revenge for the way he has screwed around with my life."

Arnold was deep in thought as he walked the familiar route home, so deep that he walked past his house to the end of the street before he became aware of where he was. He could see the dilemma was going to keep him awake most of the night. To calm his mind he retired to the porch swing and spent the next hour picking some soft jazz melodies. Finally, his father came storming out of the house demanding he come in and stop this foolishness. After all, tomorrow was an important day for him to make a good impression. Arnold stifled his reply and trudged up the stairs to his room.

The next morning he called Emma to apologize for not coming to see her last evening. He made up some flimsy excuse, which he was sure she didn't believe. He really didn't care. He had wanted to break up with her for the past six months. Now, he had found another positive aspect of the job; he had an excuse for dropping Emma. After his father had hustled off to work, he was tempted to confide to his mother about his problem, but his better judgment convinced him that such a move would not go well. He was finally resigned to his fate. In anticipation of the folks coming to pick him up, he finally assembled his gear in an orderly fashion and was ready when the two men pulled up in front of the house in a new Jeep Wagoneer and some monstrosity of a trailer tagging along behind. The driver was an older man, short, bald and considerably overweight. He introduced himself as 'Cap' and disclosed that he would be performing the cooking and looking after the camp. After an interval of silence during which his sullen young companion said nothing, Cap introduced him as Aaron, another member of the crew.

Arnold's father returned at the same time and made a big deal of welcoming the pair into the house. The third positive hit home for Arnold; he would be away from dear old Dad for an extended period. The final straw arrived fifteen minutes later with the appearance of Uncle Mervin, who immediately launched into supervising the proceedings. The collection of suitcases, trunks and various bags and valises, which littered the driveway prompted a discussion of what could be taken and what must be left. Arnold stayed out of the decision-making process until it was declared by his uncle that he would have no need of his guitar in the bush. Arnold settled the matter immediately by sitting down on the front steps and stating, "If my guitar doesn't go, I don't go."

After an hour spent sending most of his possessions back into the house, his essential gear plus guitar were loaded into the truck. Arnold quickly said his goodbyes, effectively cutting off more long-winded advice from his uncle, and they were on their way.

CAP

"When are you going to tell her?"
Cap was getting very tired of this same question every time
he visited Doc Sanders.
"I'm going to do it; I'm just waiting for the right moment.
This isn't something you happen to mention while watching
TV. I'll tell her."
"If you don't, I will," Doc responded. "She deserves to
know. And another thing, you need to pull out of this bush
job. You're too old and sick to be charging off into the wild
country."
"Can't do that. It's not a tough job. I'll just be cooking for a
bunch of fellows and looking after the camp. Besides, I
can't let Sherant down. He's having enough trouble getting
a crew together, transporting all his equipment up north and
squeezing money out of these Howe Street bandits."
'You know it will probably kill you if you go through with
this. I'll be blunt; your days are numbered, and the number
is not big, but I can see you are going to ignore my advice
as usual."
"Look, I appreciate your concern, but this tumor is going to

kill me whether I'm stuck in bed at home or breathing the
fresh mountain air. I do promise to explain it all to
Margaret before I go. Anyhow, I won't be a burden to her if
I'm away for a few months."
Cap thought about his commitment to tell his wife on the
way home and regretted it. It didn't make sense to spoil the
next few months for Margaret and the kids. There would be
time enough for all the grief at the end of the summer, if he
survived. He made up his mind to call Doc and explain his
change of mind. There was too much to do to waste time
worrying; he had to be on the road tomorrow. He was bone-
tired when he climbed into bed at sundown, and he tossed
and turned as the pain in his chest slowly grew more
intense. By two A M, he was unable to lay flat due to the
shortness of breath. He slid quietly out of bed so as not to
wake Margaret and retired to the kitchen to prepare a cup
of tea. She appeared at the doorway as he was pouring his
second cup.
"What's wrong? Are you ill?" She asked.
"No! Nothing like that, just a bit of trouble sleeping. I
guess I am anxious that all will go well tomorrow."
The temptation was strong in the early morning hours to
confess his medical condition, but he held fast, knowing it
would only alarm her and cause her to resist his going
away.
"I'm okay," he added. "Let's go back to bed."
The trailer was one of a kind. Constructed of well-
weathered wood with homemade stock racks extending
skyward from the four sides, it looked ready to topple over
in the slightest breeze. The effect of too many do-it-
yourself paint jobs, now chipped and faded, was grotesque.
The wooden spoke wheels had once adorned one of Henry
Ford's early mass-produced creations. Its attachment to the
new four-wheel drive Wagoneer gave viewers the vision of
half a century of technological progress across the length of
a trailer hitch.

Cap spent the morning carefully loading the last few items, but his mind wasn't on his work. Sweat poured from all the exposed surfaces of his body, from his baldhead to his bare legs. He was of less than medium height, but a well-rounded belly, which hung precariously over the top of his pants more than compensated for his lack of vertical stature. His eyes were clear and bright, but his skin showed the signs of seventy years and a slight jaundiced effect from the disease.

"Cap, you're a fool to try and pull that flimsy trailer all the way to Smithers. You'll be lucky to make it to the highway with that load."

"Now Margaret, I know what I'm doing. This is a good trailer, built sturdy and reinforced with iron all across the bottom. They don't build them like this any more."

Carefully, he measured around the stock racks, but his concentration was elsewhere as he continued his internal debate. He jotted down the precise length, carefully measured again and then cut the required amount of rope from the roll. However, when stretching the cut portion around the racks, he discovered he had failed to cut enough surplus to tie the two ends together. He looked at the results of his mismanaged efforts and realized he needed to focus on what he was doing and quit feeling sorry for himself if he was to have everything ready to leave later in the day.

"Consarn this fool thing!" He exclaimed, threw the rope on the ground in disgust and flopped down on the bench.

"I came to tell you," continued his wife, "that Mr. Sherant phoned to say that he won't be able to help you load up as he has to leave for the north today to make some arrangements. He apologized for the extra work, but he's sending one of the boys on the crew over to give you a hand. The young man's name is Aaron Kitchner. He should be here soon."

"Kitchner." The old man mumbled the name half to himself. "That name rings a bell. I seem to remember hearing about a young fella with a name something like that over on the Island a couple of years ago when I was cooking for that geophysical crew up near Port Hardy. He was in some kind of trouble with the police. I think he was arrested and sent to jail. I wonder if he's the same one."

"You may soon find out," his wife replied. "That's probably him coming up the lane now."

Kitch was not in the best of moods that early June morning. Saying goodbye to Julie, and another argument with Glennda had taken the edge off his spirit. It was the same old battle, but this time the finality of their situation was beginning to sink in. For the first time, he truly wondered if he would ever see his little girl again.

"Are you Mason?" Kitch's question came almost as a challenge.

"That's right," the old man replied. "Harold Mason, but most people call me Cap."

"I'm Aaron Kitchner. Sherant was supposed to phone you about me coming over. I guess I'm riding to Smithers with you."

"Yes, he phoned. It looks like a bunch of us will be driving north together. I hope we have room for everybody and their gear."

The two men looked at each other in silence for a few minutes, then conscious of nothing more to say, their eyes shifted to the trailer.

"I've never seen anything like this before," Kitch remarked as he walked around the vehicle. "Looks like your load is going to need a lot of cinching before you move it. It seems a bit top heavy."

"That's what I was about to do when you arrived."

Reluctantly following Kitch's suggestion, Cap shifted the heavier items to the bottom of the load, thus providing more stability. The two men proceeded to use up the rest of the rope, wrapping it in all directions around the trailer and its contents. As Cap pulled it tight to tie the end around the front of the rack, a wave of dizziness swept over him. He grabbed the side of the wagon for support, but his legs wouldn't hold him, and the next thing he knew, the young man had helped him to his feet and was supporting him as they walked to the bench. Cap had to sit for a few minutes before his head cleared enough to talk and his strength returned. Kitch was staring at him with a look of concern. "I guess I've had too much sun out here this morning. It made me kind of dizzy."

"Are you sure you are okay? You don't look so good. Maybe, you should go inside and lay down for a while."

"I'm fine. I've wasted enough time already. We need to get going. We have this other fellow to pick up and should be in Kamloops by evening."

"Man, I don't know about this trailer making it to Kamloops." Kitch shook his head as he surveyed the vehicle. "Couldn't Sherant afford anything better than this to move his equipment? I figured he was trying to put together a low budget operation, but this is too much. Did you build this thing?"

"Look young man, this is a good trailer. Mr. Sherant wanted me to get this equipment up there in as economical a manner as possible, and this is the way I'm going to do it."

"Okay! Okay! Let's hit the road and hope we make it."

"We go right after lunch. Where do we pick up the rest of your gear?"

"You're looking at it," Kitch replied as he pointed at the duffel bag on the ground beside him. "I travel light."

It was early afternoon before they drove out the farm lane. By then Cap had checked his list at least half a dozen times, adding additional items as he went and frustrating Kitch to the point that he had to go lie under a shade tree to get away from the confusion.

"Where do we pick up this Chipman?" Kitch asked, as he looked over the map.

"He lives somewhere over in West Vancouver. Here's the address on this paper," Cap replied, digging a torn piece of envelope from his shirt pocket. "See if you can find it on the map."

"Well, it looks like we've got a rich one on the crew," Kitch observed. "I hope he's a card player."

Finding Arnold Chipman's home was easy. Getting away from it was another matter. They arrived in the midst of a family farewell party. After an hour of food, drink, introductions, and advice from Mervin Chipman, they were able to begin loading Arnold's gear, which was piled up on the driveway.

"Well, young fella, are you all set to go?" Cap grunted as he closed the tailgate of the station wagon on the third suitcase he had jammed into a space large enough for one.

"What about my trunk and guitar?"

"Your trunk? There's no room for anything the size of a trunk on this load. What's in it that you need?"

"The trunk has all my clothes."

"What was in the suitcases?"

"Oh, that was my books, my art supplies, camera equipment and my music."

After Cap held a conference with Arnold's father and uncle, the next few minutes were spent in choosing and fitting only the essentials into the three suitcases and stuffing them back into the station wagon. It was only his guitar that Arnold refused to leave at home.

"Well, you're going to have to carry it on your lap after we pick up Tolman in Kamloops."

"I thought we were never going to get out of there; that place was like a zoo," Kitch mumbled as he slouched down in the seat.

To ease Arnold's embarrassment and help him relax, Cap hurriedly announced how much he had enjoyed meeting the boy's family. "They certainly are nice folks."

"Thank you," Arnold replied. "I guess they made too much

of a production about me leaving for the summer."
"It's better to have them care too much than not give a damn," the old man replied with a side-glance at Kitch. "What about this other fellow we're supposed to pick up? Is he the one that gets on at Kamloops?" Kitch asked.
"That's right," Cap replied. "He'll be coming in from Calgary on a flight about eight o'clock tonight. We pick him up at the airport."
"Where are we going to put him in here?" Kitch asked as he looked around the crowded interior of the station wagon.
"We'll make out," Cap replied. "Don't worry. We'll make out."

BRIAN

Brian counted the boxes along the wall for the fourth time, checking off each item on the list as he went. It had become tiresome after the second count. Now it was irritating, as he still couldn't get his tallies to agree. The old warehouse was uninsulated and cold in spite of the first traces of a Chinook wind blowing in from the snow-laden mountains to the west. It was well after nine, and the pangs of hunger were sniping at his concentration, as he tried to sort out the inventory mess inherited from the previous shift. Again, it didn't check. "No use driving myself crazy trying to deal with this now," he thought. "I had better get some dinner and give it another shot later tonight."

The only place to eat was just three blocks away, but Brian was thoroughly chilled as he slogged through the parking lot in the slush left over from a Calgary spring storm. He welcomed the steamy warmth of the diner, as he settled into a booth. Other than home, this was his refuge from the world and the personal relationship with Stephanie that was gnawing at his life.

"How's the young love of my life?" The waitress kidded him as she set out the menu. "I thought you had gone and left me to tramp around in the woods."

"Not yet, Sara, but soon. You know I'm going to miss you, especially your cooking." He smiled as he got into the mood of the moment. One of the bright spots in his day was kidding around with Sara after a day of classes and work was finally over. They had experienced a brief mutual infatuation the previous year, but it had died on the vine for all the traditional reasons: a twelve-year difference in age, the threats of a jealous ex-husband and parental displeasure. They both regretted its demise, but this time, reason had overruled emotion.

"That's not a very flattering thing to say to a beautiful woman. Be careful what you order or I may mix in a potion to make me irresistible. Oh, yes, I guess I already did that."

"I remember that stuff," Brian continued. "I think it gave me heartburn last time."

"Well, you know I'm going miss you coming in and making my day. Just promise me you won't go and marry that bitch you're engaged to. You know how I feel about her. She'll make your life miserable. She was in here an hour ago, asking if you had been in for dinner, or if I knew where you were. I gave her a 'no' on both counts, so she put her nose in the air and stomped out. For people that are supposedly engaged, you two don't communicate much."

"I'm still trying to figure how to get out of this damn engagement without angering everyone and getting my mother fired. If I dump Stephanie, old man Torren will fire mother as his office manager. It's not much of a job, but she needs it, at least until I start making good money. Stepahanie wanted to have the big wedding as soon as I graduated, but I was able to convince her to postpone it until fall. You know what she's like. Have you any ideas on how I can get free?"

"I've thought about it since the last time we talked, and the only thing that comes to mind is that somehow it needs to be her idea to end it. You and I could have a hot physical affair this time, but that would open another can of worms. I don't think either of us wants to go down that road again. Maybe she could fall for someone else while you are away. Have you got any friends that would sacrifice their summer to court her?"

"No. Most of my friends know her and what she's like. Maybe I could convince one of my enemies."

"I hope you can sort it out while you are away. I care too much for you to see you caught in her clutches. Oh! I forgot to tell you," she continued as she moved toward the kitchen. "Your sister phoned earlier this evening. She said it was important and for you to call her as soon as you came in."

"It's getting late, and I know what it's about. I'll talk to her in the morning. I need to go home and get some rest and finish the warehouse job tomorrow."

The first pink traces of morning seeped through the shutters as Brian was yanked back to reality.

"Brian, you got the job."

Brenda burst into the room and flopped down on the bed, driving out the last warm remnants of sleep.

"The letter came yesterday from that Oceanic Oil Corporation in Houston. I read it. I was too excited to wait until you got home. I phoned Sara at the restaurant for you to phone me. Anyway, it's from a Mr. Smithdale, Director of Personnel. He says they are pleased to accept your application, and all that stuff, and appreciate you wanting to finish that field job you committed to. They want you to start as soon as you get back in the fall. You get to go down to Houston for six months on a training program and then you will be working in their office here. That's great, huh?"

"I know, sis," Brian replied sleepily. "I've been hoping all year to get accepted. He phoned me yesterday at the University. I was going to tell you and Mom this morning, but I guess she's gone to work by now. I had better give her a call and let her know the news before I go back down to the warehouse. How about you fix some breakfast while I get dressed. I'm late already."

"I already told her, and she read the letter. Are you going to call Stephanie and tell her the news? Why bother going down to the warehouse, you don't need that job any more?"

"I know, but I told Mr. Rendel I would help him finish the inventory before I packed it in. Even though it's taking longer than expected, I don't want to let him down. He's been good to me, letting me work my own hours, but it will sure be nice not to have to go down there any more after today. And tomorrow night, little sister," he continued, "we are going to celebrate, the three of us, with dinner at the Palliser and a movie. Calling Stephanie can wait. I have enough to deal with right now."

Brenda thought for a minute then said, "What's with you two anyway? She calls here three or four times a day wanting to know where you are. I did what you told me and told her I didn't know, but the last time she accused me of lying. That made me angry, and I told her so. I think you need to deal with her from now on."

"Okay! Give her the warehouse number the next time she calls. I'll talk to her."

"That's great that we're going for dinner. I'm looking forward to wearing my new dress," the girl exclaimed, "but where are you going to get the money to do that, and are you going to invite Stephanie?"

"Don't worry. I have it all figured out, but I can only afford it for the three of us. Mr. Sherant sent me three hundred dollars to fly to Kamloops. If I drive my car instead, it will only cost about a hundred, so that leaves us enough for a good evening."

"Are you sure that old wreck of yours will make it out there? Every time I drive it, it leaves me stranded somewhere. That's why I quit borrowing it."

"I think so. If it doesn't, I can push it into the ditch somewhere and hitchhike the rest of the way. Anyhow, tomorrow night you have to help me talk Mom into quitting work as soon as I get my first paycheck. I am not going to marry Stephanie, but no one is to know until I start earning some real money, and Mom won't have to put up with that crap job and old man Torren any longer. Then you and her can go on a real holiday. We have it made now. I have a good deal this summer and the oil company job to go to in the Fall. She won't have to work any more, and I can get my life back. I'm telling you this in confidence, and I want you to keep it to yourself."

"That's tough. You know the problem I have keeping secrets."

"Well, just make sure you keep this one, or we'll all suffer."
As he drove to the warehouse, Brian was happy that this was to be his last shift. When he arrived at work the day shift supervisor presented him with a corrected and completed inventory.

"We got her sorted out this morning thanks to your efforts last night. We're going home, but Rendel is coming by later to pick up this list. You should have an easy shift."
Oliver Rendel showed up just after seven with a two hundred dollar bonus cheque.

"I'm sorry to lose you, Brian. I wish I had more employees like you. Good luck this summer, and if you ever need anything, let me know. I told Sara, down at the diner, to fix you up with the best steak in the house. Dinner and drinks are on me. Now, get out of here and enjoy the evening."
As Brian walked out into the twilight, he spotted Stephanie's BMW partly hidden behind some bushes beyond the driveway. She didn't pull onto the road until he was a block away. He followed her headlights passing by as he pulled into the diner parking lot. The place was almost empty. Only a couple of regulars were nursing their beers at the bar as he entered. Sara gave him a hug and led

him to one of the booths, which she had decorated for the occasion.

"Dinner is on the way, and you're getting the full treatment. Mr. Rendel told me not to worry about the expense."

As Brian was finishing his second piece of pecan pie, Sara brought him another beer and sat down across from him.

"I want you to come outside with me for a minute. Don't ask me any questions. I have a solution which could solve your problem or possibly make it worse."

Brian was a bit leery, but curiosity won out. As they stood beside the front door, she said, "Put your arms around me and hold me tight."

When she kissed him long and passionately on the lips, he saw the refection of the dying sun off a car window at the back of the lot. As he pulled away, he said, "You knew she was there didn't you?"

"I saw her drive in just after you sat down. She's been there ever since. Either you are never going to hear from her again, or all hell will break loose."

"Yeah. I'm betting on the latter."

"Well, I figured you weren't going to do anything, so I decided to spark things up."

"After that kiss, whatever happens will be worth it."

"You look after yourself and come back to me safe and single."

Brian spent the next day packing and servicing his old Mustang. There were no phone calls or appearances of an irate girlfriend at his door. That evening mother, son and daughter, dressed in their finest, enjoyed a farewell dinner. The next morning after a series of extended goodbyes, his mother requested he phone Stephanie and at least let her know he was leaving.

"I'm sure she knows. Today, she is the last person I want to talk to."

He could almost taste the sense of relief and freedom, as he headed west on the Trans-Canada toward Banff.

KAMLOOPS

Brian left Calgary with a bittersweet feeling. The day had
finally come. He knew he was going to miss his mother and
sister and all his friends, but he was overjoyed to have
Stephanie off his back for a while. Hopefully, this summer
he could sort out an honorable way of getting out of the
relationship and impending marriage. At least he could put
it out of his mind for a few weeks as he got into this new
job.
He did all the maintenance on the old Mustang that was
suggested in the ragged manual, which had come with the
car when he had purchased it the previous year. It had
served him well, but with over three hundred thousand
miles on the motor, he knew he was pushing his luck by
driving it to Kamloops. As he cruised west toward Banff,
the small vibrations and odd noises he had grown used to
over the winter seemed magnified and started to worry him.
The motor struggled on its climb to the summit of the
Rogers Pass and continued to boil over every few miles. It

seemed to Brian he had to stop at each creek he encountered along the roadway to refill the radiator.

He pulled into a truck stop at Revelstoke for an early dinner. When he came out of the cafe, the first sight that greeted him was the pool of oil spread out from under his vehicle.

"That doesn't look good," a passerby remarked. "There's a service station just down the road. I can give you a lift there if you want. They might be able to fix you up enough to keep it running."

"No, it's okay. I've got some of that real heavy oil in the trunk. I'll just fill her up with that and keep going. This isn't the first time it's happened."

The engine ran a lot quieter with this new gummy fluid and Brian was beginning to think the problem was solved until he hit the stretch of highway west of Salmon Arm. Coming down the hill into Chase, he heard a clicking noise, which progressively got louder as his speed increased. He took his foot off the accelerator and feathered the brake to slow his progress, but the noise persisted, and in fact got louder, as he coasted into town. When he tried to gain speed on the main street, the click turned to a clack then a bang, bang, bang. Brian saw the oil pressure needle drop to zero, but the Mustang kept banging along. When he pulled up to a stop light in the center of town, a man came running out of a gas station on the corner, waving his arms and yelling for Brian to turn off the motor. He coasted into the station and pulled up in front of one of the bays. The man who had called him opened the hood. It took him less than a minute to make a diagnosis.

"This car is not going any farther. Look in here," he said as he pointed to the stream of fluid seeping out of the side of the motor. "This block is cracked big time. The only way this will move on its own is with a new motor."

"Well, I don't have the time or the money to get it fixed. I need to get to the Kamloops airport this evening. Is there a bus going that way?"

"No, the last one went through at noon. I'll tell you what, I'm restoring an old Mustang about this vintage. You sign your car over to me, and I'll drive you to Kamloops."

"It's a deal," Brian replied.

It was just after eight and getting dark when the station wagon and trailer turned onto the long road into Kamloop's Fulton Field. Storm cloud had gathered overhead, and the wind had picked up, blowing drops of rain against the windshield. It had been a slow trip from the Coast dragging Cap's antique trailer. Every time they hit a bump, the load would shift, and Arnold would check behind to see if it was still attached.

"With the luck you've been having backing this thing up today, I think we had better stay out of the parking lot," Kitch said as he pointed to a widening of the road near the terminal. "Just pull up over there, and I'll check inside and see if I can find him. What was his name again?"

"Tolman, Brian Tolman," Cap replied as he squinted at another piece of battered envelope from his pocket. "Mr. Sherant said he's 23, tall, with blond hair and glasses."

"He shouldn't be too tough to find in an airport this size." Kitch was back in a few minutes soaking wet. "There's only half a dozen people in there. The Calgary plane came in about an hour ago. The guy at the desk said only a couple of women got off. He's been on since noon and hasn't seen anybody looking like our man."

"When is the next plane?" Arnold asked. "Maybe he missed his flight."

"Next one is tomorrow morning around ten," Kitch answered as he got back in the station wagon. "Anybody have any suggestions as to what we do now?"

"Well boys, we've got our orders to pick Tolman up here at the airport, so I guess we had better come back tomorrow morning when the next plane comes in."

An hour later the drizzle was much stronger as an old half-ton truck moved slowly up the airport roadway. It stopped at the terminal, and a young man got out, pulled a large backpack from the back of the truck and waved as the driver pulled away. He walked into the building, dropped his pack inside the doorway and walked over to the ticket counter.

"What time did the last plane get in from Calgary?"

"A couple of hours ago," the clerk replied. "Say, there was a fellow in here a while back looking for someone. The way he described him sure looks like you. He was quite concerned his party hadn't showed up. Were you supposed to meet some people here?"

"I guess so," Brian answered. "They were expecting me on that plane. Did he say where he was going to be tonight?"

"No, not that I can remember. He did ask me for the arrival time of the first plane from Calgary tomorrow morning."

"It looks like I'd better be here in the morning when that flight arrives in case they plan to meet it. Is it okay if I sleep here on one of the benches tonight?"

"Sorry," the clerk replied. "We're closing up, as there are no more planes today. No one is allowed to spend the night in here while we're closed. There are no more flights until that Calgary plane."

"Do you know of any campgrounds or a hostels around here? I'm just about broke and can't afford a motel."

"I don't know about any hostels, but I think there is a picnic park down by the river in the city. I don't know if it is open at night. I'm leaving in a few minutes to go home and can give you a lift if you want."

"That would be great. I'll figure out something from there."

Brian didn't find a campground or a hostel. He tried a couple of rundown motels, but they wanted more money for a night's stay than he had left in his wallet. However, he did locate a park by the river and managed to stretch his

sleeping bag out under a picnic shelter where he was partly
protected from the rain by the ground sheet he laid across
the top of the table. The ground was lumpy and littered
with small stones, which jabbed into his body as he lay
down, but he was asleep within a few minutes.
By morning the drizzle of the previous night had
progressed into a moderate but steady downpour. Cap,
Kitch, and Arnold arrived at the airport well before the
westbound plane taxied in. A dozen passengers got off, but
none of them even remotely fitted Brian's description.
"Well," Kitch shrugged. "That tears it. We can either stick
around here until the evening plane and lose another day, or
we can take off, probably make Smithers by tonight, and
let this guy find his own way up there. Chances are he
won't be on the next plane either. Maybe he decided to
cancel out of the job but didn't let Sherant know."
"I'm not sure what to do," Cap said, scratching his head.
"Mr. Sherant said we were to pick him up here."
"Yeah, but we were supposed to do that yesterday. At this
rate we could be here all summer waiting for him."
"Why don't we go back to the motel and phone Mr.
Sherant?" Arnold suggested. "We know where he's staying
in Smithers, and we have to go back and check out anyway.
It makes sense to call him from there before we make any
decisions on our own."
"That's the best idea I've heard this morning," the old man
replied. "He can tell us exactly what we're supposed to do."
As they headed back toward the City, about half a mile
from the airport they spotted a lone figure with a heavy
backpack trudging along the side of the road toward them.
"Look at this fellow coming down the road," Arnold
exclaimed. "That looks like it could be Tolman."
Cap pulled the station wagon to a stop up beside the rain-
soaked young man.
"Are you Brian Tolman?" He asked as he rolled down the
window.

Brian just nodded his head, pleased that his ordeal was coming to an end.

It took two hours at the motel, the Laundromat and the diner to get Brian fed and his clothes warm and dry. With their new arrival and his gear, they had to completely repack the station wagon before they could leave.

"I can't get over you trading your car for a ride to the airport last night." Cap said.

As they headed north from Kamloops on Highway 97, Cap turned the heater on full, and Brian was having a hard time staying awake to answer their questions.

"Like I said, I was cruising along pretty good until I rolled into Chase. The car was making a few strange noises and had lost a lot of oil, but I was beginning to think the old girl was going to take me all the way. Then there were all these new loud noises in the motor, and the oil pressure dropped to nothing. It still sort of ran, but was making a lot of racket, so I coasted into town and this guy comes running out, waving his hands in the air and yelling for me to turn the key off. He looked the motor over, but it didn't take long for him to tell me the bad news. When I asked him if he thought it would get me to Kamloops before it gave out, he just looked a little sad and shook his head. Then he offered to bring me to the airport if I would sign the car over to him. At that point I didn't think I had a lot of choices if I was going to meet up with you guys. I find out he has an old Mustang himself, about the same year, model, and everything, which he's trying to restore. So, I traded him the car for the ride. I figured we both won."

"Christ! You probably could have gotten a couple of hundred dollars for it as well if he was that quick to offer the deal," Kitch remarked. "I'm willing to bet he needed it for parts, which for that old a car are hard to come by and expensive when you can find them."

"You are probably right," Brian replied, "but the car didn't owe me anything, and it made the old man happy."

CURT

Curt was getting fed up with whole routine. It was more than a month now, and she just wouldn't leave. Last week he had gathered up all her clothes, books and other junk and deposited them in a pile in the hall. He had planned to change the locks on the apartment at his first opportunity, but since he hadn't given her a key, he wasn't too concerned that she would return this time. However, two days later, when he came back from his afternoon class, she was parked on the bed, crying and pleading with him to let her stay. He was puzzled as to how she had gained access. She finally admitted she had talked the building superintendent into letting her in.

"We are done! Can't you get it through you're thick skull that I don't want to see you around here any more. I've had enough of your immature little ways and whining. Now, get out! And, take all this junk with you or I'll call someone to haul it to the dump."

"I thought you loved me and wanted us to be together," she sobbed. "That's what you told me."

"You must be out of your mind. Why would I jeopardize my chances for a successful life by spending it with you? I'm going back to the College and get some work done. If you are still here when I come back, you and your precious possessions will spend the night out on the street."
Without waiting for a reply, Curt walked out the door.

"Come in."
Curt Schuman opened the door to the Professor's office, walked over, and stood in front of the massive, dark walnut desk. The distinguished elderly gentleman sitting behind the desk was in his eighties but had continued tenure as Department Head well past normal retirement age. He believed that as long as his mind was sharp enough to keep ahead of his graduate students, he could be effective for many years. Physically his body had not kept pace with his mind, as the ravages of age had turned his hair to white and swapped muscle for fat. He continued to peer through a microscope for a few minutes before he looked up.
"Sit down Schuman. I will be with you in a minute."
The old man was absorbed in his microscopic examination of a polished rock section. The microscope was almost hidden by the jumble of papers and books on the desk. Curt waited impatiently. He had been in this room many times during the past three years, and it had never ceased to amaze him how this man, with all the prestige of his important position as Department Head, could allow his office to continually remain in such a cluttered condition. The lack of order always had a very disquieting effect on Curt and normally made him anxious to return to the neat well-kept arrangement of his own quarters. This evening was an exception, as he was in no hurry to get back. He wanted to make sure the girl had enough time to be packed and gone before he returned.
Reports, books and maps were everywhere. Ashtrays and wastebaskets were full, and only a few square inches of

desk surface was visible. It was such a sharp contrast to his own office, which always had every item in its proper place and was swept and cleaned at least once a day.

"I want to congratulate you for the way you handled the oral examination," the Professor said, straightening up from his work. "They threw some pretty tough questions at you."

"Thank you," the young man replied. "I made sure I was fully prepared for anything they might ask. There were no surprises in their questioning." He paused, picking out the precise words in his mind. "I have come to see you this evening with regard to another matter. I wish to determine if any decision has been made on my application for a teaching position in the fall."

The professor, as his faculty advisor had come to know Curtis Shuman well. Visually, the young man's appearance and the keenness of his mind were his best attributes. He was tall, just over six foot with a slim, but well muscled body. His finely chiseled facial features were capped with abundant blond hair, combed straight back. The coeds considered him a real catch until they got to know him. The professor admired his brain but felt he had much to learn about the qualities of a successful instructor and life in general. The old man was concerned about Curt's condescending attitude toward the undergraduates, especially the women.

"The members of the Board have not reached any decision as yet. As you know, proceeding with your application would require the creation of a new position on staff. We have discussed it briefly with the Finance Committee, but since the general tendency within the University is to cut back expenditures at the present time, they were not very receptive to the idea. I think we might have a better chance for approval if we made a more concentrated effort, but that brings us to a second consideration. Some of my colleagues are not fully convinced that you are cut out for working as an instructor in this Department."

"I do not understand your concern," Curt answered as he pushed back an initial flash of anger. "My academic credentials are above reproach. I have obtained my Doctorate with first class honors and have published ten papers in the last two years, all of which have received favorable reviews. Surely this is more than sufficient."

"Let me explain." The old man settled back in his chair after picking up a folder and examining it briefly." Your knowledge of Geology, technical competency and proficiency in the course work is undoubtedly the best I have seen in some years. You would be welcomed with open arms by most large universities on that basis. This is not the problem. We have a small faculty here and, as a result, have been able to maintain relationships between staff and students that are closer and more relaxed than you find in the larger institutions. This is not a degree mill like the big schools. Our instructors are expected to have more than just a passing interest in the welfare of our scholars. Surely you have been aware of this atmosphere during the past few years."

Curt knew this to be true and it continued to irritate him. He replied, "I have noticed a number of instances when the traditional roles of instructor and student have been blurred and not strictly adhered to."

"Do you find that distasteful?"

"I feel the instructor loses respect when he becomes too familiar, and consequently his control of a class and the learning process is weakened."

"Do you think there has been too much familiarity between our staff and students?"

"In some cases I think there has been," Curt replied. He knew he was taking a chance revealing the true nature of his feelings, but this level of familiarity between staff and students was totally unacceptable to his beliefs in how a College should be run.

"This is the crux of our concern over your application. We

have had a number of indications from undergraduates in your Laboratory classes that they have been apprehensive about approaching you with questions or problems. There have been no formal complaints, you understand, but these concerns have arisen during free discussion sessions. It appears to be the more timorous, less confident students and especially the young ladies that are somewhat intimidated by you."

Curt felt no need to counter these accusations. The old man was, of course, right. He had little time for those wishy-washy types who fumbled around producing mediocre work and who were afraid to ask questions in order to improve their performance. In addition, he felt that training as a geologist was not a suitable goal for a female, and the preparation of female geologists to go out and work on field crews was totally unacceptable He did not agree with the Professor's ideas on education, but to admit this would most certainly destroy any chance he had in obtaining the appointment.

"I was not aware that some of these people found me so threatening. I would have been happy to answer their questions had I known."

"But, that is the point," the Professor continued. "Our staff endeavors to anticipate these situations. We try to know our students to the extent that we are aware of the ones needing help."

Curt was finding the conversation tiresome. He was confident that once he was functioning as a full time instructor according to his own dictates, the others would see the advantages of his methods as evidenced by superior learning results.

"I believe I detect a certain hostility to my remarks," the Professor said.

"Not hostility," Kurt replied with a forced smile. "I did not realize until today that the instructional methods used by most of the staff were an embodiment of Departmental philosophy. However, knowing this, I am sure I can adjust my teaching style accordingly. I would hope that this would be taken into account when the Board is giving further consideration to my application. Can you anticipate when I might expect a decision?"

"I am afraid we do not have a timetable for this project. I would like you to come in and meet with the Board in September if you are still interested in a position at that time. Do you have an address for this summer so that we can contact you if anything develops?"

"Not as yet. I have taken a field job in Northern British Columbia in an area with some excellent examples of geological relationships that were covered in my Thesis. I will forward an address as soon as possible."

"I expect it will be very satisfying for you to get out there and do some field geology after all these months in the classroom. This time of year I resent the infirmities of old age that keep me out of the bush."

"The geology should be interesting. Unfortunately, I do not anticipate anyone on the crew of sufficient academic background to be able to discuss my work intelligently. I was, however, able to obtain a very favorable agreement with regard to the terms of employment. I had a lawyer draw up the contract containing my demands, covering all the possible situations I could envisage. It was signed without alteration."

"You appear to have the situation under control. I wish you a successful summer."

Curt left the office with the uneasy feeling that he might have seriously jeopardized his chances by letting his attitude and irritation slip into his replies. He was further troubled when he opened the door to his apartment. Laura was gone, but she had left her mark. The place was trashed. Bookcases and cabinets were overturned , and their contents strewn about the rooms. His framed diplomas had been smashed as had pictures of other personal achievements, which he treasured. Tacked to the back of the door was a note.

'You will be truly sorry you have treated me this way. You continually deceived me with your promises and words of affection. What you see here is only a sample of my vengeance.'

Curt was livid. His anger knew no bounds, but he had no idea where to find her and take revenge. None of the folks taking an evening stroll or resting in the courtyard had seen her leave.

He knew there was nothing he could do now. His flight to Smithers was due to leave tomorrow at noon, and he still had to pack. Fortunately, he had stored most of his field gear and clothes in his locker, but there were still a few things in the mess in his apartment he needed.

He smiled as he thought, "I've got all summer to come up with a way to get back at her for this."

PRINCE GEORGE

"Does anyone have any idea where we are?" Brian asked as he sat up and rubbed the sleep from his eyes. "I can't believe I fell asleep all cramped up like this."

"I'm not exactly sure where we are, but we drove through Prince George about an hour ago," Kitch replied. "We must be about fifty miles west of there by now. That was quite a nap. You've been asleep since we pulled out of Barriere."

"Man, I was sure tired. With all that rain, I didn't get much sleep in the park last night. I'd probably still be out of it except for this bumping back here that woke me up."

"What bumping are you talking about? I can't hear anything," Kitch asked.

"I don't know how you can miss it. It feels like we're riding on a square wheel."

"Sure, I can hear it and feel the vibration when I put my ear against the door frame," Arnold exclaimed. "It sounds like it's coming from the trailer."

"Yeah, I hear it now. It doesn't sound good. I guess we better have a look," Kitch said as he pulled off onto the shoulder. "Maybe something fell off the trailer and we're dragging it. The way that load was swaying around, it wouldn't surprise me."

The source of the problem was obvious when they stopped and walked to the back. One of the trailer tires was flat.

"That tire is pretty beat up. It looks like we've been driving on it like this for quite a while," Cap said as he ran his hand around the wheel. "It's hot. Let's get her jacked up. Brian, there's a flashlight in the glove compartment, and the jack is somewhere under the front seat."

"We need to be careful getting that wheel off the ground, or this whole thing will tip over," Brian observed.

"I hope you have a spare," Kitch said as he took the flashlight from Brian and shined it on the wheel. "It looks to me like this one is finished. I don't suppose we could pile all the gear on the roof and push this hunk of junk into the ditch."

"I've got another tire buried at the bottom of the trailer," Cap replied, "but that's the only tube. There is a patching kit somewhere down there with the tire, so we should be able to fix the tube."

Working together, they soon had the jack under the axle and the trailer balanced precariously on it. Brian and Arnold steadied the trailer while Kitch forced the wheel nuts loose and finally removed the wheel. Cap rummaged around in the station wagon and came up with a couple of tire irons, a screwdriver and the patching kit.

"You've got all the modern conveniences, haven't you," Kitch observed sarcastically.

"Don't worry young fella. I was changing tires with tools like these long before you were walking."

Cap soon had one side of the tire pried away from the rim, and the tube pulled out. "We're not going to patch this one," he said as he stuck his fingers in a six-inch gash along the side of the tube. "It's done. I knew I should have hunted up another one before we left, but I forgot about it in the rush of packing. I had a couple of new ones hanging in the barn. Somehow we'll have to try and find another one up here in this country."

"That shouldn't be too tough, should it? The area is well populated. There must be a small town nearby with a garage or service station. Those wooden-spoked wheels and the size of the tires make me think it must be real old. What size is it?" Brian asked.

"Thirty by three and a half."

"That's a new one on me. What did the wheels come from?"

"They are from an old Model T Ford we had," Cap replied. "When it quit running, I rebuilt the chassis into this trailer, which has served me well through the years."

"You're kidding."

"No, unfortunately he's not," Kitch answered. "I didn't believe it either when he told me. It could be real interesting trying to find another tube that size. I doubt if there's another Model T anywhere around here."

"Our best bet in locating one is probably back in Prince George. It's the biggest place in these parts. If we have any chance at all of fixing this tire, it would be there," Brian observed.

"So, how do we get the trailer back there? Are we going to try and pull it the way it is?" Arnold asked.

"We probably could. We sure can't make it any worse unless we damage the wheel," Brian observed

"I have an idea," Kitch replied. "We unhook it and leave it here with Arnold to guard the stuff while we go find a tube. We should be back in a day or two. You're a big boy. You should be able to handle it."

"Thanks a lot. That's not going to happen," Arnold retorted.

"Naw, that's no good," said Cap. "There won't be anything open in the City by the time we get there, and we can't leave anyone out here all night on the road. Somehow we have to get the trailer back to Prince George, hopefully in one piece."

"Tell you what," Kitch said. "This tube is shot, so why don't we stuff the tire so it'll hold some kind of shape, and we can drive it back slow, hopefully without doing too much damage to the wheel. We will still have the spare tire to use when, and if, we find another tube."

"It might work. I sure don't see any other options," Brian replied. "We could take a bunch of our work socks or old shirts, stuff them with paper or grass and then fit them inside the tire. Then, if we can get the tire back on the rim, it might get us there. It's probably worth a try as we don't have any other reasonable solutions to the problem."

"And you're calling this a reasonable solution," Kitch said. "Come up with something better, and we'll do it, but until then, let's get those socks out."

The next half hour was spent digging through suitcases for socks and anything to stuff in them. Arnold searched around in the ditch and came up with some clumps of tall grass. Packages were formed and wrapped around the wheel, and using Cap's tire iron the tire was forced on the wheel to cover as much of the packing as possible. The whole thing was then wrapped with rope in hopes of holding the tire in place. The result was a well-packed tire with a tendency to develop bulges on two sides after a few rotations of the wheel down the road. Periodic stopping every mile and pounding the bulges with a hammer made the trip almost tolerable.

Their midnight arrival into the city was heralded by the flap, flap, flap of a bundle of stuffed socks that had almost worked its way to freedom.

"Christ, I'm glad that's over. I thought I was going to lose my mind from the noise," Kitch remarked as he pulled the caravan up in front of the first vacant motel. "Let's hope the rest of the summer goes better than tonight."

"You know," Brian remarked as he surveyed the misshapen wheel. "My mother is never going to believe it when I tell her how I wore out my first pair of new socks."

The next morning after much discussion they decided they would be more effective if they split up and individually attempted to cover the greatest amount of area and number of businesses in the shortest time in their search for a tube. They left the trailer at the motel and parked the station wagon in a lot near the center of the City. They agreed to meet back there at three o'clock no matter what happened. Cap chose to cover the retail auto stores, where most of the clerks had never heard of a tube that size. His frustration had him back at the truck by noon. Brian took on the various repair shops, where there was a certain level of knowledge of vintage vehicles. At one shop, the owner made a few phone calls but came up empty. Arnold hit the thrift stores. He had no success finding a tube but enjoyed trying out a few guitars and collected a small crowd at one shop to listen to his music. Kitch wandered off saying, "I've got a few ideas I want to try."

By three-thirty all had returned except Kitch, and spirits were low as nobody had any suggestions as to what to do next. No one had found a tube. Having no idea where their companion might have gone, they decided to wait until he showed up. Cap finally decided they would have to call Dusty Sherant and explain their plight. Hopefully, he would have some ideas of what they should do.

They waited as an hour passed, then two, and Kitch was nowhere to be seen. The easy bustle of afternoon shoppers strolling along the main street gave way to the harried crowd of office workers heading home, and still there was no sign of Kitch. By this time they were tired of waiting and decided to go look for him. Suddenly, a police car pulled up beside the station wagon, and two uniformed officers got out and walked over.

"Do any of you people know an Aaron Kitchner?" One of the Mounties asked through the open window.

"We sure do," Cap replied. "We've been waiting here for him most of the afternoon. We were just about ready to go looking for him. Did you pick him up? Is he in some kind of trouble?"

"He's down at the station. I suggest you come down and get him. He is a bit intoxicated, but we haven't charged him and would be glad to turn him over to your custody. He told us his story, and it was so weird we were sure he hadn't made it up. You can follow us down there."

It was a very subdued Kitch that appeared as they walked into the R.C.M.P. station.

"We picked him up outside the Inn of the North this afternoon and brought him down here to sober up. He wasn't causing any trouble but definitely had had too much to drink. He managed to tell us where you were waiting for him and this other strange story about a trailer tire. If you will look after him, he's free to go."

"We'll get him sorted out. Thank you for your help."

It took the better part of an hour before they could piece together any kind of a story. Kitch had tried a few garages and service stations in the morning without any luck. At noon he decided to hit the bars and have a beer with his lunch. He wanted to see if there were any old-timers around who might know someone with a Model T. After countless rounds of beer in a number of taverns, he found a man, whom he was sure was at least a hundred years old who actually owned a Model T, which he still drove in parades. He even had some extra tubes. Kitch was excited with the find, but the problem was that the old man wanted two bottles of whiskey for two tubes, and he was insistent that Kitch help him drink one of the bottles and listen to the story of his life. The old man had been around and told an interesting tale, but it took all afternoon to finish the story and the bottle. The police had picked Kitch up staggering along the street, as he was trying to find his way to the parking lot.

"Oh! I almost forgot," he announced suddenly, reaching inside his jacket. "Here are the tubes."

REUBEN

Reuben Delaveaux considered the last eighteen months one of the most exciting and also the most depressing periods of his life. "I'm getting too old for this crap," he thought. Two years ago he had been sitting in the bar feeling sorry for himself. It was becoming a habit, and he believed it wasn't such a bad habit, the way things were going. Most of the days then, that early in the evening, there was just he and old Skinny Ross slopping down the beer. Skinny was always there. Reuben didn't like the old man and most of the time didn't even acknowledge him as he sat down. He knew that if he even said 'Hello', the old man would start talking at him and wouldn't shut up.

That evening he needed to be alone and try to think things through. He had pulled out an old envelope from his pocket and was trying to balance out the money he would earn from his present job against what he was going to need to survive the rest of the year. At first glance, it didn't look good. While he was turning all this over in his mind, a couple of newcomers sidled up to the bar next to Skinny and started questioning him about favorable areas in which to prospect for gold.

Reuben didn't recognize either of the two men. He half-listened to the conversation, which was mostly a collection of Skinny's stories and ideas, which Reuben had heard many times before. One bit of information, however, did catch his attention. In the course of the evening he learned of a gold showing, which the old man had supposedly found, but he had gotten too sick to go out and explore any further. Reuben noted the Jenny Lake location. Even though he was on this job for Marty Kalloch, he took enough time on his weeklong break to go check out the showing. While he was prospecting south of Jenny Lake, he met the two Quebecois who had been in the bar talking to Skinny and were now staking claims. He tried to strike up a conversation, but they were so secretive about what they were doing, he figured they were probably on to something. However, the next day they were gone, leaving their staking job unfinished. He checked out the area and found nothing, but a couple of days later, he picked up some interesting gold and copper shows from a swamp area nearby. He immediately staked the surrounding ground. He sampled the veins and showed the mineralized rock to his boss, Marty Kalloch, when he got back to camp. Kalloch was interested but said he wouldn't be able to go in and have a look until the following year. Discouraged, Reuben finished the job for Kalloch, gave some of the samples to his son-in-law to shop around with the mining companies in Saskatoon and decided to go visit his brother at the Narrows. He packed his canoe and set out, but he got sick when he was halfway there. He stayed in an old trapper's cabin for three weeks until he felt better, then resumed his journey. He made it through to the Narrows but had to spend the winter with his brother's family until he was totally recovered. When he returned to LaRonge in the spring he learned that a Quebecois, Claude Rioux was looking for him.

Reuben's curiosity led him to meet with Rioux. He thought he recognized the man, but he couldn't place where he had seen him. Rioux wasted no time in making his offer. He had looked at the samples that Reuben had left with Rollie and had a couple of them assayed. He showed Reuben the results. They were interesting but not outstanding. Rioux was not discouraged. He had gone out to the claims, took his own samples from beneath the swamp and the weathered zone and had received more encouraging results from this fresh rock. He was sufficiently impressed to offer Reuben $5,000 for a three month option with the promise of a similar amount for every three month renewal. If the prospect turned into a mine, Reuben would receive a substantial purchase price and a percentage of the profits. He practically fell out of his chair agreeing to the deal. The terms of the agreement were put on paper by a lawyer the next day and signed by the two parties. Although Rioux identified himself as the principal signing the deal, he assured Reuben that he represented a group of Toronto investors who had formed a private company to start exploring and developing the property right away. Reuben couldn't believe his good fortune, but he had witnessed arrangements like this before that had gone sour when exploration results did not fulfill investor expectations. So, he paid off a few outstanding bills and put the rest of the money in the bank. He tried to keep track of Rioux's progress in exploring the claims. It was a challenge, as the man wasn't saying much or supplying written reports as he had promised. No media releases were made, and it was evident they were making a concentrated effort to keep their results and plans a secret. However, Reuben knew a large camp was being built, and a bunch of men had been moved in to the property. Unfortunately, none of the locals were being hired, so Reuben was not able to get progress reports through the grapevine. With the exception of the camp management, which was being catered by an outfit out of Saskatoon, Rioux was bringing all his employees in from Quebec. Reuben was aware of two drills having been flown into the claims and a surprising number of supply flights, both by helicopters and fixed wing aircraft.

After the three-month option period had ended, he received another cheque for $5,000, this time issued by Jenny Lake Mines. Soon after, he learned the Company had been taken public, and a prospectus had been issued to raise further monies to develop the property as a small gold mine. Reuben's mind was put at ease when he received a copy of the document, which painted a glowing report of the property potential. Rioux looked him up a couple of weeks later with a revised offer to purchase a 100% interest in the claims for an additional $10,000 and 50,000 shares of Jenny Lake stock. Reuben was tempted to take the deal on sight but decided to get an opinion from Dusty Sherant. At that point the stock was trading over-the-counter at just above a dollar. When he phoned Sherant in Calgary, he learned that Dusty had been following the progress of the Company. He advised Reuben to take the deal.

"If the plans for the mine go bust, you'll get the claims back, but no one else will touch them unless the price of gold goes up. On the other hand, if it is a mine, you win with the increase in the value of the stock. Either way, you're ahead."

Reuben took the deal and was now glad that he had. The whole operation was a scam. The Company had shown the evidence of producing gold, which was eventually discovered to have been salted in the drill core. The stock had skyrocketed to over three dollars a share, then plummeted to pennies when the fraud was discovered. Unfortunately, Reuben had held on to his shares, anticipating even greater potential profits. In addition he had spent most of the winter months convincing the authorities that he was not part of the crime. Claude Rioux had disappeared and the principals of the Company pleaded no knowledge of any illegal activity. By spring the whole affair was just an unhappy memory. Reuben felt he had to get out of LaRonge and try a new way of life.

However, there was another problem. He couldn't figure out where all the money had gone. He was so sure there was more coming after he read the prospectus that he started spending. A year ago his pockets were full of hundreds and twenties. He had bought himself a car, drove it up from the lot in Prince Albert all alone, even though he had never driven anything like that before. Then he had paid off his daughter's mortgage on her house and lent a few bucks to Rollie, his son-in-law. Even after all that he still had cash to spend on a new canoe and tent. He wasn't worried because he felt that he was set to make a bunch of money on Jenny Lake stock, but before he could put it on the market, the whole thing fell apart. He knew he should have sold it when it went over a buck, but he figured he could squeeze it for a bit more. Even when Dusty had phoned to tell him there were rumors of problems with the Company, he had held on. After all, the reported assay results were favorable, but when the fraud was discovered, this information was totally discredited. The police had initially considered Reuben as part of the illegal activities, and were still not convinced of his innocence after he had told them the whole story. However, they had insufficient evidence to lay a charge.

So, the authorities had abandoned the investigation. Since the Company was dead, and no one else had any interest in the claims, he was able to obtain all the maps and results of the work that Rioux's group had performed, but it was useless, as the reliability of all the information was suspect. When he went through the results, it wasn't that clear to Reuben why they felt the need to salt the core and falsify the results. There was gold in the rock, at least he figured, enough to justify them carrying out a legitimate program.

He could see the potential for a small profitable operation, especially if gold reached the price level the experts were predicting, but greed had been the driving force. Rioux and his partners had obviously made their plans even before they optioned his claims. The stigma of their crooked operations also made it almost impossible for him to interest other groups in the potential of the property. He knew there was little point at that time in shopping the claims around again. Regardless of this, Reuben vowed to hang onto them. The price of gold was slowly rising, and he had convinced himself that someday his property would be worth a fortune.

With his original discovery and the resulting mess, Reuben had declared he would never take on another bush job working for someone else. Especially now that he had reached his seventy-fifth birthday, the whole routine seemed to be getting tougher. However, he could see no other option. He was broke again. He was too embarrassed to ask Kalloch for summer work and was a bit relieved when Marty indicated his crews were already full for the upcoming season. He had suggested Reuben get in touch with Dusty Sherant, who was taking a crew into Northern B.C. Maybe Dusty still had a spot open. Reuben phoned Dusty, who agreed to take him on and forwarded enough money for Reuben to make the trip from Saskatoon to Smithers. Since Reuben had never flown in anything bigger than a Saskatchewan bush plane, he was excited to travel in a large jetliner. This good news was certainly worth celebrating.

According to the schedule, the daily bus for Prince Albert was supposed to leave at four. On most days, it was late and pulled out about five. Today it was early and bumped past the town limits at four-thirty.

Reuben just made it. He'd had everything ready by supper time the night before and was set to go to bed early, but Joe and Manuel had come in with a gallon of wine and then

Arthur showed up with some beer, and Reuben didn't get out of bed the next day until noon. He wasn't worried, as he still had lots of time. By two o'clock he had himself and the cabin thoroughly cleaned. He was just about ready to lock up when he saw Arthur's watch on the floor. "I'd better take it to him before I go," he muttered and went next door to Arthur's. Arthur was still asleep, but Rollie was there with a bottle of rum.

"Just got this offen those fishermen I guided out to the good fishing spots on the lake," he said as he held the bottle out to Reuben. "Come in and have a drink before you go." Certainly, Reuben had time for one drink with his son-in-law.

"That's good rum, Rollie. They must have been American fishermen."

"I thought you were not going to work for that bunch from Calgary any more. How come you're going on this job?" Rollie asked.

"I need the money. This isn't for Kalloch, it's with a crew that Dusty Sherant is putting together to go up into Northern B. C. You worked with him a couple of summers ago. He's a good guy. Besides, I've never been out of Saskatchewan, and I'd kinda like to see what it's like out there on the West Coast."

The bottle was empty at four-ten. Reuben was on the bus at four twenty-five.

MOVING IN

"I was wondering if you fellows were ever going to get here," Dusty remarked as he welcomed the last member of his crew into the hotel room. "I expected you two days ago."

"We had a few problems," Cap replied as he launched into a long-winded description of their journey. "We tried to call you last night, but you weren't in, so we just kept coming."

"I'm glad you made it," Dusty continued after listening patiently to Cap's tale. "I'm sure the four of you know each other well after that trip. These two fellows here and myself round out the party."

Dusty introduced the two other occupants of the room. Curt Shuman and Reuben Delaveaux stiffly acknowledged the introductions.

As Brian and Cap attempted to engage the two in conversation, it soon became apparent that whereas Curt's formality was bred in arrogance, Reuben's was from his limited conversational skills.

"We've got a lot of stuff to go over and plans to make in order to get this show on the road," Dusty continued. " I brought you all together here to meet each other and discuss the program. I want to hear any questions you have as we go along. We leave first thing tomorrow morning for a fishing camp up on Babine Lake, where we load the gear onto a Twin Otter for the next leg of the journey into this little lake up here." Dusty pointed to an unnamed blue patch on the topographic map on the table. "From there, we get ferried to the first campsite by chopper. Most of the camp and supplies are already sitting on the dock at Babine, just waiting for us and the rest of the stuff to get there. We're taking two vehicles tomorrow, Cap's station wagon, without the trailer and my truck, so today you'll have to pick up any last minute stuff you need and then get everything organized and loaded."

"How far is our helicopter move?" Brian asked.

"About fifty miles. We're going into a plateau area over here, just east of the main Skeena Range."

"What about communications?" Cap added. "This looks pretty remote."

"We will have radio hookup on the aviation company channel to their main office and any aircraft in the area. In addition, we'll have our own CB setup with a base station at camp and transceivers for each group in the bush."

Sensing no more questions, Dusty continued. "There will be just the seven of us. I will be running the operation. Since I am taking all the financial risk and responsibility for your welfare, I make the decisions. That is not to say that you don't have a voice in matters that pertain to you, but I must make the final judgment. If there are any complaints or disputes among yourselves, I want them brought to my attention. I want this operation to run as efficiently and smoothly as possible. There are a total of two hundred claims in three separate blocks in our work area. On the plateau, most of the ground will be rolling hills type of relief, but over to the west is a string of mountains that are rugged and rise up steeply. That part is going to be tough slogging. To get good access into the claims, we will have to move camp a couple of times. I flew over the area last weekend and picked the most favorable sites. The program is to prospect the claims and surrounding area, map the geology and run a magnetic survey. We have one known copper show in the first block, and with any luck we'll find some more. I believe you all know what your jobs and responsibilities will be. Cap will be doing the cooking and look after camp. Aaron and Reuben will be surveying in the grids, cutting lines and prospecting. Curt has been contracted to map the geology. Brian and I will be doing most of the prospecting, sampling and detailed mapping of any mineral shows. Arnold will be available to assist and learn some field geology. One thing I must stress. We will be working in groups of at least two at all times. That is wilderness country with very few trails. Anything can happen to a man out alone."

"Who will be running the magnetometer?" Brian asked.

"Reuben will at first. He used this instrument when he worked in Northern Saskatchewan a couple of years ago, but I want you to learn it as soon as possible and take it over."

"Have you selected my assistant?" Curt asked as he continued to write in his notebook.

"Arnold will be working with you," Dusty replied. "I hope you can take some time to teach him your mapping methods and answer his questions."

"As long as it does not interfere with my work," he replied coldly.

Dusty paused, and looked at his senior assistant. He was beginning to get an uneasy feeling about him, but he put it down to nervousness and shook off the concern. As the others were leaving to go to their rooms and settle in for the night, Dusty motioned to Kitch to stay behind.

"I have a good friend in the RCMP that checked you out for me. She strongly recommended that I shouldn't hire you on the basis of your problems over on the Island."

"So, why did you?" The young man asked.

"For a couple of reasons," Dusty replied. "When I heard the whole story I sensed that you were probably provoked into doing what you did, and secondly I figured you needed a chance to get your life back on track."

"I appreciate that," Kitch replied.

"All I ask is that you do your job and stay out of trouble."

The trip the next day into Babine Lake over Forestry and logging roads that were in various states of disrepair after the spring runoff, left a number of the crew members wishing they had eaten a much lighter breakfast. As they pulled in beside the dock, they observed two men busily loading the camp and provisions into the Otter. Working as a group they soon had the rest of the gear, along with the contents of the trucks, stowed in the aircraft with enough room left over for the members of the crew to complete the next leg of the journey in relative comfort.

It was mid-afternoon as the plane began to circle the small lake, checking the wind for the best landing approach. Two helicopters were perched like large shore birds on the gravel beach. The pilot ferried the Otter as close as safely possible, easing one pontoon near enough to make unloading the aircraft a relatively dry operation. The remainder of the afternoon was spent transferring everything by helicopter to the first campsite.

It was the most overwhelming experience Brian could remember, and he was living every moment to the fullest. It was his first flight in a helicopter. Riding in small fixed-wing bush planes like the Beaver and Cessnas the past summer in Northern Alberta, and the Otter trip this afternoon could not compare with the trip in the little Bell. All his senses were totally involved in the flight. The rapidly changing visual images, the steady throb of the rotor and even the smells of the cockpit contributed to the exhilaration of the moment. It was like being suspended over a precipice on a swinging rope, and even though they were flying level, every ridge they crossed felt like the high spot on a roller coaster. At first the jostling of the air currents and pressure pockets was frightening, and every time the aircraft deviated from its level course, Brian was sure they were doomed, but as each succeeding moment proved not to be his last, he began to savor and enjoy every bump, dip and roll. Arnold sat between him and the pilot in the crowded bubble. Glancing at the boy's face, Brian could see that it was white with fear.

Theirs was the final trip. The last big load of supplies and the remaining crewmembers had gone in the Jet Ranger. Brian and Arnold and a few small boxes had meant too much weight, so Lou Roman, their pilot had decided to finish the job in the smaller aircraft. By the time they lifted off, the sun was making its final descent, casting a red glow along the western horizon. In spite of the lateness of the day, when his two passengers had revealed that it was their first time up in a helicopter, Lou had diverted the flight slightly in order to take a more scenic path.

"Look over there on that peak," he shouted over the noise of the engine. The aircraft eased up barely a hundred feet above a craggy ridge. First there was a flash of movement and then half a dozen mountain goats trotted nimbly along a narrow course on the steep rock slope.

"That is probably as close as you'll get to any of those fellows all summer," Lou continued as the helicopter passed over the peak, revealing the sinuous expanse of yet another river valley.

They were traveling northwest. Darkness was beginning to obscure portions of the valley floor, and they still had about half an hour to go to the campsite. Brian began to feel apprehensive about the landing as he remembered some of the stories his classmates had narrated about helicopters setting down in the bush in the middle of nowhere.

"How are you going to land if it gets any darker than this?" He asked Lou, being careful to keep the concern from his voice.

"The boys cleared a pad down by the river," Lou replied, pointing at the map. "I asked them to set flares if it gets too dark. They should be doing that about now. I'm more concerned about getting back to Smithers after I drop you two off. By the looks of the cloud cover I may be bunking at camp tonight."

"Don't you fly at night?" Arnold asked.

"Not unless we really have to and then only if it's clear and there is lots of moonlight. It can get dangerous in this country if you have to go down in the dark."

Brian was sure he had never seen a day pass into night so quickly. Lou had been steadily lowering their cruising altitude so that, by the time they passed over a native village, they were not much more than fifty feet above the treetops. The faint yellow glow from the few cabins in the village was barely enough to silhouette the buildings against the darkening landscape.

"We can always set down here if there is any problem finding the pad at camp. It should be a couple of miles downstream. We can follow the river, and if we get a little higher we should be able to see camp in a few minutes." But there was only darkness.

"See that creek valley running off to the west over there? Isn't the camp supposed to be where that creek joins the river?" Brian pointed to a long depression to the right that was barely visible.

"Must be," Lou replied, swinging the aircraft around. "The camp should be directly ahead of us."

The rotors beat up a hurricane as the helicopter came in low over the bank. They could make out the forms of the white canvas tents on their first pass.

"Where are the lights?" Arnold asked. The smooth ride of the last half hour had almost convinced him that they were going to survive the trip, but now the fear was beginning to well up inside him again.

"I don't know," Lou replied. "Maybe they weren't quite ready for us, although we sure made enough noise getting here. I'll circle a couple of times to give them a chance to light up the landing pad."

"Look, I see a light," Arnold interrupted. "And there's another one over there, but they aren't fires. They look like flashlights."

"Somebody is flashing those lights across the landing area," Lou remarked, peering down to his left. "It looks like two flashlights is all they have, and those are spotted on either side of the pad about halfway along."

Lou Roman eased the helicopter down to treetop level right over the lights. Brian could just make out the forms of two men standing in the clearing with their lights shining weakly on the pad.

"Here we go," Lou exclaimed as he dropped the machine into the forest and settled it gently to earth.

"Sorry about the poor signals," Dusty said as they gathered in the cooktent. "We haven't got a match or lighter in camp. They are all in that last food box you just brought in."

DAY ONE

The first pink glow of sunrise was creeping over the edge of the eastern plateau when Cap bellowed out his wake-up call. Daylight revealed a massive disarray of tents and supplies spread around the camp area. Most of it was hidden under tarps for protection from rain or dew, but it had been too dark the previous night to attempt any organization, and the work of loading and unloading all day had discouraged any enthusiasm to do much except find a comfortable place to sleep. Cap had insisted that the cooktent and most of its supplies come in on the first load, and he had continually badgered the crew between flights to arrange his workplace. He had taken most of the afternoon to set up the stoves, build shelves and generally organize his empire for the maximum of efficiency. Consequently, he was probably the only one at that hour ready to face the day.

Dusty's tent, a combined office and sleeping quarters had been hung on the ridgepole, but the frame was yet to be built and staked down. The rest had pulled out their sleeping bags and spent the night under the stars. As they staggered into the early morning light and became aware of their new surroundings, the reality of their temporary new life hit them. This morning breakfast was a significant event. Cap had risen early and now presented a table laden with hotcakes, bacon, eggs and steaming cups of coffee, which the crewmembers attacked voraciously. Lou Roman had decided to wait for morning light to return to Smithers. As he rose from the table, he thanked Cap for the meal and remarked. "I guess I'll have to leave you fellows to your fun and games. I'm sure you know how much it saddens me not to be able to stay and help you put all this into some kind of livable shape. I should be back in about a week to see how you made out. Good luck."

The crew watched with mixed emotions, as he got into the helicopter and maneuvered it up over the trees and off into the horizon.

"The first thing we do this morning is get the radio working," Dusty announced, "then we need to get the rest of the tents up. Brian, you and Kitch help Reuben with the radio. The antenna is cut to the right length. Run it up as high as you can. The best way is to pick two tall trees the right distance apart and lined up in the correct direction. Cut two other trees for poles, skin the branches off, put insulators on the ends of the antenna and then tie the insulators to the tops of the poles. After that, rig up some sort of pulley system to get the poles upright and tied to the trees. Reuben has set these up before, so he will show you how it's done."

"I set this kind up over on the Island a couple of years ago," Kitch announced. "They are great if the weather is good, and there is not too many big mountains in the way, and your battery doesn't go dead and you don't have too many other camps using the same frequency. This system is not exactly state of the art for bush communications. There are types you can rent, which are much more powerful, hassle-free and don't need this kind of antenna. It looks like we're low-balling it again."

"That's true," Dusty replied with some annoyance, "but this one works fine and will do until the new one I've ordered comes in. It's bigger and more powerful. Just make sure you don't break a leg or cut your foot off until the antenna is up. Arnold, I would like you to help Cap build some more shelves and worktables. Curt and I will be gone for most of the day checking out the rocks."

The early morning promise of a sunny day had turned into a scorcher by mid-afternoon. Not a cloud in the sky, no breeze and the sun directly overhead made any kind of meaningful effort almost impossible. Erecting the antenna had taken all morning. Unfortunately, the space between two perfect trees, lined up in the right direction, lay across a small swamp, dotted with humps of marsh grass, each of which exploded into a cloud of mosquitoes when stepped on. It was a tired, hot itchy trio that sat down for lunch at the noon meal call.

"Is the radio all set to go," Cap asked as they straggled in.

"You can try it out," Kitch answered, "but I doubt if you can convince anyone to change that antenna if you can't connect."

Fortunately, the radio worked.

When Cap had finished his chores, he wandered over to watch Brian and Kitch put up the last tent.

"I heard you say you were working over on Vancouver Island a couple of years ago."

"That's right," Kitch replied.

"I was over there around that time, cooking for a camp up near Port Hardy. Were you in that part of the country?"

"Yeah. That's where I was. We had a camp over west of Port McNeil."

"Did you hear about that fellow from a mining camp that got sent to jail for stabbing a man in a barroom fight in Port Hardy that summer?"

"I was wondering when you were going to ask about that. It was me. I just got out a few weeks ago. Sherant knows all about it. You knew it before you asked me, didn't you?"
"I did. I recognized you from your picture that was in the papers then. I didn't mean to get nosy about your business, but it just had me wondering."
After Cap had shuffled off, Brian turned to Kitch and asked, "What happened? Did you really stab some guy?"
"Yeah. It was dumb, but at the time it seemed like the only thing I could do. I was in a bar by myself up in Port Hardy, while I was waiting for some of the other fellows to drive back to camp. There were these three loggers sitting over at the next table. I guess they had been there all afternoon, and they were pretty well hammered up. Anyway, like I'm sitting there with my feet up on an empty chair reading the paper and minding my own business, when one of these guys yells at me to bring the chair over to him so he can put his feet up. I just ignored him, so he yells it again, telling me what he's going to do to me if I don't bring him the chair. I still didn't pay any attention to him, so he staggers over, shoves my feet off the chair and starts pushing me around. I took it for about fifteen seconds, then I kicked him about as hard as I could in the belly, and he folded up, puking all over the floor. That's when his buddies came after me. I backed up, tripped over that damn chair that started it all and ended up against the wall with both of them closing in. I got my knife out just as one guy was grabbing at me. I started striking out with it, but he wouldn't back off. I guess I cut his arms and face up pretty bad. I got the hell out of there fast, but the cops came out and picked me up at camp. Even then I could have gotten off. The cops had had trouble with those fellows tearing up the place every time they came to town, but when they searched me they found some hash. They figured I'd bought it from somebody up there, so they kept pumping me for my source. They told me that they would drop the charges

if I would tell who sold me the stuff. I wouldn't play the game, so it was the loggers word against mine, and I drew eighteen months."
"Did they charge you with possession too?"
"No, they let that one go by."
Kitch and Brian wandered around the campsite trying to find a cool spot to relax.
"This is just too hot," Brian remarked. "There's got to be a spot on this creek where the water is deep enough to get in and cool down."
"Let's go find it," Kitch agreed.
They walked upstream toward the village in search of a likely spot. A few hundred yards from camp the stream took a sharp bend to the west forming a deep pool that showed signs of recent human activity. On the far side, opposite from the path, the ground sloped gradually up from the water forming a grassy beach. At the upper end the water cascaded down over a series of ripples. A flat, extended rock outcrop bordered the near shore with old campfire stones grouped in a ring. The pool was wide and looked deep. Brian could see the bottom, but when he dropped a stone in, it took much longer than expected to make its journey
Kitch bent over, tested the water and remarked, "It's cold, but at this point I don't give a damn."
Quickly, he stripped down and dove in.
"Come on," he hollered from the far side. "It's not bad over here out of the current."
As Brian began to peel off his shirt, a native woman came up the path from the direction of the village. She stood for a minute by the edge of the pool, then walked over and sat down on the rock next to Brian. She was tall and full-bodied with straight black hair. Brian estimated her age anywhere from fifteen to thirty. She was not pretty or cute, but she was attractive in her own way. Her mottled skin and coarse but perfectly proportioned features merged into a

unique form of beauty.

"I'm Della. You must be the miners from that new camp. We heard you come in yesterday."

Brian introduced himself and Kitch, who was watching the interplay from the creek.

"Are you going swimming?"

"I was thinking about it."

"Well, I am, " she replied as she pulled her simple cotton dress off over her head. With no other garments to shed, she dove into the water and swam with strong strokes over to where Kitch was treading water. They were facing each other until Della started splashing him and they began chasing each other in the deep end of the pool. Kitch could hardly keep up with her. Back and forth they chased each other, alternately diving and upsetting the other as they surfaced. This went on for about ten minutes until they came to the surface with their bodies tightly entwined. They kissed. Then they walked slowly to the grassy bank on the far shore and continued the embrace with increasing passion. Brian discreetly walked back to camp.

The first hint of dusk was on the horizon when Dusty and Curt returned. By then the camp had taken on a look of permanence with the tents up in a line facing the creek and all the gear unpacked and put away.

"How does it look, boss?" Brian asked as they settled in for the evening meal.

"Great," Dusty replied. "You fellows did a good job."

"My tent will have to be moved farther back into the trees," Curt announced.

"Why is that?" Dusty asked as he turned to his assistant.

"It is much too close to the other tents. I am sure there will be too much noise when I am trying to work."

"I suggest we try this arrangement out for a few days to see if there will be a problem," countered Dusty.

"No. It is totally unacceptable. The tent will have to be moved."

"Isn't that just too bad," Kitch spoke up. "Maybe there's just enough light left for you to get off your ass and go out and move it yourself." He spit out the words.

"I believe that kind of manual labor is a little more in your line," Curt replied.

"That's enough," Dusty broke in. "We'll settle this later." The men returned to their plates, but the friendly spirit of a few minutes before was gone, and the meal was finished in silence.

Later in the evening Kitch announced his presence at Dusty's tent.

"How come Brian and old Reuben had to move Shuman's tent? Why the hell couldn't he have done it himself? We put the damn thing up with absolutely no help from him." Kitch's anger was barely below the surface.

"Look," Dusty replied. "I don't blame you for being upset about what happened, but you are going to have to understand one thing. Curt Shuman is probably one of the best-qualified men in Canada to do the job that he has been hired to do here. In order to get him to agree to take on this project, I had to give him a contract that excuses him from a lot of the everyday jobs around camp and in the bush. It makes it tough to run a good camp when every one doesn't do their share of the chores, and I know you are not going to like the arrangement, but you're going to have to accept it and try not to get anything going with him like tonight. I can replace you a lot faster than I can find someone to do his job. Reuben and Cap understand the deal and have agreed to take on some of the extra chores. I would appreciate it if you could look at it the same way and stay clear of Curt. Try not to bait him into a fight."

"Well, I guess that's plain enough," Kitch replied. "It might help the situation if he wasn't such an arrogant bastard, but I guess we're not going to change that."

"Just try and be cool about it," Dusty continued. "Think of it this way. If you can learn to put up with Curt's ways and take some of his crap, maybe you won't find it so hard to stay out of fights after the summer is over."

"That's a pretty tough request," the young man replied.

BREAKING IN

The next two weeks were a nightmare of pain for Arnold. Never before had he been forced to get up so early in the morning, work so hard all day and fall willingly into bed each night after dinner. All his plans for practicing his guitar each evening and writing some new music had quickly evaporated. The instrument was still in its case, as it had been since he arrived in camp. He looked at it longingly, but he was just too tired to pick it up. A couple of nights he missed the evening meal entirely, falling onto his cot as soon as he got back to camp and sleeping right through the night. Curt had made no attempt to consider his partner's initial lack of physical conditioning in carrying out the day's work and was totally unconcerned about his welfare. Not only was Arnold responsible for carrying the heavy pack, which was usually loaded with rocks, but he was also expected to keep pace with a man who had maintained his physical condition by a winter of skiing and mountain climbing. Curt took considerable pride in his physical strength and stamina and kept a constant check that his body could perform to his expectations. He allowed himself and his partner no periods of rest during the day. Even their time for lunch was cut short by his incessant drive to forge ahead. After the ninth straight day of this routine, Arnold asked Dusty to send him home. Despite any resolve to stick it out, he had reached the end of the line. Every muscle and joint in his body ached. Every action he attempted was painful. Things like sitting down or tying a shoelace required a concentrated effort to make the muscles work in the required way. Even a simple act like bending over to pick up something necessitated a certain amount of thought as to whether the object to be retrieved was worth the pain. Dusty was well aware of the young man's discomfort and had explained to him that they were all feeling the same thing to some degree and that the soreness would soon pass once his body was accustomed to the drastic change in lifestyle. The words provided little consolation. Arnold firmly believed he would suffer in this manner all summer or until he was safely away from this place. Realizing the futility of his assurances, Dusty, with regret, finally agreed to fly him out on the next supply trip in a week, if he still wanted to go at that time.

Arnold 's spirits improved with the prospect of going home, although his days in the field with Curt continued to be a series of frustrations. Curt totally ignored him and his attempts at conversation. Arnold found that in spite of his physical discomfort, he was interested in the work, but his questions were greeted with silence and a look of disdain. From time to time he was able to read the jottings in Curt's notebook, until Curt noticed his actions and proceeded to keep the notebook to himself. He had no intention of sharing any of his knowledge or observations.

One day he asked Curt as they were preparing to sit and eat their lunches, "Why do you dislike me? Did I do something to make you angry? I have tried to follow your instructions and do my job."

Curt looked at the younger man for a minute then replied, "I'm not out here to make friends. You just continue to do your job and don't annoy me with your stupid questions." At least now it was clear to Arnold that the relationship was not going to change, strengthening his desire to be away from this man as soon as possible.

Curt enjoyed the daily expeditions and dreaded the evenings when he was forced into the company of the others. He would have preferred to conduct his mapping alone and having this kid tag along was becoming increasingly more irritating. Most of all, he resented Dusty and his position of authority. He avoided his employer as much as possible. Professionally, he was obliged to report each day's findings, but it irked him that he was forced to do this for someone whom he felt was inferior. As for Arnold, he felt he could tolerate this annoyance as long as the kid carried the gear, kept his mouth shut and stayed out of the way.

The others reacted in various ways to Curt's arrogance and antagonistic manner.

Dusty attempted to reason with the young man and pull him into scientific and technical discussions, which he felt would make Curt feel more a part of the group. He respected the young man's abilities and had no complaints about the quality of his work. His efforts to make his assistant feel more comfortable were continually unsuccessful, and the young man's total lack of respect for him came through loud and clear, so Dusty gave up and just let him do his job. At least, the quality of his efforts was above reproach. Cap tolerated him. He had inquired as to his food preferences but received no answer. Reuben had no contact with him. Kitch found great difficulty in accepting Curt's attitude and, although he was able to contain his temper, he couldn't resist trying to goad Curt into losing his. This had no effect and Curt continued to ignore him. Only Brian could be said to have any positive feelings for Curt, but this was more a result of his natural tolerance for everyone, rather than any positive responses from Curt. He made an effort to try and find and focus on favorable aspects of Curt's personality, and although he was treated with the same disregard as the others, he could accept it without concern.

Initially, Brian accompanied Dusty as his assistant on his field traverses and prospecting ventures. Dusty was surprised at the younger man's level of knowledge and the speed with which he could absorb new information. He found it a pleasure to work with someone with such a keen mind and pleasant disposition. He was such a contrast to Curt that Dusty began to regret hiring his senior assistant. Brian had mastered the magnetometer in a couple of hours and could run the instrument and interpret the results with the speed and precision of an experienced operator. His interest was sustained through all aspects of the field exploration, and Dusty often found his questions so penetrating as to force him to examine his own motives and methods of performing some of the work.

The crew had now worked twelve days with only a one-day break since setting up camp. As the weather held, and no rain was forecast, Dusty had been loath to waste a single day. But, he could sense the morale among his workers starting to slip, so there were no unhappy faces around the dinner table that night when he announced they were taking the next day off to rest. They had finished their workload early, and it was barely twilight when Brian and Kitch, attired in clean clothes, came over to Dusty 's tent.

" Since you so generously gave us the day off tomorrow, Kitch and I thought we would walk over to the village tonight. We met one of the girls from there, and she invited us to come visit. Would you like to come along?"

"Sure, that's a great idea," Dusty replied. "I'll join you. I have been meaning to go over there and talk to some of the folks to see if they know of any mineral shows around here or any other groups that have been in this area prospecting or gold-mining. I'm aware of one company that was working somewhere in this area with a small gold dredge a few years ago, but I couldn't find out much about it with my research back in Vancouver before we left. I was hoping some of the older folks in the village would remember that operation and give me some idea what creeks they were working."

The trail to the village ran back and forth in a general easterly direction along the bank of the small tributary creek that flowed by the camp until it joined the main stream a few hundred yards away. Another half mile took them to the bend in the main creek and the swimming hole. The first stretch of trail showed little evidence of regular use, and at a number of points the path disappeared entirely in a massive tangle of alder. This eventually thinned out and opened into a clear stretch, where Brian stopped suddenly and pointed toward an indentation along the side of the trail.

"What would make a track like that?"

He pointed to the outlines of a large paw or footprint in the mud. It was old, and water erosion had left little more than a featureless depression outlined in the surface, but the evidence that it was made by some large creature was clear.

"It's was probably made by a bear, but the print is too old to be sure," Dusty observed.

"If it was done by a bear, wouldn't you be able to see the impression of the claws?"

Dusty got down on his knees to examine the print more closely.

"You would think so, but there's no claw marks that I can see. They've probably been washed away."

"Or maybe the natives around here have big feet," Kitch said. "We know there are bears all over this country. I expect we have a substantial population of grizzlies. That's got to be what it is."

Beyond the point where they found the footprint, there was a wide open clearing and the trail got progressively easier to follow until they reached the pool where the boys had met Della.

"I think this may turn out to be Kitch's favorite spot. I'm sure it's a place he will remember. I know I certainly will," Brian said.

From the pool, the main trail running north was wide and well marked and showed evidence of regular use. It closely skirted the banks of the stream and appeared to have been washed away in places during periods of high water. The water in the creek ran clear and swift along the banks, Every few yards the trail passed by an old campsite or the remains of a blackened circle of stones from an old cooking fire. The profusion of second growth and tangled vegetation was now replaced by an open parkland setting of mature spruce and pine.

The setting sun had abandoned them before they reached the outskirts of the native village.

"We're going to have to clear out that first section of trail if we plan to come this way very often, especially if we plan to walk it in the dark. There's a good day of work getting rid of enough of that brush," Kitch commented.

"That was a bit rough," Dusty replied, "but there's no point in spending much effort in clearing it. We won't be at our present site long enough. I plan on moving camp in about a month if the good weather holds, and we can finish with the present block of claims."

"Where will we be going next?" Brian asked. "Will it be that tough area you were talking about along the high range to the west?"

"No, I'm going to leave that block to the last, when everyone has been toughened up enough to deal with all the climbing on those slippery slopes. The next camp is a couple of miles south of here on this main stream. It's a more open area and relatively flat with lots of rock outcrop.

It should be an interesting area to work. On the basis of what I could see from the air coming in and the old air photos I managed to assemble, the trail going south looks to be clear and open all the way to the next site."

THE VILLAGE

The village was larger than Brian had pictured it from the helicopter. He had expected only a handful of cabins gathered around the clearing but found there were more than a dozen others spread out along the banks of the creek. The moon, almost full, lit up the southern sky and scattered the night shadows of the buildings along the main street. The ground was baked and hard with years of constant use but gave up a small cloud of dust to announce their arrival. Most of the cabins were old. Originally solid structures of unpeeled logs, the effects of age and gravity had taken their toll in sagging roofs and bowed walls. Two of the newer buildings, of plywood construction, seemed out of place against this almost primitive backdrop. A number of the cabins showed a faint yellow light seeping out from the small windows, around the doors and between logs where the chinking had washed out. Half a dozen dogs set up a chorus at their approach and came to sniff their strangeness. The only signs of human activity were two small boys playing at the far end of the clearing. As the strangers came near they stopped their game and quickly ran for refuge into the nearest cabin.

"Looks like we scared them off," Brian remarked. "Do we have any idea in particular where we are going?"

"Della said that her cabin was the largest in the village, the only one with two stories," Kitch replied.

"That shouldn't be hard to find. Lou told me the chief here is an old man called Sam Jonas," Dusty said, "that he is the one to talk to. He's over eighty and has lived here all his life."

"Yeah, that's right. I forgot that. Della also told me that her grandfather was the chief," Kitch added.

"It makes sense that the chief would have the biggest house. Let's try that one over there", Brian suggested, pointing to the only two-story structure in view, where light was escaping through a half-open door.

A heavy middle-aged woman, who showed no apparent surprise at their presence, answered their knock.

"We're looking for Sam Jonas. Is this where he lives?"

The woman stepped back and motioned them into the flickering warmth. The room was large, the full size of the building. A huge stone fireplace took up half of one wall, and its crackling fire provided all the heat and most of the light for the room. Brian observed that the stones were held together with no cement or mortar, but had been carefully chipped and shaped to fit perfectly together. Along the opposite wall ran a staircase of hewn planks leading through a gap in the ceiling to an upper loft.

Most of the floor was covered with skins, many of which had the hair worn off. Throughout the room objects for cooking, hunting, trapping and fishing hung from the walls and ceiling. A large table occupied the center of the room. It was rough constructed of planks and was a contrast to the chairs, which were obviously of a long-past factory vintage. A sputtering oil lamp at one end of the table rationed its light on an old man who took no obvious notice of the visitors. He stared ahead at the fire. The woman motioned them to sit down at the table, and it was only then that the old man spoke.

"You are from the new camp by the creek."

"That's right," Dusty replied.

The old man's face was deeply wrinkled and tanned like well-folded leather. As he spoke, the lines punctuated the mood of his words, here stretching out a smile, and there transforming sadness into grief.

"I was expecting you tonight," the old man continued. "My son's wife has prepared food in the belief you would come early, but I knew it would be now, for men talk more easily when the sun has gone down."

Sam Jonas stuffed tobacco in his pipe as the woman filled their cups with strong black tea. In the flare of the match Brian took closer notice of the man. The thin lips and half-closed eye slits blended with the other creases to become almost indistinguishable. But, as the old man turned his head toward him, Brian found himself gazing into ageless, clear blue depths. Somewhere in the distance a voice was asking if the tea was to his liking. He answered with a nod as the old man drew his mesmerizing gaze away.

"None of our crew has worked in this part of the country before. It is beautiful in the early summer." Dusty spoke slowly, and Brian could sense his nervousness as he picked his words carefully.

"This is a good time of the year after the cold winter," the old man replied. "The land is waking up. I hope it welcomes you."

"We are hoping it will give up some of its secrets. We have come to look for minerals." Dusty began to feel more at ease as he continued. "We would like to hear anything your people can tell us about the rocks and where others have looked for these minerals."

"Very few men come here from the outside any more," the old man answered. "When the first snows come there are sometimes hunters who stay a few days to shoot a moose, but men do not come to look for gold as often as they did when I was a young man."

"Did they find much gold?" Brian asked.

"We all found gold. Everyone from the village would move up to the creeks as soon as the water went down, and in a few weeks we would find enough gold to buy our supplies to last us all year. When people outside found out about our gold they rushed in and staked up all the creeks and brought in machinery to work the gravels. Soon most of the gold was gone and the outsiders went home. Some of the young men still go up to the creeks, but they can make more money fighting fires or working for the logging companies."

"Then I guess you don't like seeing us come in here looking for a mine," Kitch countered.

"No, that is different," Old Sam replied. "Maybe what you are doing will someday mean jobs for people from our village."

"We would like to be successful and make that happen," Dusty added.

"Last fall there were some men in here for about a week near where your camp is set, and south of here, but they never came to the village. My son tells me they were staking claims."

"That would be the group that laid out the claims we will be exploring."

As Dusty started to describe their work to the old man, the crying of a baby from above and the activity of someone trying to quiet the child interrupted him. All of this materialized as Della came running down the stairs with the wailing infant under her arm. She stopped abruptly, as she became aware of the visitors seated around the table. She smiled at Kitch and Brian and looked uncertainly to Old Sam. He motioned her to come down and introduced her as Della, his granddaughter. Her open smile was immediate.

"Yes, I believe we've met." Kitch replied with his own inviting smile as he stood and took her hand. He hadn't realized she was so tall, towering over him by half a head. What he did remember, were the well-formed curves of her body that were not disguised by the simple loose-fitted cotton shift she wore. Silhouetted by the dim background light, she was beautiful. She held Kitch's hand a few extra seconds before letting go.

Brian could see the concern forming in Old Sam's face as he observed the interplay between his granddaughter and the young visitor.

As Old Sam began to tell of the village and his people, Della diverted her attention to dressing the child warmly for a walk outside. The old man's words echoed stories Dusty had heard all over the North. He told of how the steady advance of the white man's activities had changed their lives, mostly in a negative way. At first the influence of the missionaries and the traders, then the governments had eaten away at his heritage, while the loggers, miners and developers had ravaged the land. And again, Dusty felt guilt for the actions of his race. To Brian, however, the stories were new, a far cry from what he had read in his history and geography texts. And now, the old man added with sadness, his people must depend on those who had destroyed their way of life.

By the time he had finished his tale the evening had slipped into a moonless night. The woman had banked up the fire as a subtle hint to the visitors that the old man was tiring.

"We must go," Dusty announced, pushing his chair back from the table. "We have enjoyed this evening and would like you to know that you are welcome at our camp."

The old man nodded but did not get up.

"Brian, we had better find Kitch and head back to camp. He went out about an hour ago with Della."

It was the first Brian had noticed that his companion was missing.

The chill night air clutched at their lungs as they stepped from the soft warmth of the cabin. The village was silent. The moon was well hidden behind the clouds, and there was not enough light to even define the outlines of the buildings. Brian looked at his watch.

"Only eleven thirty," he thought. "They sure lock things up early."

He walked the length of the village calling Kitch's name softly into the night air, with no reply except the occasional call of a bird. Then he became aware of Dusty's footsteps approaching from the other end of the street.

"I think we had better head back," Dusty called. "I don't even know where to start looking. He will have to make his own way to camp. Since we are taking a break tomorrow, he has the whole day to find the trail. Unfortunately, we have a problem. Kitch is carrying our flashlight."

Kitch made it to breakfast call the next morning with less than an hour's sleep. The following morning it was the same. Each evening he went to the village to see Della, returning in the morning just before dawn. Once Brian went with him to talk with Old Sam but had to make his own way back to camp.

As the week wore on, Kitch got more and more irritable. The workload was increasing, and Reuben's patience was wearing thin as he found he was doing more than his share of the work. Kitch was just going through the motions but was so tired most of the time that he couldn't keep up with the pace of the older man. Reuben wouldn't complain, and it was only in answer to some pointed questions by Dusty that he revealed his displeasure.

"I don't mind more work," the old man replied, "I'm getting tired of finding him leaned up against a tree asleep every time I stop moving."

It was finally Brian's suggestion to Kitch that he should stay in camp one night and get some rest that lit the fuse. Kitch leaped from the bench, grabbing Brian by the shirt and pushed him back against the plywood half wall of the cooktent.

"Since when is it any of your goddamn business how I spend my time," he said threateningly.

"It was just a suggestion," Brian replied calmly. "I'm concerned about what you do to yourself and to the morale of the rest of us."

Kitch was bewildered by the relaxed reply, and his anger subsided as quickly as it had flared.

"Yeah, I guess I have been kinda jumpy. Maybe you're right. I sure am beat. That girl can wear you out real fast." After Kitch had left the tent Dusty sat down by Brian. "Thanks for solving the problem for me. I was set to have it out with him tonight, and tell him to either shape up or get out. I'm sure he wouldn't have taken the suggestion from me. I think you got through to him."

"Dusty, I think he is a good guy under all that hostility. I'm just trying to be his friend and maybe help him get things in a little better perspective. He has had a tough run just getting out of jail and then having his wife leave him. I'm sure the whole mess was probably his fault, and I think he probably knows it, but that doesn't make it go down any easier. I feel he's having a lot of trouble accepting whom he has been and what he has done. I'm willing to put up with a lot more from Kitch than from some guy like Curt, who just enjoys being miserable to people."

LISA

The arrival of June with its longer days warmed the earth. The bush was alive with creatures in search of the increasing food supply. On the slopes, pine and spruce sucked their nutrients from the earth, churning out growth in millions of tiny factories. Along the valleys the alder and willow competed for the favored spots in the sun. Upland birds were everywhere. Each breeze carried the drumming courtship of the grouse. Until he saw one of the birds beating out its call, Arnold was sure the noise was the result of a dozen chain saws that wouldn't start. Moose mothers paraded their wobbly offspring through the marshes, while the young coyotes and wolves began their serious education as hunters.

The season warmed the men's spirits as it did their bodies. Personal habits that had become irksome during the first three weeks somehow did not seem so important. The soft muscles of winter were becoming firm and the temptation to drop exhausted into bed after a day's work was becoming less. Even Arnold was beginning to feel like he might last the summer.

With the snow melting in the high country, the creeks
began to swell. The winter had been long and cold, but the
snowfall had been light. At lower altitudes only small
crusty pockets remained in the sheltered areas, while to the
west the snow line was receding rapidly up the slopes in the
direct sun.

So far, the creeks were still clear and the annual spawning
rituals were in full swing. Rainbows and grayling surged up
to lay their eggs in the graveled headwaters. The first
evening Brian and Cap had pursued the reluctant trout with
fly rods for over a mile upstream but had managed only to
lure a couple of small specimens into their creel.

"I guess the fish have too much on their minds to think
about eating," Cap retorted.

"It looks that way," Brian replied. "I think I'll try
downstream past camp for a while. There are still a couple
of hours of daylight left."

"You go ahead. I've got some cleaning to do in the
cooktent."

Flowing east from the campsite, the course of the creek
meandered across the wide quartzite platforms that formed
a series of grassy meadows. Occasionally the stream cut
down into less resistant limestone zones forming a number
of small cascading waterfalls, which ended abruptly in deep
pools of churning water.

Brian worked these pools methodically, laying the fly
precisely at the base of the falls and letting it rush out into
the turbulence of the pool.

"This is where the big ones should be," he thought.

It was difficult to see if fish were rising for the fly, but a
couple of good solid tugs suggested that he was getting
some action.

The biggest pool formed a bend in the stream just before it
emptied into the main creek. Here, the water was clear and
running fast. The deepest part of the pool closest to the

bank was shaded by clumps of bushes growing out over the water. Brian waded out onto a small gravel shoal on the opposite side and flicked his lure upstream into the center of the current. Almost at once, line tore from the reel. The rod bent close to the breaking point as the line pulled tight. Frantically he tried to loosen the tension as he ran along the shore dodging bushes and potholes and yet keeping the straining line clear of obstacles. As abruptly as it had unwound, the line went slack. Thinking his prey had tossed the hook, Brian began slowly reeling in whatever was left. Bang! Away it went again. The line screamed off the reel. He charged after it, this time fearing all his line would be stripped off before he had a chance to slow the fish down. At a small bend he dodged around a bush and stepped off the bank into ten feet of icy water. In panic he dropped his rod and took one desperate grab at the bush before the current pulled him out of reach and carried him downstream. Out of control he bobbed up and down in the fast-running water, wildly lunging for anything that came within his reach.

"Grab this branch," a voice called from just ahead of him. Brian went under, came up and turned his head to catch a glimpse of yellow before the current dragged him under again. As he resurfaced, the butt end of a branch hit him across the chest. Wildly, he wrapped his arms around it and held on. A girl held the other end as she sat with her feet braced firmly against a large rock, but the sudden force of the current dragging Brian was too strong, and she was jerked over the edge of the bank into the water.

Fifty yards downstream the rushing water willingly gave up its passengers and deposited them on a gravel bar. The young man and girl lay gasping on the bank, trying to recover from the shock of the icy water.

"That was a crazy thing to do, hanging on to that branch when it was pulling you into the water," Brian said, turning to the girl who was now shivering visibly. The thin dress clung to her slim body, outlining the full round contours of her breasts and hips.

The rest of Brian's speech was lost as he became aware of her beauty.

"I guess it was a bit foolish, but it seemed to make sense at the time," she smiled a reply. "I really thought I could pull you out. I'm sorry you lost your fish."

"It doesn't matter. I must have put on quite a show chasing down the creek after it. Were you watching?"

"Uh huh. I was sitting on the bank up there when I heard you crashing through the bush. I thought it was a moose by all the noise you were making."

"You are going to get sick if you don't get dry soon," Brian said as he took off his jacket and began wringing the water out of it. "Put this on. It might help some until you get home. Are you from the village?"

"Yes. I'm Lisa. You and your friends have been visitors in my father's house. Sam Jonas is my grandfather. Della is my sister."

Brian wondered why he had not seen her on his visits to Old Sam.

Sensing his curiosity, Lisa continued. "I have been away to school all winter and just got home yesterday. Last night I met your friend that has been visiting Della. He told me about you and your camp."

They walked along the bank for a short way looking for Brian's fishing rod but without success. By the time they reached the mouth of the creek the sun had sunk below the horizon,]099 and the chill of the night air had set in.

"It is getting dark and I have just enough time to get home while there is some light. Thank you for the use of your coat," she said as she began to slip it off.

"Please wear it home," he replied. "Then it will give me an excuse to come and visit you, if that's okay."

Brian had trouble keeping his mind on his work the next day. At least a dozen times he took magnetometer readings and forgot to write them in his notebook, forcing him to retrace his steps and do it all over again. He concentrated on concentrating, but Lisa kept edging her way into his thoughts. By noon he had decided to go to the village that night, then he wondered if it was too soon or if she even wanted to see him at all. All afternoon he continued to make firm decisions on a course of action and then change them five minutes later. However, at the evening meal, he was the first at the table with clean clothes and a freshly shaved face, a marked contrast to the rest of the dirt-stained crew.

"You look pretty fancy for going fishing tonight," Cap observed as Brian entered the cooktent. "You think maybe the fish might appreciate it and jump on the hook?"

"Well, uh, Cap, I'm, uh, not going fishing tonight."

"I expect maybe you'll be coming into the village with me," observed Kitch. "Della told me how you two fished each other out of the creek last night."

"It was something like that," replied Brian.

Halfway through the meal it started to rain. The clouds that had been slowly building up throughout the afternoon now formed a leaden blanket stretching across the sky. It started as a heavy mist sneaking across the countryside and then, with the cool evening air, turned into a steady drizzle. By the end of the meal a west wind had sprung up, sweeping down from the snowfields and pelting raindrops into anything that stood in its way.

"Doesn't look much like it's going to let up for a while," Kitch observed as he poked his head outside the tent. "If it does, I'll give you a holler. Who knows, we might make it there yet."

Brian returned discouraged to his tent and stretched out on the bunk. He tried to continue reading a book that had fascinated him two nights before, but tonight it held no interest. Every few minutes he made the trip to the tent door to look for any signs of improvement in the weather.

Arnold, who was relaxing in the other bunk, took no notice of his activities for a while. Then he became suspicious and listened for any strange sounds from outside every time Brian went to the doorway.

"What do you hear?" He asked

"Oh, nothing," Brian mumbled, "just checking the weather."

But Arnold was unconvinced and had difficulty shutting the imagined noises from his head long enough to get some sleep.

Cap's breakfast gong blasted Brian from an enchanted land full of young, scantily dressed, dark-skinned girls, gliding along on ice floes in a stream, just out of reach. As he finally was able to reach out and rescue one of these beauties, he was jerked back into reality. He had slept in his clothes on top of the sleeping bag and could barely keep from shaking from the early morning cold. The rain had stopped during the night, and the sun was trying to break a path through the remnants of the cloudbank on the horizon.

"We'll stay out of the bush until after lunch," Dusty announced at breakfast. "It was well soaked last night and will take a while to dry out this morning. We got a bit of a jump on the schedule last week so it won't hurt to slack off a bit today."

Brian went to the village that evening. Lisa was expecting him. They walked along the creek trail and talked, sharing their worlds and slowly absorbing parts of each other's life. Later they sat with Old Sam and listened to his stories. When the forgetfulness of the years repeated a tale, it didn't matter. Lisa had heard them many times, but this night they meant more because they were new to Brian.

She urged Brian to talk of his life in the city, but all the things that had been important to him there, did not seem to matter as much now. He hurried through the telling so that he could return to their world of the present. He had never felt so comfortable with a young woman. He was tempted to unload his problems about Stephanie and the supposed upcoming marriage, but his better judgment told him that such a confession would probably destroy this fragile relationship. He had not thought about Stephanie since Calgary and now, meeting Lisa, put her entirely out of his mind. He knew he would have to resolve the situation before the end of the summer, but right now he was just going to enjoy this new friendship.

The cool dampness of the night air drove away the cozy warmth of the fire as Brian opened the cabin door to leave. "I almost forgot to give you your coat. It's cold out there tonight. We dried it out. Thank you for letting me wear it the other night."

Lisa was framed in the doorway, silhouetted by the fading light from the fire. Brian had never seen any girl as beautiful.

"Thank you for putting up with me tonight. I enjoyed spending the time with you. I hope I didn't bore you."

"No, of course not. I also enjoyed this evening. I like talking with you."

The walk back to camp seemed much shorter than usual. The shadows along the trail were not as threatening and even the creaking of the long-dead branches in the wind formed a familiar chorus of night voices. So deep were his thoughts that Brian missed the branch trail and waded half a dozen steps into the creek before he realized where he was.

"Falling into this creek is becoming a habit," he muttered as he returned to the camp trail.

The moon was almost full, and he had no trouble following the flashes of fluorescent ribbon Kitch had tied to trees along this part of the trail. The camp was dark when he walked in. He was surprised at the lack of activity.

"Everyone must have gone to bed early," he thought. He wasn't a bit tired. Then he looked at his watch and realized it was two-thirty and decided maybe he was a bit weary. As he passed Kitch's tent he lifted back the flap to see if his friend had beat him back. The air was filled with Reuben's rhythmic snoring, but Kitch's cot was empty. Just as he let the door flap fall back into place a branch snapped somewhere behind the tent and his eyes caught a sudden movement in the shadows.

"Is that you Kitch?" He called softly.

There was no answer, only stillness. Brian walked slowly back to the edge of the clearing and peered intently into the foliage trying to make some sense out of the mix of shadows, but the moon had hidden its glow behind a cloud and all the shapes seemed to blend into a wall of gray.

"Must be some small animal scurrying around," he thought and turned to go to his tent. Then he stopped as the smell hit his nostrils. It was a sweet, sickly scent of something decayed.

Crack!

"Wow! That was no twig," Brian said aloud.

He could hear something crashing through the bushes on the other side of camp behind the cooktent, but by the time he got there the noises were coming from farther down the creek. They became fainter and fainter and in a few moments died away completely, and the camp was silent.

The next morning Brian reported the experience at breakfast, but no one else had heard anything.

"Everything was quiet when I got back after three," Kitch remarked. "I remember thinking I heard something down by the junction, but there are usually so many different night noises that I didn't pay much attention to it."

"It was probably just a bear," Dusty observed. "They will be nosing around camp all summer looking for food. They are not usually dangerous unless they have cubs or you come up on them unexpected."

"That's it for sure," Cap agreed. "There's some garbage from yesterday that I didn't get around to burying last night. I put it out in the bushes by the creek. I'll bet it's all over the

countryside by now."
But when Cap went down to the creek later to bury the
garbage, he found the bag in tact, where he had left it.

BEAR REPORT

The incident was quickly forgotten. Brian experienced
uneasy feelings from time to time when he returned late at
night from the village, but as no further incidents were
reported, his concern lessened, at least for a few days until
the morning Lou Roman flew into camp with supplies and
a new radio. It was the first trip in two weeks, and he was a
welcome arrival. Except for the fish Cap had managed to
catch, they had been without fresh meat for a few days.
Personal necessities such as Reuben's chewing tobacco,
Arnold's color film and everyone's mail did much to lift
their spirits. Dusty was relieved to see the new more
reliable radio with its greater transmitting power. They had
been able to call out and be heard only three times since
their arrival. Their last contact the previous night had been
a strong request for the supply flight.
"I'll bet you haven't had this many people so glad to see you
in a long time," Dusty said as the pilot stepped down from
the aircraft. "I was afraid some of these boys were going to

walk to town if you didn't come in soon. They are getting pretty sick of eating canned stew, no matter how fancy Cap fixes it."

"Well, they don't look like they're suffering that much," Lou replied as he observed the eager faces helping him unload. "Last time I saw anyone this excited was two years ago when I picked up some stranded fishermen off an island in a big lake north of here. They had been there a month living on fish and berries."

After unloading the helicopter, everyone except Curt gathered in the cooktent as Lou described some of the activities that were taking place in the area with the arrival of the warmer weather.

"Did you see any of the smoke from the fire north of here?"

"No, nothing," Dusty replied. "I haven't heard anything about fires. I thought it would be too wet this early in the season."

"This one got started about ten days ago. Last thing I heard they were getting it under control. It sure made those fellows over at Forestry red in the face for a while. You know how they are always hounding everyone about being careful with fire in the bush, well this time the Government boys were doing some kind of a tree survey and their campfire got away from them. It burned out close to ten thousand acres of good timber and almost got them too. They had to scurry to get out of its way."

"That's one way of completing their survey," Kitch replied. "I'll bet they don't have to account to anybody for it either. It's a different set of rules when they screw up."

"You're probably right," Dusty added. "When someone like myself goes into the bush to do some work, we have to carry a big insurance policy to cover fires. If you're working in an area and a fire gets started, even if you had nothing to do with it, you can still be held liable for the costs of fighting it and probably get charged for the timber that was destroyed."

"That doesn't make sense that you should have to pay when it's not your fault," said Brian.

"It doesn't have to make sense," replied Dusty. "It's the Government. Besides, how are you going to prove that you didn't have something to do with starting it. Fortunately, I don't think there has been many cases of this actually happening, but that doesn't mean much if you are the guy on the hook. What bugs me more is that you can get an operation like ours all set up and running smooth, and the Forestry can shut you down with very little notice if they decide that the bush is too dry. You have to pull out right away no matter how much it costs you."

"That's the way it works," Cap added. "Dry weather is great for working, but too much of it and you begin to wonder when you're going to have to pack up and leave."

"There's a little sidelight to this blaze up north," Lou went on. "They have been having some problems with a wounded grizzly the past few days. It cut a swath through a herd of sheep and scared hell out of the herder just south of the fire area. Then a couple of days ago a hiker was badly mauled two valleys over to the north of here. His buddies saw the bear and said it was burnt and was moving with a lot of difficulty. No way to tell which way it's headed, but a line from the fire to this last sighting comes near the village. He could be coming into this valley, so it wouldn't hurt to keep your eyes and ears open. It seems he's dragging one leg, so the tracks shouldn't be hard to spot. If you see any signs, radio in. The Fish and Wildlife boys and some professional hunters are combing the country for him, but," Lou added with a pause, "it's a big country."

Kitch was the first to break the silence.

"Whew! We sure don't need something like that for a camp mascot."

Brian was white.

"Dusty, you don't think..."

"No, what you heard the other night was probably just a

black. From the way you described it, I would say that whatever it was, it was moving at a greater speed than this grizzly is capable of."

"I hope you're right," Brian replied. "Lou, was that hiker hurt very bad?"

"He got chewed up, but it looks like he's going to recover. He told the pilot that brought them out that the bear went out of its way to come across a creek and go after him."

"Hurt bears do that sometimes," Reuben remarked. "If they got pain they strike out at anything that comes near them."

"I've heard that said before," Lou answered. "They're really dangerous when they've been hurt so bad they can't get food. They get hungry enough to eat just about any thing they can catch."

"Keep us posted on what happens and if there are any more sightings," Dusty requested as Lou picked up the outgoing mail and stuck it in his jacket pocket.

"I will. It's time to get out of here. I've got a lot of flying to do before the sun sets. You fellows can save me a stop if any of you are going over to the village in the next day or two. I think Old Sam should be told about the bear."

"We'll take care of it," Dusty replied. "We've got a couple here that seem to hike over there once in a while."

"Okay, I'll see you next trip."

They gathered on the creek bank and watched reluctantly as the aircraft diminished to a black speck in the southern sky.

"Dusty, do you think that bear is around here?" Arnold was visibly scared and having trouble controlling his voice.

"He could be, but the chances of crossing his path are slim unless he came right into camp. If you do see or hear him, I think your best bet would be to go up a tree as high as you can. Grizzlies can climb, but because of their bulk they don't do it very often, and this one is probably so weak he'd have a lot of trouble going up after you. He may try to shake you down, so pick a stout tree."

"It would be better than trying to run away," Reuben

agreed. "Even crippled, I bet he can run faster than any of us in the bush."

"I think we should be a bit more alert when we're out. Try not and get spooked but stop and take a listen and look around every so often. We are all probably going to be a little jumpy until they get him."

The mail delivery brought a mixture of emotions. Arnold's spirits took a lift from his friend Rudy's letter. They were offered a chance to audition for a small local record producer. The problem was that it had to happen in the next month. He implored Arnold to find a way to get loose from the job and come home. Another letter from his brother described to him what a great time all his friends were having. This did nothing to cheer him up.

Curt was angry that the University was still dragging their feet on his appointment. The Department secretary sent a short note indicating the job prospects did not look good, and he would probably have to return and state his case to the Board of Governors before the end of the field season.

Kitch almost broke up over a crayon-scribbled note from Julie and the news from Glennda that she was now certain she didn't want to continue their marriage.

Brian had the biggest haul with cheerful wishes from family and many of his friends. A long letter from Stephanie went into great detail about her plans for their wedding. It ended with complaints about his failure to write to her.

Cap's instructions from Margaret were to be careful and provided him with a list of all the chores to be done when he returned. He read the letter again, realizing he would probably be too sick by then to complete any of her requests.

Reuben didn't expect any mail and wasn't disappointed. Among all the invoices for supplies and services, Dusty received a long-winded request from Archie Campbell for some good news to get their dormant stock moving again.

He had been expecting that one and was still uncertain how to frame an answer that would be encouraging, even though, so far, they had found nothing.

His last letter on RCMP stationery initially took him by surprise until he realized it was from Lucie. They had spent a month together after Dusty had come off a drill job in Southern Saskatchewan. Corporal Lucie Hansen had been assigned to investigate a double murder in one of the old Moose Jaw tunnels, and with his unofficial help she had solved it. In the letter she wrote, "We got a conviction. Our villain earned a thirty-year vacation from society, and I received a commendation. Your reward will be waiting for you until our next time together."

The last sentence was a puzzler. Except for a night of passion in Northern Saskatchewan when their naked bodies entwined in a sleeping bag kept them from freezing, the relationship had been mostly platonic. They had both preferred it that way after surviving previous painful affairs. This certainly made the mid-season break something to look forward to.

The news of the bear made the boys more than a little jumpy. The pace of work slowed considerably. Each of the crew became more aware of his surroundings and alert to any unusual movements or strange sounds. Each evening a call was put in to Smithers for any news of the hunt, but although new tracks had been found, no more attacks were reported.

A few days later Dusty decided he had better make the trip to warn the villagers about the bear. He had expected Kitch or Brian to be going, but Brian was trying to stay off a sprained ankle as much as possible, and Kitch for some reason seemed reluctant to go. Dusty's concern for the villagers was unnecessary. They had known about the bear since the first incident.

"We heard from our friends to the north," Old Sam replied. "The bear is hurt and dangerous and will be that way until he gets well or holes up in the caves to the west to die. None of our people have seen him around here. We will know when he comes."

The old man went on to tell of other injured bears and how they had terrorized the country trying to survive. He related his stories without anger or resentment but simply to help Dusty understand more clearly the animal and his place in the natural world.

It was after ten when Dusty left the village. The night was overcast, and he was surprised at the utter darkness as he stepped from the cabin. All contact with time had been lost listening to the old man's stories. He had kidded Brian about his claim that it wasn't just Lisa's presence that drew him to the village. Now he could sense that the old man had an aura that transcended the present reality to a plane of natural order and well-being.

Dusty walked briskly along the trail hoping to reach camp ahead of the threatening rain. At a bend in the path near the lower end of a stretch of rapids, his eye caught a shadow movement downstream on the opposite shore. He stopped and peered into the foggy darkness, but he could only barely define a form.

"Who's down there?" He shouted and the movement stopped. Slowly, he stepped lightly down the bank to the creek. As he felt the cold clammy mist off the water he could just make out two large stump-like silhouettes above the alder tops. He was still and gazed at the two forms until suddenly a fish splashing in the rapids momentarily pulled his attention upstream. When he looked back, there was only one stump. He rubbed his jacket sleeve across his eyes as if to sweep away the haze, but only one form stood out against the darkening sky.

The creek was too wide to jump, but a few yards downstream he was able to make a dry crossing by hopping from stone to stone. As his foot hit the opposite shore the stillness was shattered by the alarmed flight of two ducks that had been nesting at the water's edge. Dusty regained his composure, then worked his way along the shore to the thicket. The skeleton of a burnt tree stood above the undergrowth, but he could see nothing else unusual. There was, however, a strong, sickly sweet odor that was overpowering. He could almost taste it and began to feel slightly nauseous as he turned to make his way back downstream to the crossing.

"I might as well go back to camp," he thought. "It's hopeless to try and find anything when it's this dark. There's lots of time tomorrow to look this place over in daylight for tracks."

That portion of the trail to camp past the creek junction was narrow, and sections were still not easy to follow even in daylight. It was primarily a game path. Kitch had cleared it to chest level for his easier access, but Dusty's additional height caused him to continually bend his tall frame in order to make any kind of painless progress. He felt some relief as his eye caught the faint light at camp. At least Cap had left a beacon to guide him in, but as he unzipped the cooktent flap he saw it wasn't Cap waiting up but Brian so deeply engrossed in a book that he didn't hear Dusty come in.

"That book must be pretty good to keep you up late after a day like today."

The young man sat up with a start.

"It's about some of the Indian legends and folklore from this whole Pacific Northwest area. Most of this material is fascinating. Some of the ideas and stories these people believe in are completely beyond my understanding, but the book is more than that. It is a record of their history, culture, and how their lives used to be before the intrusion of modern civilization. Lisa had the book sent in from her school for me."

"Are the legends the same as the stories Old Sam has been telling us?"

"Not the same, but similar. A non-native wrote the book. It was part of a Master's thesis at U.B.C., so the point of view had to be different. Many of the old legends focus on the creation of the world, and how certain mountains, rivers and lakes were formed. They have spirits everywhere and attach supernatural powers to animals like the raven, coyote and grizzly. I've been trying to find something about these large hairy wild men that Old Sam sometimes talks about, but there's nothing about them. The closest thing I could find was some stories about animal people that were supposed to have lived here before the natives came. Some were like the animals we know now, only larger, and others were supposed to have human form."

"What do you think about Old Sam's stories?"

"I just don't know," Brian replied. "Some of his ideas are so alien to what I have been taught, but I guess that works both ways. Many of the stories seem to be their logical way of explaining natural phenomenon for which we have scientific solutions, but I can't dismiss them. Old Sam is not a stupid man by far, and he has been exposed to our culture and ideas. I think he has a mind that is open enough to evaluate our explanations, yet he sees no contradictions and does not say one way is right and the other is wrong."

"I can see that. I often feel that our society has become somewhat beguiled by science, and we have lost track of this vast storehouse of knowledge accumulated over the centuries in the various cultures. It's sort of like well witching. All our scientific training tells us that it is impossible to find buried water channels by holding a willow branch in your hands, but people unaware that it's not supposed to work use it to find water where some of our more sophisticated methods fail. You just have to expose yourself to all points of view, keep an open mind and develop the ability to objectively evaluate the information."

"I'm beginning to believe that. It's only the past few weeks that I've been forced to examine my neat little package of viewpoints. I'm anxious to learn more of Lisa's and Old Sam's world, not just from them but also through the writings of others that have studied this culture. I guess I'll have to wait until mid-season break to do some serious research."

"I know it's none of my business, and I'm hesitant to even bring it up," Dusty continued, "but I'm concerned about you and Lisa and how serious it is between you. I know from what you have told me that you are supposed to marry when you get back but are not particularly excited with the prospect. I think you need to resolve this potential conflict before it goes too far. With Kitch and Della, I'm not worried. They are far from naïve and know exactly what they are doing and that their relationship, no matter how intense, is just a summer diversion. But you take things more seriously, and I hate to see you or Lisa hurt by a bond that most likely has no future."

"I think it's okay," Brian smiled. "We are good friends and care very much for each other. We have talked about it and how we feel. Right now we just want to enjoy the time we have together without making a big deal about it. I don't know what is in the future. I guess I will have to resolve this dilemma by the time the summer is over."

THE TRACK

The rain beat a heavy tattoo on the tents as they awoke to Cap's call the next morning. Most of the crew sloshed over to the cooktent just as Curt was finishing his last cup of coffee. He stood up, waited for everyone to pass through the tent door, ignored Brian's 'Good Morning', and strode out and returned to his tent.

"I see our resident asshole is in his usual good humor," Kitch observed as he forked some pancakes onto his plate. "You'd better not let him hear you say that," returned Arnold. "He gets angry with me if I even talk to him." Kitch winced as he looked at the boy across the table. "You fellows going to work in this?" Cap asked as he served up a plate of fried eggs.

"That's up to the boss," replied Brian, as Dusty entered the tent.

"The boss says no work today. The bush is much too wet to accomplish anything worthwhile," Dusty announced.

It was mid-afternoon before the storm broke. By then Dusty had partially convinced himself that last night's incident was probably the product of the old man's stories and his own vivid imagination. "I'd like to go back and have a look," he thought, "but any traces or tracks would be washed away by now."

As evening approached, the rain returned and continued for four more days. By the fourth day tempers were wearing as thin as the pack of cards that occupied most of their time during the downpour. Each night the crew would gather around the radio for any news of the bear, the fire and to catch the weather forecast. The report of a high pressure system developing over the Queen Charlotte Islands on the fifth day gave them hope for the next morning, and true to the prediction the deluge had been reduced to just a heavy cloud cover that permitted the men to return to work.

Dusty had decided to let Brian work with Kitch and Reuben for a couple of days. He still hadn't prospected the southwest corner of the block, and since it was a good three-mile walk from camp he decided, in spite of his advice to the others, that he could cover the ground faster alone. Rather than accompany the other three by the longer Jumping Rock trail, Dusty headed cross-country through the bush to his destination.

A poorly worn game trail angled south and west from the camp toward the mountain front but petered out after it crossed the creek. Dusty walked upstream to the west to where the grade was a little steeper, and the dripping vegetation wasn't as dense. By the time he had reached the base of the scree slope, the bush had thinned out enough to make hiking easier. At this point he headed south parallel to the slope.

Back and forth along the slope he worked his zigzag prospecting pattern, tying into the grid lines that Kitch and Reuben had flagged a couple of weeks previous. Rock outcrops were scarce, and most of the rocks he broke were float boulders from the high country to the west. He worked steadily, losing track of time until by mid-afternoon, when he laid his raincoat out and sat down to eat his lunch. He had covered most of the ground he had set out for the day. It was the first time he became aware that all traces of the drizzle had finally stopped and the leaden sky that had covered them for so many days was actually beginning to show hints of blue.

He finished his meal, tucking the uneaten portions back into his pack and was leaning over to wash out his cup in the small stream when he noticed the track. It had just appeared as a formless impression in the sand from where he had been sitting, but on closer inspection he could make out the shape of a foot. It wasn't a bear track. That was definite, as he saw no evidence of claw marks. It was a foot. He guessed the length at close to fifteen inches. Never before had he seen, or even heard described, the track of anything that large. He looked for signs that it had been partially washed away, making it appear larger than it actually was, but although there was a tiny stream running alongside, the foot impression was sharp and distinct, and Dusty sensed with uneasiness, recent. The imprint was clearest at the heel, suggesting that whatever had made the track was walking upright. He marked a line in the sand at the back of the depression. To find the exact length he examined the area in front of the toe marks for evidence of where the animal's claws would have made contact, but the sand was undisturbed. Searching through the bottom of his pack he found an old metal ruler, which he used to carefully measure the distance from the front of the toes to the heel mark. It was just a shade less than sixteen inches. He repeated the measurement to be sure. He would have liked to have been able to photograph it, but unfortunately, to lighten his load that morning he had left his camera in camp, so he was reduced to drawing a crude picture of the shape in his field book. A careful search of the immediate surrounding area revealed no other recognizable prints, although a line of faint depressions could be traced for a short distance adjacent to the streambed.

He took a long route, which would put him on the Jumping Rock trail for his return to camp, sticking to any clear paths he could find. The trip was unsettling. Dusty tried never to allow his imagination to become overactive in the bush, especially when he was alone, but this unusual track was beginning to bother him. It was too much of a question mark for his mind to dismiss or work around. As his imagination drifted to visualizing the size of the creature that could leave such a print, he had to force his thoughts to other subjects.

Er-er-er-er-er-er-er   Er-er-er-er-er-er-er-er

Dusty stopped suddenly and felt his body go cold at the noise. Silently, he stepped off the trail and peered into the bush around him, but he could see nothing out of place. There were no other sounds. A slight wind had picked up and its rustling passage through the trees masked the normal bush noises.

Er-er-er-er-er-er-er-er

It was directly above him. He looked up anxiously and felt the wave of relief to see two bare tree trunks being rubbed together by the wind. "This is getting silly," he thought. "I've heard that noise a hundred times." But, he couldn't shake the strange feeling that had come over him. It was like someone or something was near, watching him. He knew it was just in his mind, a result of finding the track, but the feeling persisted. Every fifty yards or so he would turn and search the woods for any movement, but all was as it should be.

His return had taken him exactly to where he wanted to go. As he emerged from a dense growth of fir, he found himself almost directly across the creek from Jumping Rock. At the same moment he heard a rippling sound down the creek. Thinking it to be only the water in the rapids, he changed his course to walk downstream with the hope of locating a narrow spot to cross to the main trail. As he got closer to the rapids the sounds became clearer and distinguishable as human voices. Kitch and Brian were sitting on the bank. Kitch had his shirt off and Brian was attempting to pull some Devil's Club thorns from his back. "You're kind of taking the long way home, aren't you?" Kitch asked, as Dusty approached on the opposite shore. "I decided to take the longer easier way back. It was rough this morning going cross country. Besides, that bush still isn't completely dry. By the way, where's Reuben?" "He went on ahead. These damn stings in my back were driving me crazy, so Brian said he'd see if he could get some of them out. You'd think I'd know better than try to walk through a patch of those plants again. They are well named. The stems run along the ground, where you don't notice them and then grow straight up with the thorny clubs on the end. Step on a stem and the club part swings around and gets you every time." "You probably won't have much luck getting relief until they fester up and you can see them. About the only thing you can do right now is slap some wet clay on the inflamed areas and hope it draws the thorns out as it dries. We've got some lotion back at camp that is supposed to relieve insect stings. It might work." Brian proceeded to plaster most of Kitch's back with mud as Dusty stood back to observe the artistry. "You sure did get into them," Dusty observed. "Your back will be a bit sore for a day or two." "I know," Kitch replied. "It's not the first time. I got caught in a patch of them a few years ago on the Island. You showing up when you did explains why it got so quiet around here all of a sudden." "That's right," Brian added. "Five or ten minutes before you arrived it got real still, not a sound. One minute the birds were singing and flying around, the chipmunks were chattering and the bush was alive. The next moment it was dead quiet, and you couldn't hear or see a creature anywhere. It was really weird."

"Come to think of it," Dusty replied, "I don't think I've seen or heard any animals or birds all afternoon."

"Do you always have this effect on the little creatures of the forest?" Brian asked with a smile.

"It's been like this since I saw the track," Dusty replied, describing his discovery of the footprint.

"That was a hell of a size," Kitch observed. "I've never heard of anything that big. It must have got hollowed out by the rain to make it look bigger. Did you get a picture?"

"No, this was the one day I left the camera back at camp to lighten my load. It didn't look washed out: the edges were still fairly sharp. What is bothering me is there were no claw marks. I don't think it was made by a bear."

Kitch thought for a minute and then replied, "It could have been our unfriendly neighborhood grizzly, and he has lost the claws to his injured foot."

"I guess that's possible, but it doesn't seem to explain what I saw."

Brian's interest quickened. "Old Sam has been telling me about some pretty big bears around here, but nothing that big. I'd sure like to see it."

"I'm almost sure it wasn't a bear track, but I can't come up with any logical explanation for it, unless someone from the village has been out there to play tricks on us. I'm not about to traipse back through that bush today to show it to you. Maybe we can get out there tomorrow. Let's get back for dinner before Cap throws it out."

The next day Dusty and Brian returned to the southwest part of the block to finish the prospecting. By noon they had covered the rest of the ground and after lunch hiked up the creek to the spot where Dusty had found the track. It was not as clearly defined as he remembered it and was rendered less distinct by the numerous tracks of shore birds that now covered the area. Brian was polite in his comments, but Dusty could see that he was not impressed.

GOLD VEIN

By the end of the week Dusty had relegated thoughts of the track to the back of his mind.

They had continuous days of fine weather and made the best of them. He had hoped to finish work on the initial block of claims by the first of July and now, on the twentieth of June they had only three or four days of work left.

That night Kitch and Reuben were later than usual getting back to camp, but when they did arrive they burst into Dusty's tent and emptied a packsack full of rocks on his bed.

"There's your mine," Kitch announced excitedly. "Reuben found the stuff in outcrop a couple of hundred yards south of Jumping Rock. What do you think? Should we phone our brokers and buy some company stock?"

Dusty went over each piece in turn with his lens. He could readily identify the copper minerals, some blackjack and a speck or two of galena embedded in the quartz. Closer examination under the microscope revealed tiny specks of another yellow mineral, which after considerable scratching with the probe, he was sure was native gold.

"It looks like it could be interesting," he finally replied.

"Could you get any idea of the size of the vein?"

"We followed it for about two hundred feet on the surface," Kitch replied. "After that it was covered with soil and moss in both directions. It goes up to six or seven feet wide in a few places, and in one spot it pinches down to about six inches. Reuben banged the samples off any outcrop that showed mineral, but there's lots of places where all you'd get is barren quartz."

"It's the best thing we've got so far," Dusty said. "I'll go out tomorrow and have a look at it."

After Reuben left to have his late dinner, Dusty began to gather up the rocks. Thinking both men had gone, he was surprised to look up and see Kitch still standing in the doorway.

"Dusty, there's something else. We found some tracks that looked an awful lot like the ones you described to us the other day. I wanted to wait for Reuben to go before I told you. Finding them had a real strange effect on him. He refuses to talk about it or even admit that he has seen them. I couldn't get a word out of him all the way back to camp. Here," he continued as he rummaged through his pack, "I made some drawings of them."

Dusty took the folded paper from the young man. On it were sketched almost exact replicas of the footmark he had seen by the creek. "This is it," he exclaimed. "It's the same damn track. You said 'them'. Were there more than one?"

"There must have been half a dozen around the outcrop and more further up the trail. It was starting to get dark when we found the vein, so we didn't have much time to look around, and Reuben wasn't anxious to stay."

"I want to go out and see this first thing in the morning. Let's hope it doesn't rain this time."

Early the next morning Dusty, Kitch and Brian took the

117

Jumping Rock trail to the new mineral show. His concern for Reuben's state of mind over the tracks prompted Dusty to assign the older man as a helper to Cap for the day. He had a good idea what to expect as far as the vein was concerned from the samples and Kitch's description. It was the fascination about seeing the new tracks that ruled his mind. This time Brian shared his enthusiasm.

They searched the area and found three groups of prints. Most of these were in the soft crumbly sand, making it difficult to determine exact size and shape, but the last group could be traced down a trail for about twenty feet and were firmly imprinted in the drying clay.

"I wish we had some plaster of Paris and could get a cast of one of these," Brian announced after comparing one of the tracks with his own foot. "Anybody that hasn't seen this isn't going to believe the size of it. I measured the distance along here between the prints, and it looks like whatever made them must have a stride of about six feet. I'm almost six feet tall and it's way longer than mine."

"Maybe it was running," Kitch replied. "You could stretch your steps out that long if you were running."

"I don't think so," Dusty said, looking at the tracks. "If it was running upright like we do, the weight would be greater on the front part of the foot, making that part of the print deeper in the mud, but these tracks don't show that. You can see in most of them the depth seems to be the same for the whole print, suggesting the weight was evenly distributed, like it was out taking a leisurely stroll."

"I wish we could get someone out here that knows more about something like this than we do. Maybe a zoologist, or an anthropologist or someone like that, who could look at these tracks and come up with a simple explanation that we haven't considered. I don't like this feeling that I'm beginning to believe that there is some kind of huge creature, that's not a bear, walking around the woods. It's not going to make getting up in the morning and going out to work any easier. It was bad enough just worrying about that grizzly."

"Brian, I think you hit it when you said there's some answer we haven't thought of," Dusty replied. "Could it be a grizzly that has lost its claws and is walking like us to avoid the pain?"

"I like your idea better than the explanation that someone in the village is laying it on us," Kitch added, " although I can see some of those bucks, who aren't too happy with us being up here, fixing up some kind of a fake foot and having a good laugh on us."

"How would they know where we were going to be?" Brian asked. "I haven't seen signs of anyone else in the bush since we got here."

"They've probably known about this mineral show for years, discovered we were working, around in this general area and decided to have some fun. I'll ask Della whom she thinks might pull a caper like this. She would know."

"Well, I guess I'd better go and have a look at that vein this morning, seeing as that's why we're out here," Dusty announced, getting to his feet.

"I'll walk over with you," said Kitch. "I've got three lines that Reuben and I didn't finish up on the east side. I might as well run them myself as long as we're out here."

"I'd like to stay and take some pictures," Brian said to Dusty. "I borrowed Arnold's new Polaroid and a couple of rolls of color film. I want to see if I can get some shots that will leave no doubt in anyone's mind about these tracks."

"Sure. You come over when you're finished. I'll be pounding away on the rocks over there, so you won't have any trouble finding me."

After Dusty and Kitch had left, Brian sat down on a log to study the camera's directions. It took a few minutes to become familiar with the instrument and load it with film. First he decided to take some shots of the best tracks. They had all made a special point of being careful during their examination to not mess up the prints, consequently he was surprised to find most of those tracks completely destroyed when he reached the upper end of the trail. Not positive he was at the right spot, he walked back and forth trying to pick out a landmark. Finally, he was sure he knew he had gone to the right place, but he walked back to the log, where he had parted company with Dusty and Kitch to make absolutely positive he was on the right branch of the trail. He carefully searched the immediate area where the tracks had been seen until finally, off to the side of the trail in the ditch, he found a well-shaped print in the soft mud that hadn't been destroyed. He shot three pictures before he noticed a white mark in the middle of the impression. With his knife he dug out a small plastic cigar holder from its muddy grave. "That's strange," he thought, "to find one of these out here. Maybe this whole thing is a big hoax someone is playing on us. I'll bet Kitch and Reuben went to all this trouble. Come to think of it, they could have easily planted that print, which Dusty found down in the southwest corner, and they had all day yesterday to make these tracks. That must be it. Kitch probably doubled back while I was trying to figure out this camera and messed these up before I had a chance to get some pictures. What a rotten trick."

"Come on out," he hollered. "I know you're out there sitting in the bush."

There was no reply.

"Look, I know you're there. This joke has gone far enough."

Then he remembered. Less than an hour ago he had seen Kitch toss the remains of his cigar into the dirt at just about this spot in the trail. He scratched around in the dirt and found little bits of tobacco and ashes mixed in with the clay. Something had stepped there since.

It seemed to Brian that he couldn't make his legs move fast enough down the trail. At the same time he realized he hadn't heard Dusty's hammer tapping on the rocks for some time.

"Dusty!"

He was running hard but stopped to listen for a reply. The bush was silent. He remembered that the two had headed east when they left him, so he continued in that direction through a small clearing by the trail. A hundred yard farther he stopped again. All he could hear was the blood pounding in his ears as he leaned against a tree and tried to get his breath.

"Dusty," he shouted. "Where are you?"

"Right over here behind you," came the soft reply. "What's the matter? I'll bet Cap could hear you yelling all the way back to camp."

"There's something strange going on in these woods. I don't know what it is, but I know it's here."

"Come on. Take it easy. Let's sit down over there and have some coffee." Dusty put his arm over the young man's shoulder and led him to a large rock beside his pack. By the time he had poured them both a cup of coffee, Brian had himself under control.

"I was just about to come over and see how you were doing," Dusty continued, "when I scared up a couple of moose, a cow and a calf, I think it was. They took off through the bush like a couple of cannon balls heading straight for where I figured you were. Didn't you hear them?"

Brian shook his head and then described finding the tracks destroyed and eventually discovering the new print. He went on to describe his suspicions as to what was going on.

"This whole thing has gone far enough," Dusty answered after a long pause. "I know Kitch didn't go back, and besides, I've known Reuben for a long time. This is not the kind of thing he would be a part of, and he'd probably tell me if Kitch was trying to pull it off himself. If it is a hoax, my vote goes for some of the young fellows from the village. On the other hand, I would like to find a way of preserving this last print until we can get some kind of an expert in here to study it."

"How are you going to do that?"

"I'm not too sure. Let's go back up there. Maybe I'll get some kind of inspiration when I see it."

Brian half expected to see the new track destroyed in the same fashion as the others, but on their return it was as clear and well-defined as he had left it.

Dusty looked closely at the impression, walked around it a few times and then hunched down on the ground beside it. "Somehow we have to try and preserve this one. I think what we might do is take my ground sheet and make a little tent over it. We can't do much if someone or something wants to destroy it, but we can keep it safe from the rain. With a cover and a little ditch around it so the runoff doesn't wash it out, we might get lucky. I'll send a radio message out to this guy I used to know at UBC. He's an archaeologist and might get interested enough to come up and have a look."

The two men spent the next hour building as much protection around the track as possible with the materials at hand.

WILD MAN

That evening Brian and Kitch took the pictures to the village. Old Sam looked at them for a long time before he spoke, "These are tracks of the Wild Man. He used to come down from the high mountains every year, and we would see tracks like this. Sometimes, after the first snow, we would see them, but four years ago the winter was very cold with deep snow, and no one has seen any tracks until now. I am happy some of our friends from the mountains are still alive."

"Has any one of your people ever seen one of them?" Brian asked.

"The old stories tell of our people seeing the Wild Man. During those times there were many more of them in this land than now. Our ancestors looked on them like we do the bear and the wolf, with respect. They were not afraid of the Wild Men because there was no reason to be. They caused us no harm. They didn't hurt anyone. There were old stories of them taking young women captive and sometimes taking fish from our nets. I have been told by people from other tribes that there are many Wild Men beyond the mountains to the west."

Later in the evening when the talk and the fire began to die out, and Old Sam had retired to his memories, Brian and Lisa walked along the creek to the little clearing above the village. They lay back against the cool earth and looked up at the flickering northern lights.

"You haven't said much since we left the cabin. Is something troubling you?" The girl asked.

"This whole thing is so strange. I guess all that has happened in the last few weeks is shaking up my world. Coming from the big city up to this country, meeting you, your grandfather's stories and now this stuff about Wild Men, I'm having a little trouble keeping my head straight. It is all very confusing."

"Do you wish you had stayed in the city?"

"No, not a chance. It is so much more exciting than chugging through the same old routine of my life back there. I just wish things would slow down a bit so I could figure out what is going on and where my life is heading. Most of all, I'm glad to be out here, so I can spend time with you. I have given it a lot of thought, and I guess it is time I should tell you about my problem. I am supposed to get married when I return, but I know it is not what I want."

"Kitch told Della a little bit about your concerns. He was hoping she would talk to me and suggest I not get too involved with you. Do you love this girl?"

"No. I am sure of that, but I feel committed to honor my promise, which was made in haste without thinking the whole thing through. Since the day the words came out of my mouth, I have regretted it."

"I don't think I should give you any advice. The only thing I can say is that I would not sacrifice my chances for a lifetime of happiness."

"How do you feel about us?" Brian asked.

"I knew I wanted us to be friends from the moment I saw

you chasing your fish down the creek. I'm glad we can be together at least for the summer. What will happen after you go back to your life in the city, and I enroll in college is the question. I guess we won't know until then."

"At least we will have this summer together," he replied.

"Something else is bothering me. I don't understand why you and Kitch find grandfather's stories of the Wild Men so hard to believe."

As Lisa cradled her head on Brian's outstretched arm, he tried to answer. "I think it's because the beliefs of your people are so different from what we've been taught. It's sort of like the tales of sea serpents, or flying saucers. Every once in a while there is a bunch of stories about someone seeing one of these things, but very few people believe they actually exist."

"Don't they believe any of the people who tell about seeing them and describe how they look and act?"

"No, not really, most people look on these people as crackpots trying to get their names in the paper or their pictures on television."

"Is that what you think of grandfather and the rest of our people?" Lisa asked sharply. "Do you think they just make up these stories to confuse those who come into our world?"

"No, I don't. It's funny, but if I was back home and read about what has happened to us in the paper, I would probably think there was a bunch of crazies loose in the bush up here, but being here myself makes it different. It makes me wonder if there isn't some mass delusion that people won't accept something as real unless they have experienced it themselves, have solid proof or can come up with a logical scientific explanation."

"If you feel that way, you'll only believe in the Wild Man when you meet him face to face. I've never seen a track or any sign myself, but I don't have to. I believe he is living in our country, because it is a truth of our people, and besides,

I know and believe those who have seen his tracks because
I know what kind of people they are, just as I believe in
what you have seen and what you tell me about the city. I
don't need proof because I know you. It is our way, just as
it is the way of your people to be suspicious."
"What do your teachers at the school say to this way of
believing in things without proof?"
"That depends on who they are and what they believe in. If
they are religious, they say it is okay to believe, except that
we are believing in the wrong things. They try to change
most of our ideas and beliefs, but we know to expect it.
While we are at the school, we let them think we accept
their ways, then discard them when we come home."
"It would probably surprise them to know they weren't
being taken seriously," Brian said, pulling his jacket up
around the girl's shoulders to keep out the cool night air.
"I think they know, most of them anyway. It's like a play
we all act out. They have their instructions to teach the stuff
that is set down by the Government and the Church, and we
believe what our people pass on to us."
They walked back to the village in silence. Brian was
acutely aware of this beautiful young woman beside him
and his growing desire for her. Each evening they spent
together he was finding it increasingly difficult to tear
himself away and return to camp. His decision regarding
Stephanie was so much easier now that he had found
someone he really cared about. He resolved to end the
marriage charade on his return home at the break. He felt
bad that his mother would probably lose her job, but he
knew he had to be true to himself.
"Would you like me to make you some tea before you go
back? The water will probably still be hot." The girl spoke
as they reached the cabin door.
"I'd like to, but I'd better not, Lisa. I've got a long walk
back, and it's getting late."
He wanted to kiss her. She moved closer and he circled his

arms gently about her shoulders as she pressed her slim body to him. The coolness of her lips surprised him, firm, yet yielding to the pressure of his.

They were silent as the yellow, flickering light poured from the open door.

"Della! Is that you out there?" Her mother's voice broke the stillness.

"No mother. It's Lisa," the girl answered.

"Have you seen your sister?"

"Only earlier this evening, but I don't expect she'll be home until later."

"You tell her to start getting home earlier if you see her," the older woman replied, pulling the door shut.

They walked slowly together down the creek trail until the lights of the village were barely visible in the distance.

"You shouldn't go any farther," Brian said. "You won't be able to see the trail back."

"When will you come to see me again soon?"

"The day after tomorrow, if I can."

Softly she slid her arms around his neck bending him down to meet her upturned face, then slipped away silently back along the dim trail.

The horror of Cap's six-thirty call was pure hell the next morning. Brian stumbled into his clothes and made his bleary way to the cooktent. The first face he saw was Kitch's, freshly shaven and wide awake.

"Man, do you look rough," Kitch remarked as Brian entered.

"I guess I didn't get much sleep last night. There was too much going through my mind. You look pretty good. What time did you get back to camp? I figured you were still at the village when I left."

"I came in about an hour ago. Della and I had a hell of a time. We went up to that old log cabin on the trail above the village. It used to belong to some relative of hers, but he died last winter and the place is still the same as the day they carted him out."

"Their mother was kind of uptight about where Della was when Lisa and I walked back to the cabin. Is that where you were the other night too?"

"Naw," Kitch shrugged. "We fell asleep on the creek bank. I guess the old lady was strung right out when Della got home. She's worried Della's going to have another kid. By the way, did Lisa tell you about her old boyfriend coming home?"

"No," Brian replied with concern. "She hasn't told me she had a boyfriend."

"He's some dude from the village who's been down to a trade school in Vancouver. Della says he wants to marry Lisa, but she doesn't want him and has been trying to break it off for the past year. She also tells me he's big and kind of mean when he gets juiced up. Maybe you should find out about him and keep your eyes open."

"Yes," Brian replied, "Maybe I should."

That evening it was a weary Kitch that trailed Reuben into camp. He was almost asleep, still in his work clothes and stretched out on his cot when Dusty looked in on his way to dinner.

"Aren't you eating with us tonight?"

"That depends on whether I can get up off this bed. Damn! That Reuben's a driver. The tireder I got, the harder he pushed. I don't think that old coot ever wears out."

"He's been like that ever since I've known him," Dusty replied. "He likes to show he can cut it just as well as the young fellows."

"How old do you think he is?"

"Damned if I can tell." Kitch thought for a moment. "I'd say somewhere between fifty-five and sixty."

"He'll be seventy-six sometime this year."

"You're kidding," Kitch exclaimed. "I hope to hell I can put out half that well if I survive to his age."

"What I stopped to tell you," Dusty continued, "is that I got a radio message off to my archaeologist friend in Vancouver, and he's going to try and get up here in two or three days to see that last track that Brian found."

The next evening when Kitch and Reuben returned to camp a new message had to be radioed out canceling the visit.

Dusty's raincoat had been pulled from its frame and ripped to shreds, and the footprint was completely destroyed.

THE HIGH COUNTRY

By the end of the month they had completed the first block of claims. Only a small area off the west edge was left untouched. Here, the frontal face of the main mountain range cut through as a limestone scarp terminating in a jagged ridge four thousand feet above the plateau floor. Although the odds of finding any minerals of value were low in that rock environment, Dusty was obliged to at least prospect the area for a complete coverage.

Reuben and Brian started out with Dusty just before dawn. The plan was to angle diagonally upslope to the northwest corner of the block and work their way individually at three relatively constant levels of elevation along slope until they reached the south boundary. Brian was looking forward to this excursion. He would be able to see some of the plants, which he had read about that lived only at the higher elevations. These were a hardier group that were content to forsake the comforts of valley life to brave the rigors of the alpine environment. He took the high traverse, Reuben the middle, and Dusty the area along the base of the slope where the chance of finding some mineralized material was the greatest. They planned to meet above the tree line, where they would be visible to each other, two miles to the south.

Brian, working his way methodically, reached the destination by early afternoon. He was soaked in perspiration, and his throat was getting raw from the continual gasping for oxygen in the thin atmosphere. His legs ached from the continual battle to keep his balance on the loose rock. As he sat down to lunch, Dusty emerged from the bushes below and made his way upslope.

"Looks like you went for a swim in your clothes. It must be nice on a hot day like this."

Brian ignored the comment as he tried to suck the last drop of liquid from his orange.

They sat in tired silence, both men savoring the rest and overdue lunch.

"Reuben should be getting here pretty soon, shouldn't he?"

"He should," Dusty replied, "although he doesn't move as well in this country as he does on flat ground. We'll give him a little longer, then if he doesn't show up, we'll work our way back along his level and meet him."

Half an hour passed and then an hour, and there was still no sign of Reuben.

"You ready to do the mountain goat bit again?" Brian asked as he adjusted his pack.

"Yes, we had better go look for him," Dusty replied. "I keep thinking every time I work this kind of country that it would be handy to be born with one leg about six inches longer than the other, so you could go along these slopes and always be walking on the level."

"Sure," Brian replied after a minute, "that would be great as long as you always went in the same direction."

They scrambled back along the talus slope for half a mile

without meeting Reuben, until a steep promontory that jutted out from the incline blocked the way.

"I guess we climb over this one," Dusty observed. "Reuben is probably up on top or on the other side. I doubt if he could hear us yell over the roar of that creek."

It took half an hour of steady climbing to reach the top of the ridge. The exertion in the thin mountain air left both men gasping.

"Reuben!" Dusty yelled. "Can you hear me?"

There was no reply. The only sounds were those of the water rushing below and the wind slicing through breaks in the ridge.

"There's no sign of him over here," Brian called from the far side as he searched the slope to the north with his field glasses.

"He should be this far by now."

"That's right. I wish I knew what has delayed him. Either he's hurt himself and is moving very slowly, or he tried to go around this face at the bottom. Maybe he felt it was just too steep for his old legs. When did you last lose sight of him?"

"I didn't see him after we climbed to his level," Brian replied. "I just hiked further up and started prospecting. I don't remember looking back down for him. What do you think we should do now?"

"About the only thing is for you to go back and wait at the meeting point, and I'll walk north along his traverse line and see if I can locate him. If I'm not back by dusk, head for camp and bring the rest of the crew with you tomorrow at dawn. It's too bad we didn't bring a radio."

"You don't suppose that he would have taken off for camp when he missed meeting us, do you?"

"No. I've known Reuben too long. If we decided we were going to meet here, he'd stay here until we met."

Brian headed back across slope to the meeting spot, while Dusty walked over to the edge of the scarp for a last look up the north slope before starting his trek. He could see nothing moving across the hundred yards that was visible. As he turned to go, a flutter of red caught his eye from below. Stretching out on his stomach on the sharp rock he could lean just far enough over the precipice to identify Reuben's red shirtsleeve. The body was sprawled on a small ledge jutting out into a crevice about a hundred feet below. It was hidden from all but a direct view by the two shear rock faces on either side. Looking through his field glasses, Dusty was reassured by the rhythmic breathing that his friend was still alive. He could also see blood collected around the body on the ledge. He yelled a couple of times, but there was no movement. Suddenly, remembering Brian, Dusty scrambled to his feet and located his companion down the slope, well out of earshot. Taking his compass, Dusty faced the mirror into the sun and flashed the reflection back and forth across the retreating figure. Brian stopped, shielded his eyes and looked back. Dusty gestured wildly and pointed to the ledge. He could just make out Brian taking his binoculars from his pack, focusing on him and then begin making his way back. Dusty returned his attention to Reuben. The body lay draped over a bush on the ledge, which jutted out to partly fill the crevice. Beyond the ledge was a straight drop for another three or four hundred feet. The rock faces on either side were vertical and smooth to the top with no visible footholds. He figured Reuben had probably slipped over the edge, bounced back and forth between the two walls and miraculously landed and stayed on the ledge. How they were going to get him safely back up was less of a certainty.

"My God! Is he hurt bad?" Brian gasped as Dusty pointed at the crumpled form.

"It looks bad. He's alive but unconscious, and he's still bleeding a bit from what I can see from here. I want you to go back to camp as fast as you can and return with Curt, Kitch and Arnold, lots of rope, a couple of blankets, some

food, a bit of whiskey, the first aid kit, the lamps and
flashlights. Bring anything else you think will help us. Curt
has done a lot of rock climbing in this kind of country.
Describe to him exactly what these rock faces are like and
have him bring all the gear he thinks he will need. I'll wait
here in case Reuben comes to."

The group returned about midnight. Dusty could see the
lights bobbing through the forest below for some distance
before they arrived. He was disappointed to see that Curt
was not with them.

"He said this type of climb is too dangerous at night and
that he would come in the morning and do it."

"Damn it," Dusty exploded. "Doesn't he realize that Reuben
could be hurt bad and needs help right now."

"I explained that to him," Brian replied, "but it didn't seem
to make any difference. He says he just won't try the climb
in the dark."

"Well, I guess we'll have to try something else," Dusty said
as he played the flashlight along the shear wall. "We've got
to find a way to get someone down there to look after him."

"I'll go down," Kitch replied. "I'm the lightest. Fasten a
rope around me and anchor it to that big boulder. Then, you
guys lower me down to the ledge. If Reuben fell through
that crevice, I sure as hell can get through it."

A rope sling was securely fastened around Kitch's slight
frame and the loose end wrapped and tied around a large
rock.

"All the trees I've sworn at this summer because they were
in my way would sure be welcome up here. I hope that
wrapping job of yours holds."

Despite the brashness of his remarks, Dusty could sense the
fear in the young man's voice and promptly replied that he
and Brian would have a secure hold on the rope. Arnold
was to shine the big flashlight over the precipice so that
Kitch could see his way to the ledge.

Cautiously, Kitch lowered himself over the edge, his

companions playing the rope out at his instructions. The
night air at the top had been warm, but now he could feel
the cold damp clamminess as he descended.

"It's straight here for a ways. You can go ahead and let rope
out slowly until I yell."

At a point about halfway down, the walls narrowed so that
he could brace his feet against one side and his back on the
other. Then, suddenly the walls opened away so that he
could touch neither side.

"I can't see him anymore," Arnold called to the others.
Before they could reply, the call came from below. "Keep
that damn light on the ledge, will you."

"It sounds like he's still there," Brian replied.

For the rest of the descent to the ledge Kitch was hanging
free, unable to touch either side unless he started himself
swinging. Arnold's light was more in his eyes and cast a
shadow of his body on the ledge.

"Take it slow," he yelled. "I'm just about there."

He could faintly make out the rock ledge coming up to
meet him just before his feet touched Reuben's still form.
He secured his footing on a level spot and loosened the
rope from his body.

He hollered up to the group above. "You can pull the rope
up and send me down some supplies. I can't see a damn
thing down here. I'll need the big lantern, some food, the
medical stuff and the whiskey. He's still out cold."

When Kitch had the lamp lit he could appreciate Reuben's
luck in landing there. The ledge jutted out no more than
eight feet from the rock face and formed a half-circular
platform of limestone sloping back into the shear wall. Two
small bushes struggled for life in an earth-filled crack
running the length of the ledge, and it was on one of these
that Reuben's body was draped. Kitch eased him off the
bush onto the level area and poured a few drops of whiskey
into the partially open mouth. The old man's body gave a
shudder, and he emitted a low moan as he tried to sit up. As

Kitch supported his head, he could feel the swelling at the base of his skull. He laid him back on the ledge, resting his head on the packsack. Kitch sensed recognition in his eyes, and another sip from the flask seemed to shake away some more of the fog. Reuben looked around, finally aware of his strange surroundings.

"You fell off the cliff," Kitch replied to his look of puzzlement. "You're going to be okay; just take it easy until I patch some of these cuts. You want some food?"

Reuben's reply was unintelligible, but he painfully shook his head and reached for the flask.

Half an hour had passed by the time Kitch had treated the more serious wounds, and Reuben was able to pull himself clumsily to his feet. Apart from the cuts, bruises and the bang on the head, the worst damage to the old man was a badly sprained ankle on which he was unable to put any weight.

The group at the top had been only vaguely aware of what was going on below. Because of the difficulty of being heard over the sound of the wind and the distance separating them, there had been little talk between Kitch and the others. Now the task at hand was how to get Reuben to the top, and this involved them all.

"We're just going to have to pull him up with the rope," Dusty shouted. "You make the sling secure around him and Brian and I will try and hoist him up."

"It won't work," Kitch replied. "Reuben weighs too much, and in the shape he is now that will be dead weight. He's not going to be able to help much more than to push away from banging into the rocks with his good leg. How about we try it another way. You haul this gear up first, except for the lamp, and then send the rope back down, and I'll make a sling around him. You anchor the rope up there, and I'll climb it. That way, with the lamp still shining down here Arnold won't have to man the flashlight, and all four of us can pull him up. We lose our lamp in the deal, but that's a

small price to pay."
Dusty thought it over for a minute and then replied. "Are you sure you can climb that far up the rope?"
"Easy. I used to do this all the time when I was a kid. It's one of the advantages of being skinny. I don't have to lift as much beef as you guys."
Kitch's solution worked. The sweat and strain showed on their faces as they finally pulled Reuben up over the edge of the precipice. As the first streaks of pink threaded the eastern sky they stretched out their exhausted bodies on the cool rock surface.
"Do you still have some food?" Reuben asked.
Although, it seemed that there wasn't a part of his body that didn't hurt, he was in better spirits. Pills had masked all but the slight throb in his head, but he was feeling the results of not having eaten since yesterday's early breakfast.
"Yes, I think we all can use some of that," Dusty replied. "Here," he said as he pulled out the thermos, "even the coffee is still hot."
"I guess our next problem is getting Reuben out," he continued. "We'll have to bring the chopper in." Turning to Reuben, he said. "I want you to go to the hospital and have the doctor check you out. I want the rest of you to go back to camp and have Cap radio in for the aircraft. I'll wait here with Reuben until it comes."
"We can do better than that," Brian replied. "I brought the walkie-talkie in the other pack. Cap figured there is enough juice left in the batteries for one call. I told him we would call in for sure this morning, and he said he'd sleep with the receiver by his ear so we could call anytime."
The first try brought Cap's anxious voice, and two and a half hours later Lou Roman set the little Bell down gently on top of the scarp, loaded Reuben in the bubble and headed for town.
"I don't know about you fellows," Kitch said as the red speck disappeared down the valley, "but I'm going back to

camp and sleep all day."
At camp the first one they met was Curt, standing outside his tent, expecting an explanation of what had happened. The four walked by him into the cooktent, without a word.

MOVING CAMP

Moving camp is an event either anticipated favorably or dreaded, depending on the person and a comparison of the old and new camp sites. To Brian and Arnold it was a new experience and was exciting. It meant a new area to explore and fresh fishing holes. Being at a lower elevation and on the bank of the main river, it provided a new community of forest life for Brian to study. To Cap and Kitch the move was a pain in the neck. Cap had everything finally arranged around the camp to suit him, but his daily supply of energy was steadily diminishing. He wasn't looking forward to the effort required in starting all over. His habit was to set out a proper place for everything within his kingdom, and he badgered everyone to fit into his system. Now it all had to be torn down, packed up and set up again somewhere else. Most of the work involved in the move fell to Kitch, especially with Reuben in the hospital for a few days. Just a slight concussion and pulled leg ligaments was the report, but it was enough to keep the old man on his back until camp was set in the new location. To Dusty the move was

GUY ALLEN

just something that had to be done. It always meant extra expense, but he had taken that into account in his original bid. They had finished the first block of claims on schedule with nothing more interesting being found than Kitch and Reuben's quartz vein. Prospecting had proven the mineral deposit to be small, and the assays showed only meager amounts of gold.

The move took three days. One day was needed to pack up, another for the actual move and the third to set up camp again at the new location. Because the move was short, only three miles, they used the little Bell with slings. However, this involved the extra work of everything being packed into boxes and tied together and then untied and unpacked and put into use in the new location.

The new site was on the riverbank in an area of mature forest. Large balsam fir and white spruce towered above the tents. The area had been missed by past fires, leaving a ground surface free of deadfall and underbrush with a few grassy patches along the river shore. Shielded by the forest, the cold winds off the western glaciers, which cut through the morning mists at the old camp, were missing, making the prospect of abandoning the sleeping bag's warmth in the morning a little easier to bear. They were now due south of the village, just as far away, but the trail along the river was well marked and easier to travel.

"Just another week and we go out." Arnold had been marking the days off on Cap's cooktent calendar. He was anxious for the audition and had been working on his guitar riffs every evening. His muscle soreness and fatigue at the end of the working day was getting easier to bear, just as Dusty had predicted. Others in the crew had questioned his sudden dedication, but when he explained about the audition and the chance to record, all except Curt were supportive. Curt continued to complain that the noise was disturbing his concentration, but no one paid any attention to him. Only Kitch suggested he go find someone who

140

cared about his problems. Arnold was sure he wasn't homesick, but he was willing to admit he was beginning to get a little sick of where he was.

"You know, young fellow, I'm beginning to think you're getting tired of our company," Cap said as he looked up to see Arnold run a large black cross through yesterday's date.

"No, it's not that," Arnold replied quickly. "I'm just really excited about this chance to play our music for someone who can help us. Also, I'd like to go to a movie, have a milkshake and a pizza, sleep between some sheets for a change, watch television until midnight, and go to bed knowing I don't have to go charging off into the bush at dawn or climb another damn mountain for a while. I'm beginning to appreciate my life at home. I guess I needed this experience to find that out."

"That sounds pretty good," Dusty said as he zipped up the tent flap. "I could add another, and that would be getting away from these bugs."

"They're sure beginning to take over the country," Arnold observed. "You would think with all the great advances made in science they would have come up with something that would keep these creatures away. I've tried all the kinds of bug dope we have here, but none seem to do much good. Last few days I've been using Reuben's system of grinding up orange peel and rubbing it on my skin. It seems to work better than anything else."

"You'll have to go to the village and get some bear grease. That's supposed to work real good, although I've never tried it." Cap replied.

"The trouble is," Dusty added, "it stinks so bad that nothing else will come near you either."

"Well," Cap replied, "that would be one way of keeping those two young fellows in camp in the evenings."

"You guys can kid," said Arnold, "but these bugs are really beginning to get to me. I've never seen so many jumping, flying, crawling, and biting creatures in my life. They get

inside your clothes and get trapped in your hair. They drive
me nuts out there, and what irritates me even more is that
Curt seems completely oblivious to them."

"You'd better get used to them," Dusty replied. "They won't
let up until the first frost. They are much worse in Northern
Saskatchewan. I try to do any work up there in late
September or October."

A week to go and Dusty could see that they were all
looking forward to the break. It bothered him to lose the
time and good weather in the middle of the season, but he
had tried breaking a project into two parts a couple of years
before on a similar type of job and found that the crew had
actually gotten more work done in fewer days. It helped
keep up the men's spirits and this, Dusty believed, was
more important than how quickly the work was completed.
Besides, he needed to get back to Vancouver and resolve
further financing concerns with Campbell. He had decided
that unless the second payment was forthcoming, he was
prepared to shut the program down, in spite of his contract
with Curt.

There hadn't been much talk about the bear during the past
few days. It was still in the back of everyone's mind, but no
reported sightings had been announced in almost two
weeks. They had daily radio communication between the
camp and town, and the word was now that the
Government was calling off the hunt. Everyone figured that
the bear had died or was living like a normal grizzly
should. Only Reuben was dubious. "Old bears are tough.
He's probably hiding out somewhere until his wounds heal.
We will hear about him again."

The next day was hot. After the crew was gone and he had
finished his morning chores, as was his custom, Cap went
back to bed for a few hours sleep before getting organized
for the evening meal. These naps were becoming longer
and more regular as his condition worsened. The pain had
steadily become more difficult to bear, and the pills were

less effective in easing his discomfort. Today, however, it was too hot for sleep. He lay on his cot for an hour watching a big deerfly drone away in the corners of the tent and then finally gave up and went outside to find some cool spot in the shade. Reuben had been flown back to camp the previous day and was able to hobble out and spread a blanket under some willows by the river where a slight breeze was wafting off the water. Cap went down to join him and the two men carried on a desultory conversation for a few minutes, finally giving it up as too much of an effort in the heat.

Reuben was the first to break the silence. "There's somebody walking along the top of the ridge over there." He pointed toward a long quartzite outcrop that rose to a scarp about two hundred feet above the valley floor and ran to the north and south parallel to the river.

Cap shielded his eyes from the sun and stared in the direction of Reuben's point. He could just make out a figure moving at a steady pace along the crest of the scarp. As close as he could determine, it was almost a quarter of a mile away, too far to recognize who it was.

His feelings were voiced by Reuben. "I can't tell who it is. It's too far, but I don't think it's one of our crew. There's nobody supposed to be working over there. All the claims are on this side of the river. It must be somebody from the village."

"He's a big fellow. It looks like he has to bend to get under some of those branches." Cap's eyes hadn't left the figure. He began to feel a bit uneasy. "Have you got a pair of binoculars?"

"There in my pack," Reuben replied as he started to get up.

"You stay there," Cap said. "I'll get them. You're supposed to stay off that leg. Where's your pack?"

"It's in my tent under the cot."

By the time Cap had rummaged around under the cot, dug the glasses out of the pack and returned to the riverbank, the figure had disappeared.

"As soon as you got up and moved, he headed back into the trees."

Cap scanned the ridge hoping for some sign of movement, but only the undisturbed wilderness met his eye.

The two older men had a captive audience at the supper table as they described the event. For once, Cap felt no need to embellish the truth to hold his listeners' attention. Arnold was the first to comment. "Are you sure it wasn't a bear you saw instead of a human?"

"Bears don't walk on their hind legs when they're taking a leisurely stroll," Kitch replied with disgust. "It's only when they sense something or are preparing to attack that they stand."

"We've got enough light left," Brian observed. "Why don't we go over and see if we can find some tracks."

"Sure, I'll go," Kitch replied, "but it's probably just that local legend coming back to haunt us again. At least I would be able to compare any tracks with ones we found over by the gold vein."

"I wish you wouldn't joke about that," Brian commented uneasily. "I'm not so sure it's just a legend. All these stories, and the tracks we been finding are beginning to freak me out."

All but Curt, who made a point of taking no interest in any of the concerns of the others, gathered outside the tent as Cap and Reuben pointed out exactly where they had seen the figure.

Brian and Kitch were back by dark. They burst into the cooktent as Cap and Dusty were sitting down to steaming mugs of hot chocolate.

"We looked all along the ridge, but there were no tracks," Kitch announced. "It's bare rock and moss up on that scarp, and back in the forest it's just a bed of pine needles."

"There's one thing though." Brian looked perplexed. "Are you sure that figure was bending down to get under some

of those tree branches near the edge?"
"That's what it looked like from here," Cap replied.
"Well, I'm almost six foot and it's all I can do to reach up
and grab any of those branches. We checked the trees
along the scarp, and there were fresh branches broken
eight feet above the ground. "

JUMPING ROCK

The pain in his chest was turning into a dull ache. All afternoon he had been trying to keep up with Curt but continued to fall behind. He was sure that Curt was pushing him harder today. "He probably knows I'm feeling lousy," thought Arnold. "The bastard is trying to drive me into the ground." Arnold tried to make his legs move faster, but they couldn't match Curt's longer strides. "If I could just get my breath. Maybe I should have tried to get into shape before coming out here."

"Come on punk! I cannot wait all day for you."

Arnold tried to speed up and stumbled over an exposed root. Frantically he grabbed at a dead branch, which promptly broke and sent him sprawling into the damp moss. He looked up to see Curt, hands on hips, standing over him.

"Give me my pack. I have a job to do and I cannot wait around while you learn to stay on your feet. I'm going to map around the back side of this cliff and then head for camp. You can follow me or head back across country. I don't care. I am not going to wait for you to catch up from now on."

Without waiting for an answer, Curt disappeared into the bush.

"Wait!" Arnold cried. "I don't know the way back."

There was no answer. Arnold scrambled up and ran to the place where Curt had left the trail, but the bush was thick with small spruce and tangled second growth. Panic began to creep in as he searched unsuccessfully for a passageway with no success. He forced his way through the dense foliage for a few yards and listened intently, but all he could hear was his own breathing. Slowly, he made his way to the trail and sat down.

"Christ! Why couldn't he wait for me?" He sobbed.

As the feelings of panic passed he began to assess his situation and try to reason how he was going to get back to camp. His first positive thoughts of finding his way back with the compass were discouraged when he remembered the instrument was with Curt in his pack.

"Let's see," he reasoned. "We walked upstream to Jumping Rock and then left the creek to go cross country. That was about an hour ago, and the sun's been at our back since then. If I walk toward the sun I should come back to the creek. Then, if I walk downstream I should come back to the Rock or, if I'm past it, I should eventually come to the Forks and the main trail to camp."

With a lighter heart, he set out squinting into the sun. An hour and a half brought him to the creek, and a hundred yards downstream he spotted the Rock.

"Maybe I'm not so useless out here after all," he thought. He ran down the trail and scrambled up the backside to the top of the Rock. At trail level the bush was too dense to see very far, but from his vantage point on the Rock he could trace the creek, and the trail that led eventually to camp.

He settled on the flat surface and closed his eyes. He soon lost track of how long he had been sitting on the Rock. "I

must have fallen asleep," he thought, as he noticed the lengthening shadows and the sun hanging lower in the sky. Realizing his watch was also in the pack, he could only guess at the time. "I'd better get going if I'm going to make it to camp before dark."
As he got up and tried to stretch out some of the stiffness, his foot slipped on the moss-covered edge and he began to slide down the steep front face of the Rock, grabbing frantically at anything that might afford a handhold on the slippery slope. The last thing he remembered was the incline giving way to a shear drop.

Reuben and Kitch were the last to come in for supper.
"You guys stink like a swamp," exclaimed Cap as they sat down.
"That's where we've been most of the day," Kitch replied.
"We didn't clean up because we thought you'd enjoy a little change from the smell of your cooking."
Dusty was just finishing his meal as the pair came in.
"Isn't young Chipman gonna eat tonight?" Cap asked.
"Hasn't he been in?"
"No, not yet."
"Go have a look in his tent and see if he's there," Dusty nodded to Kitch. "Has Curt eaten yet?"
"Yes, he was in early," Cap replied.
"He's not in his tent," Kitch announced when he returned.
"Brian says he hasn't seen him either."
Dusty headed for Curt's tent, which was set off by itself back from the creek. He found him seated on the bed copying out his field notes.
"Where's Arnold?"
"I don't know."
"He was with you. Didn't you two come back together?"
"No. He couldn't keep up, so I left him to make his own way back to camp."
"Damn it man! You know he's not used to the bush and

might have trouble getting back."

"That is not my problem. I was hired to map geology, not baby sit. I didn't want him along in the first place. I put up with him for a while, but that's over. There is no way I can carry out my duties properly if I have to wait for this kid every other step."

"You know damn well I'm not sending you or anyone else out alone in this country," Dusty replied, "but that's not important now. Where did you last see him?"

"About a mile and a half east of that big rock by the creek, on the flank of the anticline that outcrops there."

"We're going out to look for him. Are you coming?"

"No. I have work to do. I have no doubts that he will come dragging his tail into camp sometime tonight."

Dusty left the tent without voicing his next thought. The rest of the crew was gathered in the cooktent when he returned.

"What happened?" Kitch asked.

"Curt left him in the bush because he couldn't keep up."

"That's about what I figured."

The group, aided by lanterns and flashlights, made their way along the trail to Jumping Rock, calling Arnold's name every few yards. They were surrounded by darkness by the time they got to the Rock. The pace had been stiff and Cap was exhausted. He knew he shouldn't have come. He could feel his body getting weaker with every step.

"This is hard going for these old bones of mine. You fellows go ahead on up to the ridge and pick me up on the way back."

"Sure," Dusty replied. "I think we had better split up here anyway and ...."

"He's up here."

Brian had crawled up on the Rock and was standing at the edge shouting to the group below.

"Arnold's up here, on top."

The boy was stretched out on the flat part of the surface on his back with a pile of moss under his head. He was unconscious.

"Better bring the First Aid kit," Brian continued. "He's cut up pretty bad."

It took a few minutes for Dusty to bring the boy back to consciousness.

"What happened?" Arnold looked up at his companions.

"We were wondering the same thing."

"I remember slipping off the edge and falling."

"How did you get back on top?"

"I don't know." He paused for a moment, then shook his head.

"It's getting late," Dusty announced. "Let's get back to camp. Do you think you can walk?"

"I think so," Arnold replied.

Brian and Reuben gently helped the boy to his feet and supported him for the first few shaky steps. They eased his climb down off the Rock.

"I can walk okay, but my head hurts like hell."

"We'll get you fixed up back at camp," Dusty replied.

The return to camp was slower. It was a black night and Brian had to pick out the trail with his flashlight before they could proceed.

"That was a weird scene," Kitch said as he dropped back to walk with Dusty.

"It was a little strange. What especially are you referring to?"

"He couldn't have pulled himself back up on that rock. I looked over the edge. It must be about a twenty-foot drop."

"Maybe he came to for a while and doesn't remember it."

"Come on! Are you trying to tell me a little guy in his shape, all cut up and banged around, is going to climb up that slope and stretch himself out with a nice little moss pillow. If he had been able to do that he would more likely have tried to make his way to camp."

"Well, what's the alternative?"

"I don't know. That's what blows my mind. I'm trying very hard to think of some logical possibilities."

At camp, closer examination showed Arnold to be suffering from a number of deep cuts and scratches and a substantial lump on the head. Cap dressed the wounds, administered a healthy portion of his private stock and put the boy to bed. Reuben had turned in, but the soft June night kept the others out for that extra cup of hot chocolate. It was the first really warm night since their arrival. A gentle breeze from the creek was playing through the trees carrying hints of pungent evergreen smells about the camp. A chorus of crickets, punctuated by the throaty call of a bullfrog combined to form the evening symphony.

"This country can be so soft and gentle at times and so puzzling at others. Just when you think you begin to understand and feel in harmony with nature, things happen, or you find something out of place, and you realize how little you really know. These events of the last few days," Dusty continued, "don't fit, and I don't have a rational explanation. It would be comfortable to accept Sam's view of his world, but maybe that's a luxury that comes from not quite enough knowledge, or too much. I wish I could be sure whether it is he or I that is the uninformed. Apart from the threat of that wounded bear, I can't even be sure how much risk we are taking working this area. I definitely will understand if anyone wants to pull out. You have that choice at any time. What Curt did today was inexcusable. I will talk with him and hopefully he will accept the error of his action. He is a proud man, and it will be difficult. I don't want to send Arnold out with him again.

Brian, do you think you can handle working as his assistant?"

"Yes, I can do it, but it's not something I'm looking forward to."

"I know," Dusty replied, "and I appreciate your effort. If it's any consolation, remember one thing, he's one of the best field geologists in the business. You pay attention to what he's doing, and you'll learn more than you'll ever get from a university course. If it gets to the point where you can't take him any longer, come and talk to me first. I want to keep this operation running as smoothly as possible."

"That's fair enough," Brian replied.

The new arrangement worked well. Brian had no trouble keeping up with Curt, and though he would have liked a friendlier relationship, he wasn't particularly bothered by the lack of communication. He busied himself prospecting while Curt meticulously mapped the details of the rocks. On occasion he would point out hidden rock exposures that Curt had missed, and would take secret pleasure when his partner's actions would admit the error. Brian found he was also becoming very interested in the plant, animal and especially the insect life of the area, and by constant reference to his field guidebooks, was soon able to identify the various species and their characteristics at will. The whole countryside took on a new dimension, and with this new knowledge, he came to feel a fellowship with the creatures of the woods. To watch the birds and be able to understand and predict their actions for that time of the year, to catch a glimpse of the animals training their young, to see and identify the flowers that bloomed together and know which ones would be coming out next and understand why they grew where they did: all of it filled him with a feeling of belonging to something that was good and worthwhile. When he tried to share this new awareness with the others, only Dusty and Reuben had any kind of appreciation of what he felt. But Lisa knew, and so did Old Sam. In the evenings they talked of it, and the old man told him of the ways of the creatures that he hadn't seen, like the wolverine, the marten and the timber wolf. He told Brian of how it was different in the high country and how the land had changed since he was a boy. Later during the warm evenings, Lisa would lie by his side on the creek bank and tell of their life in the winter, how the animals survived and how things could be very bad for all when the winter was long and cold. As he learned more, he found there was so much he wanted to know of the world now around him. Arnold was also learning. Working with Dusty, all the questions that had been suppressed by Curt's attitude came tumbling forth. He had watched long enough in silence to become interested in the work so that everything Dusty did was greeted with whys and hows. Dusty explained it all, to the point that it was beginning to take twice the time to perform every task. However, after a few days the questions eased off as Arnold found he was able to confidently carry out his assigned work.

GUY ALLEN

THE BREAK

A few days later Lou Roman eased the big chopper in
through a break in the trees and hovered it a few feet above
the pad before setting gently down on the row of skinned
pine logs. The throb of the engine echoed off the ridge and
down the valley as the prop slowed its arc. The forest wore
a cloak of early morning stillness without a breath of
breeze. It was going to be another hot one. A few wisps of
horsetails on the eastern horizon were the only breaks in the
blue expanse. The sun, four hours from its zenith, was
steaming the dew off the rocks, and most of the crew had
already discarded their shirts, an event usually reserved for
the afternoon. They were out by the pad, bodies and clothes
scrubbed, ready to go. Roman surveyed the array of
suitcases, duffel bags and boxes arranged in a pile beside
the clearing and announced, "You fellows are going to have
to travel lighter than that or I might not be able to get you
out in one trip. Is everyone going?"
"No," Dusty replied. "Reuben wants to stay in camp and
keep an eye on things. It's too long a trip for him to go
home. He'll need some supplies in about a week and might
decide to go to town then for a couple of days until the rest

of us get back. He's got orders to check in with you people by radio each day."

"Okay. Oh, I almost forgot. Here's the mail. I don't suppose you've got a spare sandwich in there," Lou motioned to the cooktent. "I hustled out too early this morning and missed breakfast. I don't want to pass out from hunger on the way back."

Dusty and Lou Roman headed toward the cooktent and the increasing sound of Cap's cursing and pot-banging.

"He doesn't sound very happy," the pilot remarked.

"Don't let it bother you," Dusty replied. "He gets that way when anything disturbs his routine or doesn't go exactly the way he planned, but he gets over it fast. What worries me some is that he is becoming increasingly irritable and appears to be steadily losing weight. I've postponed mentioning it to him in hopes this break in the routine will cheer him up."

"I'm sorry to hear that. He runs a good camp, way better than most of the ones I service. I'd hate to have him angry at me while he's fixing my food."

Lou busied himself at the platter of bacon and eggs. "Isn't anyone going to join me?"

"I guess I will," Dusty replied. "These guys were up at five o'clock hassling Cap for breakfast so they'd be sure to be ready when you got here. I wish they were that enthusiastic to go to work in the mornings."

Lou scraped the last crumbs from his plate and sat back in satisfaction. "That was great." Then, leaning forward on the table toward Dusty, he continued, "I guess you heard on the radio about the new fires that broke out over to the west."

"We were listening last night. I got the impression that it's pretty well under control."

"Well, it is and it isn't. What you heard is the official report from Forestry downplaying the seriousness of the situation," the pilot replied. "I flew over the area the day before yesterday. The blazes are small, and the Forestry seems to have them pretty well contained, but that bush is dry as a bone. All they need is a good wind and they are in trouble."

"What's the weather outlook? Is there any chance of some rain?"

"Not much. There's nothing forecasted and no signs of any new pressure systems building up. But, the thing is, the winds are predicted to increase, and if the fire does get out of control, it could blow into this area with less than a day's notice."

Now concerned, Dusty got up from the table. "I'll go get a map. I want you to spot just where the fires are."

Using his fork as a pointer, Lou outlined the burning areas, which formed an arc three valleys over from their present location.

"It'll take a pretty good wind to bring that fire over the mountains."

"I know, but I've seen it happen," Lou replied. "What could take place if we don't get some relief from this heat is that the Government may close off your area. So far they haven't said anything, but they are getting jumpy. It wouldn't take much for them to shut you down."

Dusty thought for a minute. "Maybe this is the right time for us to be taking this break, but I'm kind of worried about Reuben being in here alone. I need you to come in quickly and get him if things go bad."

"He won't be alone," Brian, who had been listening with interest for the past few minutes, announced. "Kitch is staying too."

"I thought he was going down to Vancouver to see his wife and little girl."

"He was, but he got a letter this morning. She got their divorce finalized and is getting married again. She doesn't want him to come. He doesn't see any point in going back now."

"Is he taking it hard?" Dusty asked.

"I don't know. With him, it's really hard to tell. He bottles things up pretty good."

"I'll go and talk to him," Dusty replied. "Lou, will you keep in touch with them by radio and pull them out if there's any sign of danger. I'll call you from the city every other day to check on the situation."

"No problem," Lou replied. "I'll look after them."

Kitch still had two full bottles of rye whiskey dug in under an old stump behind camp. It was enough to get him thoroughly drunk and stay that way for the better part of three days. Finally, on the third day, Reuben rescued him from falling into the river, filled him with soup and coffee and put him to bed. By the next morning Kitch's mind had accepted the end of his relationship with Glennda and Julie, and they were beginning to slowly fade into the background of his consciousness. It seemed that his life could be summed up as a collection of disasters, punctuating interminable periods of basic survival. As long as he could remember, booze had been the medicine to dilute the pain. Unfortunately, it didn't seem to be working this time.

"I cooked some stew," Reuben poked his head through the tent door. "You want some?"

"Sure," Kitch replied, rising up on his elbows, then slumping back as the pain drove his head down to seek the coolness of the pillow. "That is, if I can walk and make it as far as the cooktent."

"I'll wait until I see you before I serve it," the old man replied.

Kitch stumbled to the cooktent, banged his head on a shelf and sunk onto the wooden bench.

"What's today?"

"Tuesday."

"Guess I lost a day or two somewhere. Christ! I feel awful."
He looked at the old man sitting across from him. "You're

looking pretty smug with your hair combed and a clean shirt. Why didn't you tie one on with me?"

"You didn't offer me any."

"Oh shit!" Kitch started to say something else, but decided he wasn't up to pursuing the topic any further. It was too painful to even think of a suitable reply.

Another ten minutes of silence and Kitch tried again.

"What do you plan to do until the rest of them get back?"

"I'm going to town tomorrow and drink my own whiskey."

Kitch gave up. He walked to the rear of the tent and flipped on the radio transmitter.

"Well, let's see when your ride is coming in."

It took him half a dozen tries to raise an unrecognizable voice through the static. After numerous requests to repeat the message, Kitch was finally able to make sense of the answers to learn that Lou had left word that he would be in to camp about noon, and because of the fire danger, Dusty had phoned and requested that Kitch come out also.

"Looks like you're going to have company, whether you want it or not," Kitch said as he hung up. "I think I'll lock you in your hotel room, take all your money, and spend it on drink and fast women."

The old man got up, looked at his partner, spat on the floor and walked out.

The day seemed even hotter than those before. Lou voiced his worry as they moved up over the trees.

"The fires are getting bad. A bit of wind picked up last night and sent part of the blaze over the ridge. It's about twenty miles from your camp and appears to be moving this way."

"I guess Dusty was right to pull us out," Kitch replied. "It could get scary."

"He didn't have any choice. The Forestry ordered everybody out of the area."

Kitch was suddenly concerned. "What about the village?"

"Most of the men are out fighting the fire," Lou answered.

"The Government flew the rest of them into town. Say, do you want to fight fire? They're grabbing everybody they can get their hands on to go out there."

"I don't know. What's the deal?"

"A few bucks a day and all the smoke you can eat. It's a lot of hard work and can be dangerous if the fire goes wild. Most of the folks in town try and avoid getting involved."

"That does not sound like a great deal. What if I don't want to go?"

"Then you'd better stay away from the bars or any places where people gather, because they can make you go if they figure they are understaffed."

"Well, I guess I might as well learn to be a firefighter. There's not much else to do in town, and it'll sure beat the hell out of spending all week in town keeping Reuben out of trouble."

No time was wasted on the ground. A Government chopper was sitting at the airport warming up with a group gathered around waiting to get on board. An hour after setting down, Kitch found himself sitting with six others in the helicopter heading for the fire area. He was settling back ready to endure the monotony of another boring chopper ride when a voice beside him asked, "Want some chicken?"

The man next to him had pulled a big box of fried chicken from his knapsack and was passing it around to the rest of the men. He had turned to Kitch.

"I'm Martin, and these are John and Gabriel." The other two nodded a greeting. "I don't know those other fellows. They're from another village somewhere to the north and don't seem very friendly."

Kitch introduced himself and had a piece of chicken.

"We've been out on that fire for over a week now, and all I could think about for the last three days was fried chicken, so we kinda hitched a ride back into town and ... I forgot the wine."

Martin pulled a gallon of red wine from the knapsack.

"Can't eat chicken without wine," he mumbled as he tilted the bottle back and took it down well over a pint on the first pull. He passed the bottle on to the others, settled back on his bedroll and drifted off to sleep.

Kitch observed the man as he slept. Somehow, he seemed strangely familiar, but he couldn't remember running into him on his visit to the village. He was Kitch's height, but wider and well muscled. He had long black hair, braided near the end. The features of his face were finely chiseled and delicate with an oriental cast. He wore a loosely knotted Apache headband with faded and ragged-edged denim jacket and pants, with charred cuffs and small burn holes.

THE FIRE

Kitch could see the fire from about twenty miles out. It was actually a number of blazes dotted along the west slope of a broad forested valley. There was no wind and the smoke rose straight up almost blotting out the sun. As they dropped over the ridge he could make out a road being bulldozed in from the north along the valley bottom. Every few minutes a water bomber would come in along the treetops and empty its belly into the blaze. As they hovered over the pad to set down, Kitch became aware of Martin watching him.

"This your first fire?"

Kitch nodded.

"You stay with us and you'll do alright."

On the ground there were a dozen or so men standing around not seeming to know what to do.

"C'mon," Martin called from the cab of a truck." We'll go up the line and see what's going on."

John and Gabriel had already tossed their gear in the back, so Kitch did likewise and climbed in. Martin took the truck down the dozed track without easing his foot off the accelerator for an instant.

"Those men will be standing back there until someone comes down, takes them by the hand and tells them what to do," he yelled above the roar of the motor. "And, that could be some time from now."

The three miles they covered lasted somewhere between an instant and an eternity for Kitch. Martin screeched the truck up beside a parked dozer and jumped out.

"Where's John?"

"You bounced him out about a mile back," Gabriel replied, gingerly easing his body out over the tailgate.

"He'll show up. Leave your packs here, and we'll see what they want us to do."

A short way up the track were half a dozen men, their skin and clothes blackened with soot, stretched out on the bank with big steaming mugs of coffee. As they approached, a tall gray-haired man in a Forestry uniform got up.

"Martin, where the hell have you been all day? I need you to organize some men down at the south end of the fire break."

"I went to town for some fried chicken."

The older man didn't reply, but Kitch could guess from his expression that anything Martin did probably wouldn't surprise him.

"And the young paleface here is called Kitch. He's with that mining crew working down south of our village."

The man shook Kitch's hand and introduced himself as Fred. He inquired as to Kitch's fire-fighting experience and then suggested that he stick with Martin until he learned the ropes. Turning to Martin, he added. "You take these two down on the break, and I'll send the rest of them at the pad to you."

Kitch asked the question as they walked down the track.

"How did you know I was with a mining crew? I didn't tell you that."

"I recognized you when you got on the helicopter. I saw you the last time I was at the village, one night you came in to see Della."

"You know Della?"

"I'm her father."

Nothing was said for ten seconds and then Martin started to laugh. He looked at Kitch and laughed all the harder until he had to sit down in the middle of the trail and hold his sides.

"Don't look so worried. Hell, I know you two been spending your nights in that old cabin north of the village." For one of the few times he could remember, Kitch didn't know what to say.

The firebreak on one side was a track the dozer had widened for about a hundred yards along the valley bottom. On the west slope the fire blazed in the still air, sending up streams of smoke. Men worked their way back and forth along the break and up the other side putting out the little blazes as they caught from the settling sparks. The bush was dry, and the brown clumps of grass burned quickly when ignited. Kitch had moved farther up the valley after he had learned from Martin what he was supposed to do. There, the crackle of the fire was mingled with the roar of the bulldozers, which were working their way up the slope along the edges of the blaze, attempting to confine it to a smaller area. He joined two others patrolling behind the dozers and learned that the worst of the battle was over and that the entire blaze was now confined to this mile-long stretch of slope.

It was hot, dirty and exhausting work, and Kitch was bone-tired when another crew relieved them at dusk. A camp kitchen had been set up near the trucks, and it was here that he found Martin and the others just finishing their meal.

"Thought we were going to have to go looking for you," Martin grunted. "I'll bet you liked that job so well you were thinking of taking another shift."

Kitch pulled a couple of scoops of stew out of the kettle onto his pan and leaned back on the grassy slope.

"Here, start with this," Martin said as he pulled a half-filled bottle of wine out of his pack. "It makes even that stew

taste better."
Kitch took a long pull, coughed and spit half the liquid back on the ground.
"My God! What is that stuff?" He sputtered.
"Just a little juice we make back in the village," Martin replied. "It's good for you, toughens up your body."
"Sure," Kitch said, handing back the bottle.
Shadows probed their dark forms across the valley as the sun settled behind the burning slope. Through the smoky haze it appeared larger, diffuse and blood red. Cinders and ashes sprinkled through the still air. Mostly they were burned out, but occasionally a live spark had to be stomped on before it had a chance to feed on the parched vegetation. All the normal night sounds were masked by the noise of the fire. No animals could be heard scurrying about, and the only birds to be seen were the crows waiting around the cooking area for handouts.
Kitch walked back to the truck, retrieved his pack and climbed up the east slope to a level area. Here and there on the hillside flickering points of light marked small groups of men settling in for the night. Kitch picked a clearing near Martin and his friends, who were playing cards on an old chunk of plywood. Kitch looked on for a few minutes but was too sleepy to follow the course of the game. Along the slope were stands of young fir and jack pine, and he soon had enough of the full-needled lower branches to form a spongy mattress. He stretched out his sleeping bag and settled back to the panorama of stars dimly visible through the haze. There were no clouds and the northern lights projected a fiery display as if in answer to the blaze below.
Kitch awoke with a start. At first he was conscious of the daylight, but suddenly he realized it was still night and the light was coming from the fire, which was burning much brighter. He could feel a soft wind fanning the heat and ashes up from the valley. Small blazes were springing up on the hillside, as men ran about attempting to put them

out. Kitch watched in fascination until he realized the danger of his position. There was bush burning on all sides of him. As he frantically gathered his few possessions into his bedroll, he was unaware of his name being called until Martin grabbed him by the arm and motioned him to follow. They scrambled up to the crest of the knoll where a small group of men had gathered. Below, they could see the blaze inching its way up the slope, jumping from tree to tree with the gentle prod of the wind.

Although it seemed to Kitch that everyone was running around in a state of confusion, Fred appeared to be in control of the situation. He communicated continually on the radio, attempting to coordinate the activities of the various crews. Kitch was able to gather through the static and crackle of transmission that one dozer had been caught in the blaze and had to be abandoned, but that the other one had worked its way to the top of the ridge and was attempting to clear a wide break where the trees were not as dense.

"If he can get that cat through here and clear out the trees, we might be able to keep the burning down in this valley." Fred was talking to no one in particular. Then he turned and yelled to Martin. "You string your men out along the top and kill any sparks that get over to the other side." The rest of his words were lost to the roar of the dozer as it swept a path through the stunted forest.

"It looks like a long night," Martin said as he tried to light the stub end of a cigarette he had fished out of his pocket. "Here," Kitch motioned, tossing him a pouch and papers. "Roll a new one before you burn the end off your nose." Martin stationed a man every hundred yards along the ridge. Kitch's position was at the south end of the line, a bit beyond the projected course of the fire. Here, the noise was less intense, and for the first time he felt the chill of the night air. He hadn't realized until then how really tired he was. An hour later he was dozing as Martin came along with some coffee.

"Looks like I was just in time with this."

"Yeah, it's getting tough to sit here and stay awake," Kitch replied.

"S'been a tough day. Had to shake a couple fellas awake, but the fire's letting up, at least the wind died down. You might get to your bed yet tonight."

The two men sat and smoked in silence, each in his own thoughts. The fire noises had lessened, and only once in a while a faint whisper of the wind could be heard rustling through the pines.

"Every year there's at least one big bush fire in this country," Martin observed. "Back in my grandfather's time, and when my father was a young man these fires would start from lightning or somebody's cooking fire when the bush got real dry like this. A whole bunch of bush would burn and then the rain or the wind blowing it back on itself would put it out. Nobody tried to stop it . They saw no cause to. It was just another normal event. If the fire got too close to their homes, they got out of the way and moved to another spot. Now the Government spends all this money to fight the fires, and it doesn't seem to make much difference. They still burn their way through the country until it rains or there is nothing left to burn. It seems like a hell of a waste."

"That's the feeling I get about us being here," Kitch replied. "I can't see where we've had any control over this blaze."

"I've argued this with some of the fellas from the Forestry, but they figure I'm just a dumb Indian who doesn't know anything about the bush, because I haven't read the books that tell what it's all about, but damn it, I've lived all my life here." He sat silent for a few moments, drawing the last bit of smoke from his cigarette. "The forest, to me, is like a person and has a life with different ages. You can walk through the bush and tell whether it's young, or middle-aged or old by the kinds of trees and bushes, which ones are together and how big they are. And you can tell what kind of a life it's having. The trees may be bent over by the winds as a man becomes stooped by too much work or worry, and the marks of fires on the forest aren't much different from the scars people carry from getting hurt. And just as people can make a new life so can a forest, but somewhere death must occur either by old age or by fire so that a new group of trees can be born and grow."

By noon of the next day the fresh Pacific breeze had carried in the rain clouds. The wind had kicked the fire up a bit, but with the drizzle that followed, the burning decreased.

Except for a few smoldering spots, the blaze was out by midnight, and the men on the hillside had an uninterrupted sleep.

The first chopper load took off as Kitch finished his breakfast. The 'Cat' driver had left much earlier to walk his machine on the long trail out to the road. It was a beautiful morning. The fresh crisp air with a taste of salt bathed the land and helped erase the last traces of fatigue from the men's minds.

THE LONG HIKE

"Let's walk back."
The yell came from across the clearing.
Kitch looked around, decided that Martin was talking to him, and answered. "To where? The village?"
"Sure," Martin replied, seating himself on a partly burned log. "It's only about fifty miles cross country, and there's a good fishing hole on the way. You still got some time off, haven't you?"
"Yeah, about five or six days," he thought for a moment, "What the hell, let's go."
"We'll take off as soon as Gabriel gets back. He's going too. He's over trying to talk Fred out of some of the leftover food. Here he comes now, looks like he did okay."
"Hope you liked that stew," Gabriel said. "I got twenty cans."
"If it's that stuff we had the other night," Kitch replied, "I hope the fishing's as good as you say it is."
They walked until sundown, keeping a pace along the narrow trail that was steady, but not tiring. It was a glorious day, warm, with a gentle breeze from the west. Kitch's only complaint was the weight of his pack on some unused muscles. Gabriel, though carrying more on his homemade pack board, showed no signs of strain. Kitch could

understand Martin's broad shoulders easily taking the burden, but Gabriel, though an inch or two taller than Kitch, was certainly no heavier. Kitch studied the man, trying to determine his age. So far, he had pinned it down to somewhere between thirty and sixty. Gabriel spoke very little, and when he did, the words came slow and haltingly as if chosen carefully to convey a message. At first Kitch had thought he was a bit simple and had paid little attention to him, but now their close contact brought on a new awareness. Where Martin was boisterous and joking, always at ease among men, Gabriel was quiet and reserved. He was at home with the plants and animals of the forest. He found game trail where Kitch saw nothing. Broken branches in a patch of wild raspberries told him that a bear had fed on the fruit, and the slight dampness of the broken canes revealed that it had happened only a few hours before. He showed Kitch rabbit paths and dens in the thick underbrush, and from partly dried droppings, knew that the rabbit had been there that morning. From the number, size and shape of the tracks farther on, he could tell that three rabbits had passed that way since last evening's rain. Kitch was fascinated. All the time he had worked in the bush he had been only vaguely aware of its life. When Brian had tried to share his excitement, Kitch had been only mildly interested. Brian's approach had been too scientific. Gabriel showed Kitch how to tell the mushrooms he could eat from the ones that were poisonous. He pointed out plants that would provide food from their leaves, roots or young shoots: and the trees of which the inner bark could be eaten. In the days that followed, Kitch was to learn more from this man of few words than he thought possible.

They made camp by a stream where the water tumbled over the rocks to form a deep pool. Martin caught some grasshoppers along the bank and with one firmly attached to a fishhook, he let the current wash his line into the pool.

Four grasshoppers brought four trout, enough for dinner.
Fried with the wild mushrooms and washed down with hot
tea, it was the best meal Kitch had eaten in some time.
The next morning came early with the midsummer heat, but
the three men had been awakened long before dawn. In the
early darkness, animal cries had filled the air with fear. The
sounds were too close. Gabriel sat listening intently. The
puzzlement he felt showed in the firelight, causing his
companions to feel all the more uneasy.
"There's a bear and a wolf, but only one wolf. That's
strange. Both animals are in pain."
Then, as suddenly as it had begun, the noise stopped and
there was silence. The whole forest held its breath. Kitch
was certain he could hear something breathing heavily on
the opposite bank, but there was not enough light to make
out any shapes.
"Do you hear something moving over there?" He asked.
"Can't tell," Martin replied. "The creek's making too much
noise."
"There is something there," Gabriel announced. "See those
willows moving just back from shore."
His companions strained their eyes to the opposite bank but
could see nothing.
"One of us better stay awake the rest of the night in case
anything else happens," Martin suggested. "You two catch
some sleep, and I'll stay up."
But neither man was able to sleep. At first light they ate a
quick breakfast, giving the sun time to melt the river mist.
After packing up camp the three men slowly forded the
stream keeping an eye on the far thicket for any unusual
movements. There were none. It seemed quiet enough as
they skirted the area of dense growth.
"Almost too quiet," Kitch thought. "No birds. Nothing."
As they approached higher ground there were larger trees,
and the second growth had thinned out. Charred logs,
reminders of past fires covered the ground, piled upon one

another in all directions, making walking difficult. They made slow progress hopping from log to log or walking the length of one if it pointed in the direction they were going. The wood was still wet and slippery in the shaded areas, resulting in a number of falls. The men were not sorry to pick up a well-used game trail that followed the easiest route through the tangle. A few paces along the trail Gabriel slowed and looked carefully at the ground.

"A bear used this trail last night. Here are tracks going in both directions. He went this way and then came back. See here, where one track is over the other. This is a big grizzly, but something is wrong with him, with the way he walks. Here, the footmark is crooked, and here, and here. He's dragging a back foot."

For Kitch the explanation turned a hopeless mess of tracks into a clear record.

Farther along the trail was the explanation. The burned, half-eaten body of a large timber wolf lay in a small clearing beside the trail. The scorched flesh, which had been slashed and torn away by the bear, had deformed the animal's body to the point that it was barely recognizable.

Martin was the first to speak. "I think we'd better get out of here. He'll probably be back for another feed."

"Not for a while," Gabriel replied. "He ate pretty good last night. This wolf must have been burned bad to be away from the pack and not able to run from a lame grizzly."

Kitch stared thoughtfully at the scene of the struggle. "About a month ago there was a lot of talk about an injured grizzly that was supposed to have attacked somebody. Do you think this could be the same bear?"

"Could be," Martin replied. "It's hard to know. That bear was way south of here. They don't usually stray much out of their own part of the country."

"They will if something crowds them out," said Gabriel. "If there's a fire or he's hurt and can't catch game he'll go farther away to look for food."

The men were more on guard to the noises of the forest as they moved south that day. By mid-afternoon they had come to the headwaters of the watercourse that flowed by the village. Here, in its upper reaches, it was a shallow stream that could easily be crossed on foot. As they continued along its rocky shores through a series of canyons cut into bedrock, it became deep and faster. Just before sundown Martin found the spot he was looking for. For a mile they had followed a trail by the stream as it meandered through a series of sandstone ridges finally cascading into a deep pool cut into the softer shale beds. The shore formed an arc, gently sloping up to a grassy platform where the remnants of past camps were scattered over the green expanse. Charred stones lined cooking-pits, and the skinned tent-pole tripods and drying racks remained as sentries between the yearly fish-gathering parties. Martin tossed his pack on the grass and began looking closely into the dense foliage at the edge of the clearing.

"Ha! Here they are."

Scratching away the cover of leaves and twigs, he pulled a wine bottle from under a tree root.

"Tonight we eat the biggest trout and drink the best wine in British Columbia." He held up the bottle. "I supply the wine, you two catch the fish."

Kitch eyed the bottle suspiciously.

"That's not the same swill you tried to feed me the other night, is it?"

"No! No! This is the honey of the Gods. It's from huckleberries. Lisa made it last year when we were here for the salmon run. Here. Try it."

It was noon before Martin or Kitch stirred from their sleeping bags. Both men suffered the effects of last night and stumbled about mumbling incoherently until Gabriel filled them with coffee and stew.

"How did I get wet?" Martin grumbled as he poured water out of his boots.

"You tried to jump over to the other side of the creek last night," Gabriel answered.

"What! You must be crazy. I can't jump that far."

"You thought you could last night."

"No, that's foolish." Then, turning to Kitch, he asked. "Why didn't you stop me?"

"He thought he could do it too," Gabriel replied. "I had to pull you both out."

"Well, there's no point in going any farther today," Kitch said. "We might as well dry out our clothes in this sun and get an early start tomorrow morning. Besides, I don't feel that great."

After the wet clothes and sleeping bags had been laid out, Kitch and Martin stretched out in the afternoon sun. Gabriel sat smoking his pipe on an old river bank log, every so often flipping a dropline into the current, letting the bait swirl into the eddies and backwaters of the pool.

"The bear was around last night."

His remark immediately caught his companions' attention.

"I took a walk early this morning," Gabriel continued. "I crossed a trail back in the woods west of here and found his tracks. There were two sets of them again, one going and one coming. I followed them a ways in both directions, but they just kept going. It was the same bear."

"Did he come close to where we are now?" Kitch asked.

"Near as I can tell he never left the trail. Maybe all the hollering you two did last night scared him away."

"It sounds like he's sticking around this area," Martin replied. "Does that trail head toward the village?"

"It goes in that direction, but I don't remember it from being here before. It's mostly a game trail. Been a bunch of moose over it since the rains."

"Where do you think the bear is now, ahead or behind us?"

"I don't know. Couldn't tell which set of tracks was older. My guess is he's behind us, and I hope going the other way. But, we better be looking out for him and keep watch tonight."

"It's spooky," Kitch observed, "almost like he's keeping track of us."

"He knows we're here," Gabriel replied.

Gabriel agreed to stay awake the first half of the night, deciding that his companions needed the sleep. He got no argument. Fortunately, the night was uneventful as Kitch and Martin both slept through most of their watches.

The early morning dew was heavy. Silver droplets glistened on leaves and sparkled where caught on the spiders' webs. The trees and bushes showered on anything that disturbed the stillness, and even the slightest noise crackled in the crisp dawn air. Pant legs and boots passing through the tall grass were soon soaked, and attempts to dry out clothes and bedrolls were only partly successful.

THE CAVE

The morning sun tried to warm the land as the three men
trudged south along the path, but by noon fluffy white
cloud banks had built up from the west, turned gray, and a
rain-soaked wind soon had them shrinking into the
protection of their upturned collars. By mid-afternoon the
rain had increased from a blowing mist to a steady
downpour, soaking everything. The men were miserable.
Their clothing was suited for normal July weather, not this
preview of winter. The cold evening meal of stew was
eaten in silence, as each man tried to hide his thoughts from
the wet and chill.
"This has got the makings of a hell of a miserable night,"
Kitch observed. "Have either of you got any ideas where
we can camp to get out of this?"
"No, I don't know of any good cover between here and the
village," Martin replied.
The men were soaked clear through. The prospect of trying
to get some sleep in their wet bags was not an option, and
the idea of trying to continue along the trail in the darkness
was even less appealing.
"There is a cave," Gabriel added hesitantly. "It's about a
mile or two west of here, I think. I was only there once, and
that was quite a few years ago. It would be big enough for

us if we can find it. I would probably have no trouble spotting it if I was coming north from the village. That's how I found it, but from here, I don't know."

They sat quietly for a few minutes thinking about their options before Kitch asked, "How far to the village?"

"About a day and a half walk," Gabriel replied.

"How long do you think it would take us to reach the cave?"

"Bout an hour if we don't have trouble finding it."

"Let's go look for it. Maybe we'll get lucky," Kitch suggested, as he began tying his pack together. "It sure won't be any worse than what we got now."

The search took two hours. After a few wrong turns, then retracing their steps, Gabriel was able to spot some familiar landmarks, and they managed to pick their way to the entrance at the base of a low hill, just as the last traces of daylight were soaked up in the soggy dusk.

"This looks pretty good," Kitch said as he flicked on a match with his thumbnail. "There's even some dry wood back there."

A few minutes later a roaring blaze was scorching the chill from their wet, huddled bodies, and the heat soon had them all dozing.

Kitch awoke suddenly and sat up. It was late. Only a few embers were left of the fire, and the cold blackness of the night had seeped in around them. He didn't know what had awakened him, but he was vaguely aware of an unfamiliar noise. He thought he had heard something running, but that could have been part of the dream, which was rapidly slipping from his consciousness. The only sound was Martin's rhythmic snoring from the other side of the cave. Beyond the bed of the dying fire and the mouth of the cave, it was totally dark, and he could see nothing. He lay back, trying to summon the release of sleep, but it was no use. He was wide-awake. He crawled out of the still damp sleeping bag to fetch some sticks to rekindle the fire. He was uneasy, but shrugging his shoulders he put it down to the lingering memory of the dream. The fire caught easily and soon flooded the entrance with warmth and its flickering light. Kitch sat thoughtfully chewing a piece of smoked fish and staring out into the darkness. The rain had stopped, and the occasional glimpse of a star marked the passage of the clouds. A soft breeze from the south had picked up and rustled the leaves along the front of the cave. His thoughts were interrupted, as he sensed an unpleasant smell. Suddenly his eye caught a movement to the left. At first glance he thought it was the wind buffeting the line of small trees, but it was out of place. He stared hard at the spot for a few moments but could see nothing out of the ordinary. He pulled his eyes away at the same moment a branch snapped directly in front of him. It broke the stillness like a shot and startled Kitch to his feet. A momentary icy chill swept his body as he stared in the direction of the noise, but there was still nothing to see. He picked up a burning branch from the fire and hurled it in the direction of the noise. The glowing brand arced over and over in the air and landed with a shower of sparks in the wet thicket. That feeble light, however, had been enough.

Kitch caught a quick glimpse of the movement. It was only a form, a shadow momentarily slipping between the trees. He picked up another burning branch, tossing it in the same direction, but this time there was nothing. Kitch felt his muscles slowly beginning to relax only to hear the scratch of steps on the loose rock to his left. Before he could react, Gabriel appeared in the small circle of light.

"Christ! You scared me," Kitch exclaimed. "What the hell were you doing creeping around out there."

Gabriel turned his head to look out into the bush, saying nothing. Then he walked over to Kitch and hunched down by the fire. He replied in a hoarse whisper.

"Tell me what you saw out there."

Kitch described the noise and the moving figure.

"I saw it too, from over there. It ran by me when you threw the fire. It came so close, but I could not see it clearly because of the dark."

"Was it the bear?"

Gabriel sat staring into the fire until Kitch began to wonder if he had heard his question. Suddenly, he spoke, "No! It wasn't the bear."

"Well, what the hell was it?"

Gabriel looked at Kitch thoughtfully, then answered slowly, testing the effect of each word on his companion. "I'm not sure, but I think it was a Wild Man. I've never seen one, but this could be as the old men tell about them. The stories tell of him living in this area. I think this might be his cave, and he was surprised to see us here."

"I've heard about some of the stories that Martin's father tells. Are you saying they're true?"

"I don't know. For those who believe in the Wild Men, like Martin and Sam Jonas, they live. All my life since I was a small boy and first heard the old stories, I've wanted to see one so I could know if they did exist. I don't know. I just don't know." Gabriel sat with his head lowered, looking into the fire. He was still sitting there motionless in the morning when Kitch and Martin awoke to the sun's first rays.

Through another breakfast of stew, they recounted the night's events to Martin. There was no doubt in his mind as to what they had seen.

"Let's go down and see if we can find some tracks. Maybe we can trail him," Martin said excitedly.

The bush was still wet from yesterday's rain. Tracking would have been impossible for anyone else, but Gabriel picked up the trail right away. Broken branches, low plants crushed under foot, and other less obvious signs led them through the mass of undergrowth and up the side of the hill above the cave. But, nowhere could the outline of a footprint be identified in the spongy turf. Gabriel moved more slowly now, ferreting his way up the slope, occasionally picking up threads of the trail. His companions moved quietly behind him, careful not to disturb his concentration until they reached the summit of the knoll, where they stopped to catch their breath. Along the top, the ground cover was thinner, and the surface was dry and rocky. Gabriel walked carefully around the surface then stopped and peered out to the west.

"No trail I can follow up here," he remarked as Kitch came alongside. "It looks like he headed for the mountains. That's where I think he would want to go. If he stayed on the high ground we can't track him."

"Did you see anything to tell what we're following?" Kitch asked.

"No. Whatever it was, it was moving fast, and running upright at least part of the way. Down below there were branches broken off higher than my head."

"Hell! We know what it is," Martin interrupted. "Let's keep going."

By circling back and forth Gabriel was able to pick out fragments of a trail in the soft earth down to a creek on the backside of the hill, at which point all signs of the creature's passage disappeared completely. They searched the opposite shore without success.

"Might as well go back to the main trail," Gabriel sighed as he eased down on a log and let the cold mountain water run across his feet. "I lost him. He must have walked the creek a ways before he headed west again."

The journey back to the main trail was much more pleasant than yesterday's trip searching for the cave. The main trail was wide and well used. It was a beautiful July evening when they stopped to make camp, but the disappointment caused by the failure of the hunt tempered their mood. Martin and Kitch were bone tired and fell into their sleeping bags with little talk after the usual filling of stew.

Both were asleep by the time Gabriel washed the pots and plates. He was still awake when Kitch got up around midnight to have a cigarette. He rolled an extra one for his friend and pulled his bed closer to the warmth.

"Can't you sleep?" He asked, handing Gabriel the cigarette.

"No, it's time for me to do some thinking. Sometimes things make more sense late at night."

"Last night and today has really gotten to you, hasn't it?"

"Huh?"

"While we were tracking this creature today, I got the feeling that if there had been a trail, you would have followed it all the way to the mountains or until you dropped."

"I would, or at least until I found what made the trail."

"Why? Does it really matter that much?"

"To me, it matters very much. I have to know if he is real. The old stories are not enough. I have to see him with my eyes. There is no other way I can believe he exists."

"Old Sam at the village says he saw one when he was a kid and tells stories about others he knows who have seen them."

"I know," Gabriel replied. "Sam Jonas is a great man, but he is old and sometimes get confused. I have heard his stories, and most are mixtures of tales that have come down from the past and things that have happened in his lifetime. I wonder if he can tell the difference now."

"You think he gets mixed up about what is real?"

"I don't know, maybe sometimes. When I used to ask him questions about the Wild Men, he'd look at me in that way he has of seeing right through you and give me the same old stories. We'd all heard them, ever since we were small. Martin has heard them all and has no doubts that they are real, but he has been taught these things since he was a baby. For me, my family came to the village when I was ten. We came from farther to the south where we had not heard any tales of these wild creatures. The idea of large wild man-like creatures living amongst us was frightening, but as I grew older without seeing any of them, I began to doubt."

GABRIEL'S STORY

"One day, when I was about thirteen or fourteen, a man
from the village came back from hunting, telling everyone
that he'd seen one of these big men. This man used to drink
all the time so no one took him seriously about anything.
He wanted someone to go back with him and maybe find
some sign, so he could show everyone that he was telling
the truth, but nobody was interested in going except me. I
said I'd travel with him. We packed some gear and left that
same day. We walked west toward the mountains for three
days. He was half drunk all the way but seemed to know
where he was going. On the evening of the last day, he got
jumpy and didn't seem to want to go any farther. I talked
him in to continuing on, so he took me to the spot where he
claimed he saw the big man. There wasn't much to see, but
we searched around for a while, and I found what I thought
was a footprint. It wasn't very clear, and it was getting
dark, so we bedded down there. When I awoke the next
morning, he was gone, took off in the middle of the night. I
wasn't surprised, the way he'd been acting. I figured I'd
look around some more before I went back to the village.
That morning I found a fresh track in the mud where we'd
been looking the previous day. It was a big one, and farther
on there were half a dozen more. They were not so clear

but were good enough to make me want to keep looking, but I was suspicious. I began to wonder if the man had made these tracks the night he left and was sitting back in the village laughing at me. I decided to stay. I searched around the hills for a week and found just enough signs, or what I though were signs, to keep me going. This took me right up to the mountains where I could see the trails up into the high country and the many caves above tree line. It was a long tough climb, so when I reached the caves, I decided to stay and explore them. They were all shapes and sizes. Bears and small animals lived in a few. I grew to like it up there. It was all different from what I had known of the valley and the land around the village. I spent a lot of days looking around in all those caves searching for signs of the big people. Then, this one day, back up in a narrow canyon I found a big cave. It was well hidden by an overhanging rock ledge and bushes, and unless you walked along a steep slope you couldn't see it. When I climbed down to the mouth of the cave I really got excited. The ground was all tramped down, and it was clear that the cave was being used. At first I thought it was another bear den, but inside there were signs that I didn't find in any of the other caves. There were rocks piled up in mounds, some of the rocks so heavy I couldn't move them. And there were spots where branches had been laid out on the ground like a bed. I was convinced that I had found what I was looking for and that it would be just a matter of time until the people of the cave came back."

Gabriel paused in his story, took a long pull on the remains of his cigarette, and stared thoughtfully into the fire.

"I found a secluded spot to hide on the other side of the draw where I had a clear view of the cave. I had enough food, so I figured I could stay hidden for at least a week without coming out, but I was sure I'd see something long before then. I stayed in there nine days and saw nothing. All the while I was there, I had this feeling I was being watched. I'd stretched my food out and could have stayed another few days, but I felt I had to get out of there or go crazy. Toward the end of my stay I couldn't sleep. All the time I felt these eyes on me, but never did I see anything. When I finally came out and went back to the cave, there was grass and green shoots sprouting up where it had been tramped flat before. They had obviously been aware that I was spying on them and decided not to return. The whole thing made me even more eager to see one of these creatures, but it caused me to change my ideas about how to hunt them. Up till then I had gone about it the way you would hunt for bear or deer. Now I had the feeling I was after something very wise in the forest, and I would have to learn to live in their land as they do in order to make contact with them. I made up my mind not to return to the village. For a while I searched around the canyon, but there was nothing. I had the strong feeling the creatures had cleared out of the area. It was getting on in the season. The larch had turned and the birch and poplar had lost their leaves. Then the snow came. In a way I welcomed it because I thought it would make tracking easier, but there were no signs of any tracks, and finally the cold drove me out of the high country. Instead of coming back to the village I knew, I headed west into the Nass River valley. That was wild country back then, and I guess it still is for the white man. One day I came upon two women and a man going south. The man had a broken leg, and the women had tied him to two poles and were dragging him along behind this skinny old horse. They were having a hell of a time. I offered to help them get him back to their cabin in trade for some food. It was about thirty miles and we damn near killed the old man with pain getting him there. One of the women took a liking to me and decided to teach me all about being with a woman, so I stayed with them most of the winter until the man was up and about and strong enough to run me off. All winter they'd been telling me the stories, which they claimed came from some of their people who lived to the west. This encouraged me to head in that direction. I traveled down the Skeena River and talked to a lot of people and heard a lot of stories, but I never saw any sign myself. About that time there was a report of some fellows seeing what they called Sasquatch running around on a beach near Bella Coola. I was able to get work with a fisherman, and as pay, convinced him to take me down there. These folks around Bella Coola had a lot of these stories too, and I spent a couple of months chasing around trying to find out all I could. Finally I got fed up with people and went up and lived in the mountains. It was a beautiful part of the country, and I felt at peace all the time I was up there. It was over a year before I came back out to civilization. During that time I learned to get everything I needed from the land as I moved about. Most of my efforts were spent on staying alive, but always the creatures were in the back of my mind. Most of the winter I had that old feeling, like up in the high country, that I was being watched, but like before, I could never see any signs of what was doing the watching. Then, in the early spring after a new snow, I finally found tracks. They were the best I'd ever seen. I followed them for well over a half a mile until they got lost on a bare rock slope. They were clear and distinct, no more than a couple of hours old when I found them. I searched all over the mountain to try and pick them up again, but there were no more. I saw and explored a lot of caves up there, but there were no indications of any of them being occupied by the big people. The tracks could have been going anywhere. They did convince me that there was something to the stories, but I felt that my searching was over for a while. I figured I had seen all I was meant to see for then, so I started walking for home."

"You walked all the way from Bella Coola!" Kitch exclaimed. "Why did you come back here? That must be a good four or five hundred miles."

"Yes, it was a long trip, but it was my home, and I missed my family. It was the year we had the big floods. I had a hell of a time crossing some of those creeks and rivers. I got back to the village that fall. It was quite a surprise, as I'd been gone over three years, and everybody thought I was dead." Gabriel stopped and looked at his companion. "One other funny thing was that the fellow that I went out with to look at those tracks in the first place never did come back to the village. I get wondering sometimes what happened to him."

The first threads of pink were pushing into the eastern sky as Gabriel snaked an ember from the dying fire to light his pipe. Kitch reached over to the pile of dry wood and threw on a few branches to catch a blaze and drive out the early morning chill. The light of the flame danced on the older man's thin features. Kitch was about to ask some of the obvious questions that were in his mind, but the look of concentration on Gabriel's face stopped him. As if he was reading his companion's thoughts, Gabriel continued, "When I saw those clear tracks, I was convinced. There was no doubt because I couldn't figure anything else that could have made them, but I never did see the creature. The doubts have returned, so now I wonder if I imagined what I had seen or if the tracks were really as good as their picture in my mind. Yesterday I got that feeling again that I have to know the truth."

"Are you going to hunt them again?"

"Yes. I feel the pull to go back and live in the mountains and look for the big people. This time I will stay until I know the truth."

As dawn brightened the sky Kitch sat alone with his thoughts. Gabriel had been a stranger not much more than a week ago and then, in a few days, a friend. But, this obsession set him apart. Kitch could not understand and was suspicious, as he was with anything that did not fit with his world. They smoked quietly as the fire built up heat under the coffee can. Neither spoke. Half a dozen times Kitch opened his mouth to voice a question that would rationalize an explanation, but they remained unspoken. Kitch sensed that it was a gulf that would separate them until he could feel that strongly about something himself.

They started early on the trail. Kitch and Gabriel ate their breakfast, packed the gear, and shook Martin out of his bedroll, in that order. The day was a repeat of yesterday, warm with a clear sky and a soft ground breeze blowing out of the south. Walking all day, they figured to make the village by nightfall. The trail was clear, and as Martin announced, it would get better as they neared the village. Around noon their path swung back to the river at a point where the banks dropped away to form a wide pool of still clear water. With a yell Martin and Kitch tossed off their packs and dived into the pool. The water was cold and quickly drove off the heat of the trail. Kitch swam to the middle and floated on his back soaking in the rays of the noonday sun.

GUY ALLEN

BEAR ATTACK

"Bear!"
Kitch snapped around to see Gabriel pointing up to the opposite shore. A large silvertip was limping rapidly down a draw about seventy-five yards from the edge of the water. Gabriel and Martin were both on shore.
"Get out! Fast!" Gabriel yelled. "Get up a tree! He's coming!"
Kitch pumped his legs hard, but his boots kept slipping on the river bottom stones. Twice, three times he fell, scrambling up the bank, the last time on all fours. He grabbed at a small bunch of willow but missed and slid back down the muddy bank on his belly.
"Run! Get the hell out of the water!" Martin yelled as he disappeared into the trees.
Kitch doubled his legs under him and drove his feet as hard as he could into the bank, at the same time lunging at the bush. This time he caught it and squirmed up on top at the same instant as the bear hit the water.
Martin's yells aimed Kitch toward a large birch near the edge of the woods. He felt like he was moving in slow motion as his wet clothes and the slippery ground held him back. He could see the branches of the birch shaking as Martin climbed to a higher position, and he could hear the

bear splashing through the pool behind him. He looked
back just as the animal scrambled up the bank. Kitch
searched frantically for a tree he could climb.
"He's right behind you," Martin yelled from his perch.
Kitch barely heard the warning as his friend's yell was
mixed with the panting and grunts of his pursuer. At once
he spotted a branch just above his reach jutting out from a
large pine. With a leap he lunged upward and wrapped his
fingers around the rough bark, but with a sharp crack the
branch broke sending him sprawling into a clump of
bushes. He hit hard. His head snapped back against the
edge of a rock and everything went black for an instant. He
rolled over and tried to get up. His mind was frantically
telling his body to move, but it wouldn't respond. The bear
was about thirty feet away but had stopped and was
swaying from side to side with its nose in the air, trying to
search out its prey. Kitch's senses were shaken, and the
image of the bear kept coming in and out of focus. He tried
to get up again but fell drunkenly back into the bushes.
Sensing the movement, the bear stopped swaying and
arched its back. The gray hairs on its neck stood straight up
in a hump. Off to the side Kitch detected movement out of
the corner of his eye. His mind registered the scene but
wouldn't let him believe it. Gabriel had come out of a
thicket beside the bear carrying a good-sized club. With all
his strength, he swung the club to catch the bear at the base
of the skull. The bear shuddered, dropped to all fours,
grabbed the club, thrust it away and with the same motion
took a swipe at Gabriel's retreating form. It sent the man
hurtling back into his thicket hideaway where he lay
without movement. The bear scrambled over to the still
form and gave it a few perfunctory shakes. It looked down
at its prey, shook Gabriel's body again and then lumbered
back out of the woods toward the river. It was a slow
motion dream that Kitch couldn't accept as reality. His
body was so heavy that he couldn't get up. He just wanted

to go to sleep, but he knew that was a bad idea, and some part of his consciousness wouldn't let him. Suddenly he was freezing cold. Martin was shaking him violently and then there was nothing but the soft black warmth of unconsciousness.

When Kitch awoke the sun was on its descent in the western sky, and the shadows were growing long. He lay out in the open beside the trail with his pack supporting his head and his sleeping bag covering him. There was no one in sight. He tried to sit up, but the sudden stab of pain in his head stopped him. He got on his hands and knees slowly and forced his body to an upright position. As his head began to clear he heard noises in the bush. He staggered to the edge of the trail in time to see Martin struggling with a makeshift stretcher, trying to drag it with Gabriel strapped on, out of the woods and on to the trail.

"You stay out there," Martin called. "I'll get him out. You take it easy. You're in no shape to help."

Kitch's head hurt too much to argue, as he watched Martin struggle with his burden into the clearing. Martin had taken a bunch of saplings and laced them together with strips of blanket to make a sort of hammock. Two longer poles were tied to either side. He had the ends of these tied to his waist. Gabriel was stretched out on the bed and was barely conscious. Martin had tried to repair the battered body as best he could. He had wrapped Gabriel's chest and right shoulder and arm with the remains of the blanket, most of his own pant legs, his spare shirt and every other bit of cloth he could find. With all this, Kitch could still see areas that were completely blood-soaked. The left arm was in a splint and a tourniquet was wrapped around the right arm just below the shoulder.

"He looks pretty bad," Kitch observed.

"We need help for him, and soon," Martin replied. "He lost a lot of blood and is still bleeding a bit. I got most of it stopped, but we've got to get him to the village. There's

doctor stuff there and Lisa will know what to do for him."
Then, as an afterthought, he added. "Are you okay to make
it?"

"Yeah, let's go. I'll carry the other end of this rig. He's
going to get bumped around too much with you dragging
him, and it'll start the bleeding worse. How far do you
figure we're from the village?"

"About three miles, maybe a little more. It's good open
trail."

It was a rough trip. Every step brought a jolt of pain to
Kitch's body. Half a dozen times he had to stop for a few
minutes to regain his strength and clear his head.
Mercifully for Gabriel, he was unconscious for most of the
trek. They finally arrived at the village just after dark. By
now, the pain in Kitch's head was blinding, and he had to
go strictly on nerve to finish the last half-mile.

Lisa took over as soon as they brought Gabriel in. She
redressed all the wounds and finally stopped the last trickle
of blood. Martin was stretched out on a cot in the corner
and Kitch was slumped over on a chair with his head
cradled in Della's lap. When she had finished with the
dressings, Lisa quickly crossed the room and shook her
father awake.

"We've got to get him to the hospital and doctors. He's lost
too much blood and I don't know what else to do." Tears
were beginning to well up in her eyes as she spoke.

Martin stumbled to his feet and tried to clear the cobwebs
from his brain.

"Someone will have to go down to the head of the lake to
the store. They can radio out from there. We'll send one of
the young fellows by horse. If he leaves right away he
should get there by noon."

Kitch caught the last few words and sat up. "We've got a
radio in camp, and I can get there a lot sooner than that."

"You stay here and rest," Lisa said. "I'll go. Brian is in
camp and can send the message."

Kitch protested feebly, but the pain in his head had returned and he was relieved not to make the trip.

The chopper came in an hour after daybreak with a doctor, who was visibly impressed with Lisa's patch job. They loaded Gabriel on the aircraft as the doctor assured them that, although their patient was going to be laid up for some time, he was going to be all right.

After the aircraft had gone, it took only the familiar sound of Della's voice and the warmth of her body to waken Kitch. In the soft early dawn the pain and fatigue of last night seemed remote. At first, he wondered where he was. The strange house and the people's voices were unfamiliar. Then reality shattered the haze and concern for his injured friend took over. Brian, Lisa and the girls' mother were at the big table downstairs. As he climbed down and lurched over to the bench, Della thrust a mug of hot tea in front of him and busied herself frying a batch of hotcakes.

Kitch wolfed down his breakfast as Brian related what the doctor had said about Gabriel's condition.

"I guess we'd better get back to camp and go to work," Kitch finally announced. "Is everybody back?"

"No, just Dusty, Reuben and myself. The rest are supposed to come in today. Dusty says we're free until tomorrow."

"That's good," Kitch replied. "I think I can sleep until then."

Brian had looked forward to the days off and the opportunity to go home with mixed feelings. He missed his mother and sister, but he dreaded the confrontation with Stephanie and her father. He had written to his mother to prepare her for the possibility of losing her job. She replied that was no longer a concern as she had lined up another better position. He knew he would miss Lisa and being away from her for even a few days, and this dampened his enthusiasm. Home seemed different somehow, or maybe it was he that had changed. His family was overjoyed to see him and have him back, but they were caught up in their lives, and their interest in his new activities didn't extend much beyond their concern for his well-being or the fear that the work might be too demanding or dangerous. They asked about his tasks, but when he described the wonderful world that had been opened up to him and launched enthusiastically into descriptions of what he had seen and learned, he found they could not relate and were bored and easily distracted. With his friends the reaction was the same, only they lacked the concern for his feelings to let him ramble on. After four days at home Brian was ready to return to camp. He had it out with Stephanie and endured her anger, her threats and her tears without any feelings of guilt or regret. He knew his mother wouldn't understand and would be hurt if he left early, so he divided his time between home and trips to the library. Greedily, he explored all the books he could find about the tribes of the Pacific Northwest and their customs and legends, especially those dealing with wild man-like creatures. Interwoven through these tales were similarities to Old Sam's stories, leading Brian, at one point, to wonder if Old Sam had a similar supply of books stashed somewhere, providing him with a source for his narratives. These investigations led to a survey of more modern reports of sightings of Sasquatch, the Yeti of Tibet and the Russian accounts of strange manlike creatures roaming some of their less-populated areas. Brian's interest grew with each new bit of information. There were too many similar reports to totally dismiss them all as fantasy. His longing to be with Lisa and hear the stories again in the light of his new knowledge brought him back to camp two days early.

He was anxious to discuss this new material with the others at camp. He was becoming convinced that this was more than just another old native legend. Now, sitting beside the fire in the cabin with Lisa and Old Sam, he described the recent Sasquatch sightings to the old man. Sam Jonas was not surprised, but listened carefully to Brian's report.

BACK TO CAMP

Cap returned to camp, again against his doctor's warnings. He wasn't feeling any better, but he was dedicated to finishing the job. He couldn't accept the stigma of being a quitter. Margaret had not been told about his condition, but she was now suspicious that something was wrong. He had lost almost thirty pounds, and his spark, energy and enthusiasm for life was gone. It was a radical change in his personality. Her questions were met with denials that anything had changed. He tried to explain her concerns away by saying he had just been working too hard. He also used this excuse for his continual need for sleep. When he arrived back on the job, it was evident that the break had been of little benefit to him. Dusty was becoming increasingly worried about the old man's health but received the same denials when he raised the subject.

Arnold was certainly in a better frame of mind than when he had left, as he had been successful in avoiding his Uncle Mervin. All indications suggested the audition had gone well. He and Rudy had given it their best shot, and although his partner was discouraged by not being immediately signed up to do a record, Arnold argued that the people who listened to them were not high enough up the corporate ladder to make that decision. His suspicions were confirmed when he received a letter before he returned to the bush, stating that the group was impressed, and their demo disk had been passed on to management.

Dusty had flown to Vancouver and made an appointment with Archie Campbell for the morning after his arrival. He had warned all of the crew except Curt that their term of employment may be cut short if Campbell failed to make the second required payment. He was as apprehensive about this meeting as he had been for their first encounter. His first shock was the change in attitude shown by Suzanne. She seemed almost happy to see him, and proceeded to ask him questions about the summer work. When Campbell finally arrived for their meeting half an hour late, he was less friendly than his secretary.

"I suppose you're here for some more money. Have you brought all the reports?"

"They're all here. Unfortunately, we haven't located a mineable deposit, but we are hoping for some better results in the new area."

"Well, you'd better find something to give our stock a boost. Our shareholders are getting impatient to see some action."

"As soon as I receive payment, we'll get the project back on track."

Dusty was surprised when Campbell handed him a cheque for the full amount owing without hesitation.

On his way out he stopped to say goodbye to Suzanne, who replied, "We're coming up to see you in a few weeks. The boss wanted to make it a surprise, but I figured you needed a bit of warning."

"Who is coming?" Dusty asked.

"The boss, Mervin Chipman, me and probably a
photographer. I reserved a helicopter yesterday to take us
in. I'm kind of looking forward to the trip."
"Thank you for the heads up. We'll be expecting you,"
Dusty said without conviction.

Curt's return to the city had not gone well. He had written
to the head of the Geology Department requesting an
appointment to present his application for a teaching
position in person. The interview had been granted. He
made a well-organized, professional presentation to the
Committee, who appeared totally uninterested in what he
had to say. As he began to suspect, his application was
immediately denied without a clear explanation of the basis
for the decision. Curt had come to the school for the
appointment directly from the airport. He was in a foul
mood as he entered his apartment. The first thing he saw
was Laura seated on the sofa waiting for him. She had
cleaned up the mess she had created before he left and had
bought new frames for his awards and diplomas.
"What are you doing here?"
"I called the Department and they said you were coming
back today, so I thought I'd surprise you. I hope there are
no hard feelings for what I did before," she said as she
walked toward him. When she got close, Curt hit her hard
across the face. She fell to the floor and started to sob.
"I told you before to get out of here and stay away. Now,
get up and go if you know what's good for you."
She got to her feet slowly and said, "I don't want to leave.
I'm sorry for what I did. I just want us to be like we were
before when you told me you loved me."
Curt was getting madder by the minute. As he walked
toward her, she could sense the anger and slowly backed
away. As she stepped out on the narrow patio, her foot
caught on the doorjamb, and she fell against the old
wooden railing, which surrounded the platform. The railing

started to give way as she struggled to get her balance. Curt grabbed for her as the support broke free and she began to fall. His grip on her shirt held for a few seconds before it slipped from his hand, and she fell screaming for four stories to the pavement below.

Curt rushed down the stairs. He was the first to arrive before the crowd gathered around her crumpled lifeless body. Someone phoned 911, and the paramedics arrived with a doctor within minutes. The police followed a short time later. Everyone was questioned, and Curt was asked for a complete statement. They examined the broken railing and appeared to accept his versions of the events leading up to her fall. They requested he remain in the city in case they had further questions. He agreed but stipulated he was required to return to his job soon.

Back at camp there was still considerable doubt about the results of Brian's research. After supper one evening he had asked the others to stay and hear what he had discovered, and with the exception of Curt, who had stomped off to his tent without a word to anyone, all were agreeable. Quickly he recited some of Old Sam's stories about the wild men in the high country and how Old Sam's ancestors had seen them. Then he told of the stories and recent sightings that he had read about.

"It's as if Old Sam had read the same books before we came up here."

"Or that the writers have visited with the natives in this part of the Province," Dusty replied. "I've heard some of these tales with slightly different form and characters over on the Island."

"That's right," Kitch added. "Some of the Haida legends are similar, although I can't remember any about the wild men. Maybe our own legend of a week ago will add some fuel to the fire burning inside you," Kitch proceeded to describe the night and following day that he, Gabriel and Martin had

GUY ALLEN

spent at the cave.

"It's the same old story," Dusty replied when he had
finished. "All these stories are told, but no one around here
has actually seen one of these creatures."
"What about the newspaper reports?" Arnold asked.
"That's just it," Brian replied. "They are third and fourth
hand stories. Some fellow tells another fellow, who maybe
tells a policeman or local reporter, and it gets in the local
paper and then the wire service picks it up, and someone
rewrites the story and finally the rest of the world gets it.
It's the same with the stuff from Europe and Asia. Some of
these sightings were back in the last century, and we're just
hearing about them now because some scholars took the
trouble to translate."
"Most of us are not going to be convinced unless one of
these big fellows walks up and shakes our hand someday,"
Kitch replied. "Even with what happened at the cave, I'm
still doubtful. I suppose if I saw one, I probably still
wouldn't believe it. I'd just figure I was having some kind
of a drug flashback.
"This is what Lisa can't understand, why I just can't accept
their existence without direct proof. She does. She's never
seen one. She just believes the stories are true. Maybe her
culture makes it easier to believe."
"I don't think so," Kitch replied. "Gabriel spent a few years
trying to get a look at one because of this same feeling."
"But suppose you see a Sasquatch," Arnold put in. "So
what. People are going to believe you about as much as you
believe the native stories. Even with us in camp, if you
come in some night with a story of meeting a wild man in
the bush, everybody is going to sort of agree with you and
then keep watching you out of the corner of their eye to see
in what other ways you've gone strange."
"That's crap," Kitch replied. "We've all seen enough weird

things around here and know each other well enough not to take that attitude."

"Maybe so," the young man replied, "but it's a hell of a lot easier for me to accept that there's no basis for the stories. Maybe the world needs a real clear photograph or movie of one of these creatures."

"There is a short film taken down in the States, but most people figure it's a fake. I've seen it, and it leaves a lot of room for doubt," Brian replied, "but the thing that really strikes me is how the descriptions of eyewitnesses from such widely separated parts of the world, and at different times in history have been so similar. Surely they can't all be derived from one original fantasy."

Dusty thought for a minute and then replied. "What troubles a lot of people is that they can't see how a creature so large can be totally elusive in a world so densely inhabited. But, this is a matter of perspective. Most of the world's population is confined to the limited areas of habitable land. Few people have any concept of the tremendous spaces on all the continents that contain only a scattering of people or that are empty most of the time. Look at this country. We're part of only a handful of white men that have ever visited this section of the Province, and the high rock country to the west is even more remote. Take any valley or mountain range along the whole Pacific Northwest and try to imagine the number of humans that visit it in a lifetime. You could lose a whole tribe of man-like creatures in this country, especially if they lived in small groups and made an effort not to be seen. I'm not saying they are here. I just feel they could be here and yet remain the mystery they presently are."

"But, most of this country is continually being covered by aircraft. It seems that everyday at some time you hear an airplane or a helicopter. I would think that if these Sasquatch did exist they would be spotted from the air now and then."

"Sure, that sounds reasonable," Dusty replied. "But it is surprising how difficult it is to see things from the air even when you are looking for them. There are lots of grizzlies in this country. We know that, but they are almost never seen from aircraft, and when planes go down and the searchers know where they crashed, they can still fly over the area and not see them. This country can hide anything, especially like I said, if it doesn't want to be seen."

"So it boils down to the same old story," Brian observed. "You decide to believe or not on the basis of all the reported evidence until the day you meet one face to face or someone captures one and the whole world is forced to accept it."

MEETING ON THE TRAIL

The next day was ungodly hot, the hottest of the summer, at least that was the general opinion around the table at dinner. The heat had sucked the last bit of spare energy, causing the normal evening chatter to be listless and spaced with great gaps of silence. The hot air was still, and the cooling night breezes off the high mountains to the west seemed unwilling to make their presence felt. Only Brian and Kitch were able to ease the discomfort by a teeth-chattering plunge into the icy water of the river.

The mosquitoes were out in abundance. With no wind to blow them off target, they were scoring on anyone who ventured outside. The sun lay on the horizon, a huge angry red ball pushing its last oppressive rays through the muggy sky. The air lay heavy along the ground leaving little droplets here and there as it crept into the shaded cooler areas. When the darkness had blotted out the last trace of pink in the west, flashes of heat lightning lit the horizon like footlights on a vast stage.

There was little interest in any form of activity. Cap had cleaned up quickly, even though he was getting weaker by the day. He dragged himself outside, and he and Reuben pulled their camp chairs up to the riverbank in order to catch any breezes that might be lurking nearby. They smoked in silence. Dusty , as was his custom most evenings, worked away steadily on his maps, plotting the information gained that day. Curt presumably was engaged in the same activity, but since he went directly to his tent after the evening meal and zipped the flap shut, no one knew for sure what he was doing. Arnold was curled up on his cot picking out some new tunes on his guitar and leafing through a batch of magazines. Kitch and Brian dried themselves off and put on clean jeans and shirts in preparation to go to the village.

The air lay still along the trail, making it a hot walk. By the time they reached the village, they were both soaking wet again, this time with perspiration and in a poor mood brought on by the discomfort. But, this was short-lived. One look at the unhappy pair, and Lisa suggested they go swimming.

The favorite swimming hole was a short distance upstream from the village on a bend in the river with a bit of a backwater, which formed a wide deep hole away from the main current. Quite a few years before, the girls explained, a dredge had been brought in to process the river gravels for gold. This spot was the only one worked, as the miners had gone broke before they could recover any gold. Of course, the villagers knew it wasn't a good place for gold, but nobody had asked them. Most of the machinery had long since been broken up and the parts carried off for a number of uses.

The river was low, and the pool was almost without current. Warmed by the sun, the top layer of water was much easier to take than the icy current of the main channel. They had to pick their way along the path in the moonless dark to a flat grassy area between the rocks, where the shore sloped gradually to the water. After the first shock of cool water against his skin, Brian finally enjoyed complete relief from the oppressive heat. They splashed water in the direction of each other's voices and at shadows they could barely see in the darkness. Catching a glimpse of movement near the rock wall, Brian swam in that direction with strong easy strokes, only to have his head pushed deftly under the surface as he reached for the elusive form. Coming up coughing and sputtering, his hands grasped out and closed on Lisa's arm as she tried to swim away. She struggled to free herself, but Brian wouldn't let go.

"Now you're going to get a dunking," he said as he grabbed her about the waist and tried to upend her, but she moved closer reaching her arms around his neck. He was surprised and entranced by her nakedness as he held her firmly in his arms. Her struggling stopped as he released his hold, but she didn't move away. As they embraced, the soft silky warmth of her skin filled Brian with overwhelming feelings of desire. Slowly she took his hand and led him through the darkness out of the water and up the grassy bank. They found a level spot where Lisa lay down on the cool damp turf and pulled Brian down to her. She kissed him with unexpected passion. As he started to get up, she held him more tightly and wriggled her body beneath him.

It was late when they strolled back to the village. They walked slowly, trying to stretch out the night, savoring the last tastes of their lovemaking. The lights in the cabin had long since been put out and the village street was quiet. Brian was the first to break their silence. "I wonder if Della and Kitch are back yet. I wouldn't mind having company and some light on the walk back to camp. He has the only flashlight again."

"Wait," Lisa replied. "I'll go in and see if Della is home." She slipped quietly into the darkness and returned almost immediately.

"She hasn't used her bed. They must still be out."

"I guess I'd better make the trip now rather than wait for him. It might be morning before he gets back. I wish I could stay with you all night and not have to go out and work tomorrow."

"I know," Lisa replied. "So do I. Maybe, when you have a day off we can stay together longer. I have a small light you can take with you. I don't want you falling in the river again."

By the time Brian left the village a faint image of the moon was partly visible above the treetops, but it did nothing to make hiking any easier along the river trail. He was tired but moved at a good pace. He eagerly sought at least a couple of hours in the sack before Cap started pounding on the dishpan.

As he came around a slight bend in the trail, he caught a quick movement out of the corner of his eye, and his nose picked up a strange odor just before the blow fell and everything went black.

When consciousness returned, he could just barely make out the sound of voices, which seemed to come from a distance. They were threatening voices, and the first feelings, of which he was aware, were alarm and fear. He had been propped up and tied tightly to a tree. A young native man stood over him, weaving drunkenly and waving a hunting knife dangerously close to Brian's throat as he tried to keep his balance. Brian recognized it was the odor of whiskey, which he had smelled just before he was hit. It was now being expelled upon him in great force. He tried to focus on what the young man was yelling, but the pain in his head made it difficult. The man was telling Brian to leave his woman alone and that he would kill him if he didn't stay away from her. Each stumbling word was punctuated by the point of the knife being pressed against Brian's chest, here and there tearing the cloth of his shirt. As the young man continued his harangue, another figure emerged from the bushes. This man was a bit older and stockier and was also drunk. He lunged toward Brian and struck him hard across the mouth with the back of his hand. Brian's legs were free enough to kick and catch his attacker in the knee. Brian struggled hard to loosen himself from the rope but could not, and the newcomer struggled to his feet, limped toward Brian and struck him again across the side of the head. As he raised his hand the third time, Brian started to move his head to deflect the blow. The man stopped when he saw the younger man stiffen, and they all heard the warning voice behind him.

"Drop your knife and tell your friend to back off and untie the ropes, or I'll stick this right into your spine."

Brian was overjoyed to hear Kitch's voice. The young man stood with his knife hanging loosely in his hand and then dropped it quickly with a scream of pain. The older of the two turned and crouched as if to spring at Kitch, but another scream from his friend made him back off. Kitch walked over to Brian's attacker and hit him with the full force of his body behind the blow. The man went down and stayed down.

"I'm not kidding," Kitch snarled. "I'll cut him in half if you don't get those ropes untied."

Reluctantly, the older man scrambled over and loosened the bounds.

"Now, both of you lie down on your bellies." Kitch's voice came across cold and hard as the two lay down on the ground.

"Throw me their rope," he motioned to Brian. "We'll tie them to the tree and let the wolves play with them tonight." Kitch lashed both men by wrists and ankles to opposite sides of a large pine beside the trail, making the ropes as tight as possible. Then, leaning over the older of the two men with the tip of his knife against the man's throat, he growled. "If either of you gives us any more trouble, I'll cut you up and feed you to the fish. If you want your knife back, go see Martin Jonas. I'm giving it to him for safekeeping."

While they walked along the trail, Brian was still shaking as he voiced his concern.

"Were you serious about the wolves attacking them?"

Kitch laughed and shrugged his shoulders. "No wolf with any self-respect could stand the smell of those two, but our unfriendly neighborhood grizzly might be in the area to give them some excitement. I do think that neither of us should be around the village alone for a while.By morning they'll be sobered up and over being scared. I don't think they're brave enough to try and take their anger out on us, but we need to be aware if they're still around."

"Did you just happen to come along when you did?" Brian asked.

"No. Della warned me about them. She said they'd probably try and cause trouble when they found out Lisa was with you. The young fellow claims she's his woman. The other one's his brother. They live up north, not always in the village. When I took Della home, Lisa told me you had just left. I had a feeling something might happen, so I tried to catch up with you and got there just as the older fellow was getting ready to take another swing at you."

"I wonder why Lisa didn't tell me about them. She has never made any mention of having a boyfriend."

"From what Della says, she doesn't consider him a boyfriend. To her he is just a fellow she knows from school. They are supposedly great fellows around Lisa, but with anyone else they are just plain mean. She probably doesn't think they'd cause any harm. I guess she and Della argued about it before we came. She says Lisa is worried about you not wanting to visit her if you think she is involved with someone else."

"Well, I sure think the brother was ready to do me in back there before you arrived."

"Naw. They just wanted to scare you, but that might have changed when you kicked the brother. My concern was they were drunk enough to have cut you up badly by accident."

THE VISIT

Ten days later Dusty received a radio message that Archie
Campbell was flying into camp the next day. There were no
indications of the purpose of the trip, but Dusty had a few
suspicions. He had been keeping track of Wildwood's press
releases and was aware of the very erratic behavior of the
Company's stock on the Vancouver Board. It had dropped
from a high of a dollar twelve, when the field program was
announced in the early summer to the present low of twenty
cents a share with very little trading volume. When the
small mineral vein had been discovered, Dusty had wired
the news to Campbell, who had immediately informed the
press. This had been good for a few cents increase on
moderate volume, but when the assays came back, the
public interest cooled and the stock resumed its slide.
Campbell needed some kind of positive news to whip up
the interest and get his stock trading again at better prices.
So Archie Campbell was in hot pursuit of some feed for the
publicity mill. Dusty debated whether to warn the crew to
watch what they said around the man on the possibility that
some remarks might be taken out of context and publicized.

Eventually he decided that Campbell would only be interested in what he, or possibly Curt, had to say. The radio message had added that there would be four persons in the party including Campbell, his private secretary, the Company's consulting engineer and a photographer, just as Suzanne had alerted him previously. It was expected that the party would be staying overnight, and it was requested that suitable accommodations be provided.

Only Arnold totally dreaded the visit. The consulting engineer would be his Uncle Mervin. One of the few things Arnold had really enjoyed about the summer was the absence of Mervin Chipman from his life. He had hoped he would not have to put up with his uncle, at least for a few more weeks.

The chopper set the visitors down in the heat of early afternoon. The group emerging, with their clean well-pressed clothes, was in marked contrast to the camp surroundings and the casual dress of its inhabitants.

Archie Campbell immediately made his presence felt. He was a big imposing man in his early fifties. The physical power gained in his early years in the logging camps was giving way to executive flabbiness. Intermittent attempts to keep fit were becoming less frequent and the enjoyment of a life of plenty, which he had missed in his youth had become a dominant force in his day-to-day routine. He had made it the hard way, the story of which was readily loosened from his tongue by a drink or two. Twenty years in the logging camps, starting as a cook's helper in his teens and finally as owner of his own rig, trucking logs to the mills, had toughened him to the ways of the world. Then one day on a job in the Slocan, where a new timber area had been opened up, he'd found some pieces of rock that looked like they had gold. He showed them to a friend, who sent them to another friend that did a bit of prospecting. Together they staked some claims and then took the samples to an engineer and a lawyer. Archie had been amazed at how fast the whole thing grew. A company was formed and people began buying stock in this company before anyone knew whether it was good enough to be a mine. It wasn't a mine, and later Archie learned that the engineer and the lawyer had never expected it to be an operating mine. Archie was disappointed. He had made some money from the venture, not nearly as much as the engineer and the lawyer, but what was of greater value was the education he had gained. He was fascinated by the whole process and realized it offered a means of becoming truly rich. He sold his truck and spent the next year scouting the Province for some good prospects. He took courses in prospecting, geology and mining and read every book about the stock market that he could lay his hands on. Finally, an old prospector near Dawson Creek brought him some asbestos samples from an area where the mineral had never been previously reported, and Wildwood Exploration Ltd. was born with Archie Campbell in complete control. He had staked some more claims around the showing, gotten some good grade assays and then gone to the brokers. His timing was perfect. The market was hot. Speculator interest was high, and the brokers were short on product. The first brokerage house underwrote 300,000 shares with future options on another 600,000. At one stroke he had his minimum subscription and the money. Then the news of the asbestos discovery swept the industry, sparking a staking rush in the area and a sharp rise in the price of the Wildwood stock. Almost over night Archie Campbell was a millionaire, at least on paper. It was a heady experience. At last, he could pay himself a good salary for managing the company, and every time he wanted some extra cash all he had to do was peel off a few shares and put them on the market.

But, that was three years ago, and the Company's fortunes, along with Archie's had deteriorated. Every time the stock dropped a penny Archie's paper value went down $7,000. For a man to whom this figure had once represented a couple of month's wages the loss was hard to take. The staking rush had died as suddenly as it had begun. Some work was done that first summer, but the only asbestos found was in a small deposit on Wildwood's ground. A year later most of the other claims had been dropped, and the area was quiet once more.

By last fall Archie knew he had to do something to get the Company active again. He needed another property or a new idea to get people interested in Wildwood. Eventually, he had gone to see Mervin Chipman, who he knew by reputation as an engineer who either had claims to sell or knew where properties could be picked up cheap by people in Campbell's situation.

Mervin Chipman was an enigma to Archie Campbell. Chipman was the product of three generations of Chipmans who had exerted strong influences in the local business community. Since birth, he had had all the benefits of money and the right connections, but his ego and his greed prevented him from leading a life of total leisure and comfort, and as a result he was compelled to put in long hours of work. Where Archie Campbell accumulated money for the enjoyment it brought him, Mervin Chipman gathered it in simply for the sake of having more as a measure of his business success.

Most people meeting Mervin Chipman for the first time took a mild dislike to the man, which only intensified if they made an effort to know him better. He was tall and angular. In contrast, he had the moon shaped face that was a trademark of the Chipman clan. This feature, which was in harmony with the stockiness of his nephew was almost grotesque perched on his lanky body. The dark, pencil-thin mustache that lined his upper lip and curled at the corners suggested a perpetual 'Have a nice day' type of face, a direct contradiction to the dour critical nature of its owner.

Chipman had come up with a prospect for Archie. It was an old obscure showing in an unexplored area, but the price was right and Archie grabbed it. With the first snow, he sent a planeload of stakers to this quiet plateau to mark out the boundaries for Wildwood's next discovery. Campbell had the claims staked in his name and sold them to the Company for his cash back and an extensive block of stock. The news had edged the stock price up, the brokers raised some more money for the Company, a field program was announced, the stock went up a little more, and everyone was happy for a while.

But, soon the situation again became critical for Archie Campbell. The Securities Commission required that part of the monies raised be used to evaluate the property for which it was subscribed, so Archie had to shop around and see where he could get the minimum amount of required work done at the cheapest price. Most of the big contractors wouldn't give him a quote. They were too busy, or the job was too small, or they had some other reason for not wanting to take on the work. And, so again, Archie had gone to see Mervin Chipman, and Chipman had suggested Dusty Sherant, a small contractor who was honest and could complete the program inexpensively.

Archie had, however, expected more. He had offered Dusty some Wildwood stock in addition to the quoted price to do the job. He figured if Sherant had part of the Company he would make sure the field results were encouraging, but Dusty had turned down the offer, and in fact threatened not to take the job on at all. This attitude confused Archie, but with no one else in sight to do the work, he agreed to Dusty's terms.

The results so far were discouraging. One lousy mineral show, which wasn't good for much more than a week's action on the market was the only useful news he had received. Lots of stuff about bears and fires and such, but this didn't help the stock, and hence, was of no interest to

Archie Campbell.

He had brought Chipman along on the trip hoping to get some useful press material translated out of all the scientific talk. Although they hadn't discussed it, he was sure Chipman knew the score. He also knew Chipman controlled a block of Company shares through relatives and dummy corporations in Calgary, a definite conflict of interest that was buried under so many layers that it had been difficult to trace. That information had cost Archie a few well-spent dollars, but it was his ace in the hole to control Chipman if he ever needed it. They had talked about the mineral showing and Chipman had indicated that in many of these cases important factors, which may suggest greater value are often overlooked and that he himself should visit the occurrence.

The third man in the party was the photographer, a young man who appeared to be terrified of the helicopter and his new surroundings. He mumbled his greetings as he stumbled out of the chopper and disappeared into what seemed to be the only safe refuge, the cooktent. The general consensus was that he had given his name as Dennis.

Suzanne was the last person to emerge from the aircraft. Either she was much more beautiful than Dusty remembered, or he had been too long in the bush. Dressed in a brief khaki skirt and low-cut flowered blouse, she immediately brightened the atmosphere of the camp. In contrast to the original cold greeting Dusty had received from her the first time they met, today she was friendly with everyone.

Dusty was wary with Campbell and Chipman as they gathered in the office tent to discuss the program. He fenced successfully with Chipman's brusque formal manner, but Archie Campbell's bluff and hearty ways put him off guard. He had not known the older man long enough to realize that the friendlier he became, the more dangerous he was. They went over the results in detail. In spite of Chipman's long-winded scientific explanations, Archie Campbell was quick to realize nothing had been found, not even to the point that it could be altered and used in a positive way to stimulate the market. The discussions continued through dinner and well into the evening. At Chipman's suggestion it was decided they would make an early start and visit the mineral show as well as a number of other points of geological interest the next day. Campbell agreed without enthusiasm. He was ready to go home.

Mervin Chipman was up and ready to charge into the bush at six. While the majority of the visitors and crew stared morosely into their plates, he babbled on with scientific theory. His attempts to stimulate table talk ended in monologues of his past bush adventures. Brian was interested, the rest were not, and Arnold had heard all the stories at least a dozen times before.

SUZANNE

Although he wasn't looking forward to it, Dusty had decided to spend the morning with the group at the mineral show, taking Brian and Arnold along to help. He planned on Curt showing the other areas of geological interest after lunch. Since they would end up in a section of the claims only Kitch and Reuben had prospected, these two would go along to show them the way. It would be an all day tour with some of the trails passing through areas of thick bush. The visitors were advised to dress accordingly and be prepared for a long day. To everyone's surprise, Suzanne decided to go along too. Dusty was puzzled. He observed she had been acting strangely. She tried to start a conversation with him a couple of times while they were on the trail but stopped suddenly on each occasion, as Campbell moved up to join them. Dusty had the feeling she wanted to tell him something away from her boss. When they reached the mineral showing, his attention was diverted from these concerns, as he attempted to interest Campbell and Chipman in their discovery.

Dusty was in camp working on his field notes when Reuben returned with Suzanne in late afternoon. When asked what had happened to the rest of the group, Reuben explained that since the girl was getting a little tired of just standing around with nothing to do, Kitch had taken her down river to the swimming hole to cool off and then had asked him to bring her back, while he guided the rest of the group on their return to camp

As far as the rest of the party was concerned when they finally returned, Mervin Chipman's enthusiasm had gone, Archie Campbell was physically exhausted, Curt was mad, and Dennis, the young photographer, shook with discomfort. In spite of the blistering heat and the lack of rain that day, they were all soaking wet.

Only Kitch seemed in good spirits when they finally made their way into the cooktent just before dark. Earlier in the afternoon he had taken Suzanne along the creek trail past Jumping Rock to the swimming hole, where he had first met Della. It was a longer route but much easier going. Suzanne pranced along the trail happy to be away from the boredom of the morning. At a low spot along the bank, she tested the water.

"I thought you said we were going swimming," she said. "This water's too cold."

"Don't worry. It gets warmer up ahead where the river slows down. We go swimming there all the time. Besides, you didn't bring a bathing suit," he replied.

"Neither did you."

"That's not a problem. I'm not shy like you girls. I don't need a suit."

They reached the spot above the rapids where the water was barely moving.

"This isn't bad," she said, as she ran her hand through the water, stood up and peeled off her shirt and jeans.

"You think I'm shy, do you?" She asked as she slipped out of her bra and panties and stood mockingly naked in front of Kitch.

As he grabbed for her, she turned and dove into the pool.

Kitch rapidly undressed, tossed his clothes in a pile and
followed her in.

Suzanne was a strong swimmer, and try as he would he
couldn't catch her. Every time he got close she would dive
deep and surface on the other side. Finally Kitch gave up,
climbed out of the water and stretched out on the grass.. He
watched her as she swam back and forth in front of him,
but he must have fallen asleep, for the next thing he knew
she was sitting on the grass beside him. She had dressed,
brushed her hair, put on a touch of makeup and looked
especially beautiful.

"We need to talk," she said. "I tried to get Dusty alone,
away from the boss, but Campbell was sticking to us like
glue. I need to get a warning to him. I think it is important,
and it looks like you will have to be the messenger."

"This sounds heavy. What's going on?"

"I'm not sure, but I have a strong feeling Mr. Campbell is
making plans to bail."

"What do you mean? Is he planning to shut down this field
operation? It was very evident he was disappointed we
haven't found something to make him a mine."

"No, that's not all of it. He has bigger plans. I think he's
planning to clean out the Treasury and take off somewhere.
Last month he took on a new project. The Company bought
an equipment rental business that was in financial trouble.
He gave the owners a little bit of cash and a bunch of
Wildwood shares for their interest. Then he had me stall off
all their creditors with promises that they would all be paid
as soon as he got this rental business on its feet. Instead, he
put all the equipment up for sale. Well, the machines are
gone and so is the money. As far as I can tell he made all
cash sales and put the funds in his personal account. He
wouldn't let me handle any of this, but I hacked into his
personal computer and had a look at his bank account. It
has grown rapidly with a number of large recent deposits.
Finally, last week Chipman came in with another of his hot

mining prospects. This one is in Mexico. I left the intercom open while they were in conference and heard Chipman tell him they could make a whole pile of money with this one. They plan to take the deal to one of the shadier brokerage houses to raise the money."

Kitch listened intently while she unfolded her story.

"I have some questions," he said. "Why are you telling me all this, and how does it affect us? I don't understand some of this and will probably forget most of it by the time we get to camp. Why don't you write it all down and pass the note to Dusty before you leave?"

"I did. It's here in my pack, but since I haven't been able to get him alone, I decided to explain it to you, so maybe you could answer any questions he comes up with. I want you to give this letter to him. As for this project, I'm sure Dusty will not see another cent in payment. Campbell is paying none of the outstanding bills coming from this work, or in fact, any of the other expenses of the Company."

"So, why did he haul all you folks up here?"

"He wants some kind of news he can spin to raise the price of the shares, so he can sell the rest of his holdings. In fact, he already has a sell order out at a price above the present market."

"So, then what? If he sells all his stock, he no longer controls the Company and would have no interest in what happens to it."

"Bingo! Now you're catching on. He won't care because he'll be gone with all the money."

"How do you know all this stuff? I thought you were just a secretary."

"Thanks a lot! In fact, I have a Masters in Business Administration. I took on this job as a favor to a friend of mine who works for the Securities Commission. They've been suspicious of Campbell for some time but have been unable to pin anything on him. I have the feeling he suspects I am not who I claim to be and is getting jumpy."

"It sounds like you're ready to blow the whistle on him. Do you plan to help the Commission and the cops take him down?"

"Absolutely! The bastard has it coming for all the crooked stuff he's been pulling, and I'd love to see that creep Chipman take the fall with him."

"Wow! Remind me never to get on the wrong side of you."

"It's Dusty's decision as to what he is going to do with this. If he has questions tell him to call me at home at this number after six."

After a couple of hours and another swim they got dressed and strolled back to where the rest of the group were still looking at rocks. Kitch asked Reuben to escort the girl back to camp.

"I'll look after the rest of them. I want to take them back by the short cut."

As Dusty had watched the others drag into camp, the traces of a knowing smile caught the corners of his mouth. After a subdued evening meal the newcomers fell into their bunks, and Kitch came strolling into Dusty's tent."

"Just what happened out there? It's a long time since I've seen an unhappier group."

"Listen," Kitch replied. "That has to be the biggest collection of assholes on the continent. All I heard most of the afternoon was Campbell's bitching, Chipman's bullshit, Curt's insults and Dennis' whining. I finally had enough and talked Suzanne into going swimming in the creek. We had a very interesting discussion, which I am about to lay out for you. That is one intriguing lady, both beautiful and intelligent. When we returned I asked Reuben to bring her back to camp. The group kicked rocks for another half hour, then Curt told me to guide them back to camp if I thought I was bright enough to find the way. That tore it. I brought them back over the most direct route."

"You mean through the swamp?"

"Yeah, and across the creek five times. It sure shut them

up. I don't think I heard a word spoken that last half mile."

"Well, thank you for that. I was getting fed up with the bunch all day."

Kitch pulled Suzanne's letter from his pocket and handed it to Dusty. "I think you'd better read this before we send them home. She explained the situation to me while we were at the swimming hole. She felt you shouldn't question her about it now, as she is certain Campbell is suspicious she is up to something, but I have her home number for you to call."

Dusty read through the letter quickly as he sat on his bunk. Then he read it again.

"This doesn't surprise me," he said, "although I sure read Suzanne wrong. I figured her for just another blond airhead."

"She's far from that. I didn't understand half the stuff she told me until she broke it down."

"Is she going to alert the Commission to his little escapades?"

" She already has and is evidently working with them to get the proof they need. She didn't have any suggestions as to what you should do, except to assure you that you won't receive any more payments."

"That's a tough one. Campbell reluctantly stuck to the contract and paid me another twenty-five percent of the bid price when I was in Vancouver at the break. He isn't obliged to pay any more until the project is completed, and he has received all the maps and reports. If I pull us all out now, I would be breaking the contract, and I'm sure he would waste no time in suing me."

"It sounds like your only solution is to lowball the rest of the operation and get it done as soon as possible. Maybe, you should send some of us out to cut expenses."

"No, I can't do that," Dusty replied. "I promised you all a season's employment, and I plan to stick to that. I'm just getting sick of dealing with all the crooks in this business.

One thing though, I would like you to keep all of this to yourself. I need the rest of the crew to focus on the work to be done."

Kitch got up to leave. At the tent door he turned to Dusty. "I don't know if you've ever wondered about it, but that girl definitely has an all-body tan."

WILDWOOD EXPLORATION.

The visitors left the next morning. Everyone was happy to see them go. In spite of commendations on the good work and assurances by Campbell that he was pleased with the progress, Dusty knew, thanks to Suzanne, what to expect. After they had gone, he radioed a friend in Vancouver asking him to relay any press releases Wildwood was putting out. He was interested to see what kind of a spin Campbell was going to put on the visit.

That evening the tone was more relaxed. Even Curt had cooled down enough to be civil to everyone except Kitch. Brian voiced the thoughts that had been troubling him throughout the day.

"After the last couple of days, I'm a bit confused about why we are doing this work. I got the feeling that Mr. Campbell isn't very concerned whether we find a mine or not and that he and Arnold's uncle didn't really expect us to discover anything worthwhile. If that is the case, the whole thing doesn't make sense."

"That's not exactly true," Dusty answered. "Granted, they realized there is little probability of locating a mineable deposit, however, they are focused on how they can structure news releases from our project in such a manner as to raise the price of their stock."

"So, all the trouble and expense of having us up here wandering around in the bush is strictly a ploy to work their stock."

"That's essentially it, and because of the way it is set up, Campbell stands to make a lot of money."

"I still don't get it. If we don't find anything here, it means the property is worthless. If this property is all that Wildwood owns, then the Company must also be worthless."

"That's right, but even so, I'll bet that when this happens and everyone knows the property is worthless, the stock will still trade around a dime a share, and with two and a half million shares out, that means the public is putting a quarter of a million dollars value on a worthless company. They are giving it value with hope that the Company will get into something else that proves to be valuable. Campbell is in the process of attempting to acquire more assets. If these pan out, people still holding the stock stand to make a profit, or at least get their original investment back."

"I get that," Kitch remarked. "I just don't see how Campbell stands to make a bundle if the price goes down."

Only Dusty, Kitch and Brian remained in the cooktent, as the rest of the crew had lost interest in the discussion. Dusty decided to reveal Suzanne's story to Brian.

"So, it's just a big crooked game for him," Brian observed.

"Yes and a very lucrative game. Let's look at it this way," Dusty answered as he poured some coffee from the steaming pot. "I know a little bit about the history of this property from the few remarks I overheard. The rest I can guess. Evidently Campbell got the idea for these claims from Chipman. Chipman contracted to have them staked, and Campbell paid him for that as well as for finding the property, presumably with cash, if the whole thing was done properly. Campbell paid for this with his own money and the claims were registered in his name. He then turns around and sells them to Wildwood for his money back and a good-sized block of stock. He may have had a little bit of work done on them while they were in his name in order to justify a value increase. Anyway, say he paid $10,000 to some relative or friend of Chipman to get the claims; he then commissions Chipman to write an engineering report extolling the virtues of the property. When he sells to Wildwood he gets the $10,000 and maybe $75,000 worth of shares that are trading at around a dime, which gives him a paper profit of seven hundred and fifty thousand shares. After the Company does a bit more work on them, he gets Chipman to write a qualifying report recommending an exploration program costing three hundred thousand dollars spread over two stages. If this is done in the right form, the Securities Commission will okay it and Campbell goes to the brokers and gets them to raise the money, giving them some incentive through options on further shares or a gift of some of his own shares. The brokers can underwrite the stock at the agreed on price and take up to 25% of the proceeds as commission. They sell direct to their own client accounts. As a result, the brokers make money and Wildwood gets roughly two hundred and twenty-five thousand dollars into the treasury. Now, Campbell has a few options. If he's lucky, and the property appears to have potential, he can find another company with some money to spend, who will take over his exploration obligations for an interest in the property. This would allow Wildwood to keep its money and have the obligations for which it was raised fulfilled by someone else. If no company is interested, then he has to do what was done in this case, find someone to do the minimum amount of work recommended for the first stage of the program at the lowest price, which will keep the Commission off his back. If nothing is discovered on the property, Chipman is commissioned to write a report to that effect, recommending no further work. If the property is a good one, an interested outside party can then probably be found to finish off the work commitment. Either way, Wildwood keeps the rest of the money."

"But how does Campbell directly make his bundle from that scenario?" Brian asked.

"I think that's the easy part," Kitch put in. "Try this. First of all, Campbell has Company money for a big salary and lots of liquid lunches. Secondly, if the brokers stay on top of it they can keep the price up, trading between themselves and publishing lots of phony news from Campbell's office. This gives Campbell time to feed his stock into the market at a good price. Is that about the way it works, Dusty?"

"That's it. You figure, if the stock can be kept at a dollar, Campbell can look at a paper profit of ninety cents a share, or six hundred and seventy-five thousand dollars, depending on how many shares he can unload, and if they can keep the price up there long enough for him to cash out. If Campbell, Chipman and the brokers do all this with care, no one has broken the law."

"So, everyone wins except the folks that eventually end up with the stock, because they believed all the stories," Brian observed with disgust.

"That's right," Dusty continued. "There's the odd case where a company really did hit it big, and the investors made a bundle, but those are few and far between. The odds are probably about the same as a lottery. Anyway, the big reason Campbell came up here was that we haven't been providing him with the exciting news he needs to keep the share price up. That theoretically is the reason he is expanding the Company's interests in acquiring this equipment leasing company and a Mexican prospect. Where he has gone wrong, according to Suzanne, is in pocketing the money from the equipment sales in his personal account. She also figures he's up to something shady with the Mexican deal, but she's in the dark about that one. She has a contact in the Commission and plans to help them lay charges against him."

"Why aren't the people who invest in these things told how the system really works?"

"They are continually being told. There are a few books on the market dealing with the subject, and occasionally there are articles in newspapers and trade journals exposing another stock scam, but people don't really want to believe that the system works that way. They are usually convinced that the company they bought stock in is one of the honest ones. Either that, or they think they have some kind of inside knowledge that gives them an edge. The people who really know what is going on aren't going to make any noise because they are the ones that are making the profit."

"So, what does Campbell do now since we haven't given him the news he needs?" Kitch asked.

"That's what bothers me," Dusty replied. "Suzanne thinks he's about ready to grab all the funds and take off to somewhere warm. He's not stupid. He has to know he can't wriggle out of this mess. He got nothing out of the visit that he can use, unless he makes it up, which no doubt is his plan. If he has a bunch of sell orders for his stock above market price, he must plan on publishing something that will drive it up. He will have to exercise some care in what he puts out, as I think Chipman is still concerned enough about his own reputation to blow the whistle on him if he goes too far. He doesn't care if we keep going, as he has no intention in paying any of our bills, but he believes he has to keep up appearances so that the Commission and the brokers don't come down on him. However, I did get my money for this next stage, so I'm obliged to complete the Project."

"Well, that's not very reassuring, I guess," Brian replied hesitantly. "So we just go on doing what we've been doing. Knowing all this kind of kills my enthusiasm. Dusty, did you know how this whole thing was structured when you took on this contract?"

"No, but I had some early suspicions, especially after Campbell started giving me the run around about paying the first installment. I'd heard some bad talk about him around Vancouver, but it was Chipman that lined me up for this job, and at that time I thought he operated straight. I've radically changed my opinion about that man in the last month. I guess my personal financial situation originally overrode any reservations I might have had about taking the job."

"I got bad vibes these past two days from both of them," Kitch put in. "They're hustlers and there's no way I'd trust either one very far. So, you pretty well know from what Suzanne said that you're not going to get the rest of your money?"

"I have no illusions about it," Dusty replied. "I was able to get half of the contract price after a lot of hassle at the start before we moved in. All the flying costs went direct to Wildwood, and up to the time of the visit, Campbell had paid all their bills, but that has stopped. The money for supplies and to pay the crew comes from my account. I made out a bill to Wildwood for another twenty-five percent of my contracted price before I went to Vancouver at the break. Campbell put it in my account right away."

"When are you supposed to get the final payment?" Brian asked.

"When all the claims have been prospected and mapped, and the job is complete. They are not obliged to make the final payment until they have received all the maps and reports, and I suspect Campbell will be long gone by then."

"So, he has lots of time to complete his plans and take off."

"Not if Suzanne blows the whistle and brings it all down on his head," Dusty replied.

A few days later the supply flight brought in the mail. As usual, the dinner table was quiet on mail day as reminders

GUY ALLEN

of the outside world brought on feelings of homesickness. Usually Kitch would try and get some talk going, but tonight he and Reuben were unusually late coming in, and the meal had started without them.

CURT'S PROBLEM

The early morning call came in over the radio for Dusty to
be ready for an unexpected helicopter flight due into camp
in less than an hour. The call was from Lou Roman. Dusty
was to expect a visit from the RCMP. Lou didn't know the
purpose of the trip, but he suggested Dusty keep all the
crew in camp until it was sorted out.
The big chopper landed as predicted, and two uniformed
Mounties jumped out, ducking under the circling blades.
The older officer strode purposely toward the group
gathered around the pad. He was followed by a younger
female officer. Dusty met them at the edge of the pad as the
rest of the crew crowded around to hear what was going on.
"We're here to talk to Curt Shumann," the older Inspector,
who appeared to be the leader, announced. "We have a few
questions for him. Is he here in camp?"
As he spoke, Curt emerged from his tent and walked over
to the group.
"I'm Shumann. What's the problem?" He asked before
Dusty could reply to the officer's question.
"We have a few questions to ask you in regards to the death

of the young lady, Laura Reston." Turning to Dusty, he asked, "Is there somewhere we could speak with this young man in private?"

"Are you arresting me?" Curt interrupted, making no attempt to move away. "I am not prepared to answer your questions without a lawyer present, which we obviously don't have out here. So, you either leave me here to finish my work or arrest me and take me in to the city and allow me to find legal counsel before I discuss any of this with you."

"You realize you may be making this more difficult for yourself by taking that attitude," the Inspector replied. "We can take you in for questioning as a material witness without issuing an arrest warrant. There are only a couple of small items we need to ask you about."

"It appears you don't understand what I just told you; I am not saying anything without a lawyer present."

The Inspector was visibly irritated. He discussed the problem with his partner away from the group.

In the meantime, Dusty tried to reason with Curt. "If you have nothing to hide, I would advise you to talk with these officers and get the matter cleared up so we can get back to work."

Curt looked at his employer but made no reply.

Finally, the Inspector announced, "If that's the case, I'm afraid you will have to return to the City and find yourself a lawyer."

The rest of the crew crowded around Dusty after the helicopter had taken off, peppering him with questions.

"I don't know what is going on. All I got out of that is Curt is somehow involved in the death of a young woman. There is evidently some question as to whether it was an accident."

Curt's journey with the officers took place without any discussion. The female Corporal tried, without success, to get him to open up, but Curt ignored her. In spite of his outwardly calm demeanor, his mind was working overtime constructing an acceptable version of the accident. As a consequence of his temper, he had experienced contact with the police on a number of occasions in his youth. He had learned early how to maneuver his way successfully through an investigative process. His self-assurance that he would be dealing with persons of lesser intelligence negated any anxiety. He felt no guilt regarding Laura's death and was certain he could convince these people of his innocence.

Curt returned to camp two days later. Dusty met him at the landing and invited him into the tent, where he seated himself on the spare bed. Dusty observed the tightness of the muscles in the young man's face and body. He sat stiffly on the bed waiting for Dusty's questions.

"Do you want to talk about what is going on?"

"Not really, but I guess I owe you some kind of an explanation. The police suspect me of causing the death of a young woman, who fell from my apartment balcony. It was an accident, and I have attempted to assure them of that, but my lawyer thinks, as I do, that they don't believe my story. They evidently found her diary in which she wrote that she feared me and thought I might threaten her life. That is ridiculous, of course, but they appear to believe it. In addition, my neighbors were eager to report our argument before her accident. However, they didn't have enough evidence to arrest me. They told me I can come back to work, but I must report in to them by radio every week. I expect they will contact you as well."

"They already have," Dusty announced. I'm supposed to let them know if you take off. Are you prepared to fulfill your contract obligations, or do you wish to be released from our agreement."

"No. I'll do my job and clear this mess up when I get back in the Fall."

"Did you kill the girl?"

"No, as I have continually repeated, it was an accident. It is my problem. It won't have any effect on my work, and I don't see where it is necessarily your concern," Curt spit the words out in a staccato burst, his face reddening with anger. Dusty could sense the mounting agitation and the test of wills the young man was attempting to enforce. When he first heard about the charges against his assistant, he had anticipated that somewhere down the line something like this was going to happen, but he had been hoping to postpone it until the project was completed.

"Well, I'm afraid it doesn't work quite that way. What you do or have done does concern me. Your actions and attitude have an effect on the morale of the rest of the crew. Ever since you arrived here, you have made a point of working strictly to contract, a contract, which you had written and insisted on being put into effect. You have made sure that I could find no point for criticism within this agreement, but you've also made no extra effort or attempt to get along with the crew. Okay! That's the way you have wanted it, and that's the way it is going to be." Dusty could feel his temper rising to meet the occasion. "There is no provision for any additional time off or terminating our agreement without sufficient notice under your contract, and I'll be damned if I'm going to release you from it in your present frame of mind or to sort out your personal problems. You pull out now, for any reason, before this job is over and you have broken the contract. If you do I will notify the police, forward a letter to the head of your university and sue you for non-performance."

Curt's face went white. He hadn't counted on this reaction, and a fear of loss began to creep into his consciousness. He was not as confident as he appeared that this dilemma would resolve itself in his favor, but it wasn't his nature to let down his guard and reveal his inner thoughts to anyone. Quickly, he weighed the alternatives in his mind. He was very tempted to walk out right now, get away from this job and this collection of morons he was forced to live and work with and disappear, but it was also not his nature to walk away from his problems, whether they were his fault or inflicted upon him by others. He didn't think Sherant had enough influence with anyone to affect his career, but he wasn't sure and, most important, Curt had to be totally sure of his position before he acted. He knew his chances of landing the teaching job at the University were dead, but there were other schools where his academic credentials would override any concerns about incidents in his past. He despised indecision in others and would not tolerate it in himself. It was the sign of a weak and undisciplined mind. He knew he must cool down and take control. Though he hated doing it he had to play this man's game temporarily, hoping the results would justify his momentary submission to authority.

"I will stay and complete the work I committed to. I shall also keep my distance from the others and try not to antagonize them," he answered slowly. "My problem with the police is my problem, and I will give you no cause to contact them. Whether you believe me or not is of no matter, I did not kill that girl. It was simply an accident."

When he returned to his tent, he knew what he must do. He fully expected the accusations to snowball when he returned home, and the local press began to focus on the story. There had been no mention of his name so far in the local paper. It simply described her accident as occurring after an altercation with a friend. His lawyer had made efforts in his behalf to keep his name out of the press. He knew the accident was to some degree his fault, but he didn't push her over the railing. He needed to construct a story relating the chain of events leading up to her death that would be believable in line with the known facts. It would be helpful if he had a copy of her journal. Laura had been trouble from the day they met. He had told her what

233

she wanted to hear, and she believed him and had this ridiculous idea that he would marry her. Most of the other young women he romanced were aware the relationships were temporary and showed little resistance to breaking up when the affairs were over. His goal was clear in his mind. He needed to present his case in such a manner as to totally clear his name of any wrongdoing. Fortunately, she was no longer around to disagree with his story.

Cap was in extreme pain. As he went about his daily chores, it increased to the point he had to go to his tent and lay down long before his work was done. His meager supply of prescription pain pills had run out and the over-the-counter remedies had little effect. By mid-afternoon he could find no position, which offered any release and sleep was impossible. He needed help, but if he went to Dusty with his tale of woe, he was afraid he would be sent home and not be able to finish the job. His dilemma was heightened as the time for the evening meal approached. He knew he was incapable of preparing a decent dinner. Fortunately, Brian came back to camp early. He found Cap lying on the floor of the cooktent in obvious agony and carried him to his bunk. The old man had confided in him earlier about his condition, which he reluctantly agreed not to reveal.

"You try and rest. I'll fix the meal and come and get you when the rest of the crew returns. I do think you need to tell Dusty about your illness. At least he could bring a doctor in or have some pain medication as part of the next supply trip. No one will fault you if you want to go home now."

"No! There's nothing they can do. All the doctors who have examined me say the same thing. This is the end of the line for me. I just want to get through this one last job, go home and die. This pain will ease off, and I will be okay tomorrow. Please don't say anything to Dusty yet. I will tell him when the time is right, and I can no longer do my job."

THE DISCOVERY

Dusty settled back to his letters and reports, but by nine-thirty he had had enough. He strolled over to the cooktent and was surprised to find Kitch and Reuben in the middle of supper and Brian closing up for the night. There was no sign of Cap.

"What happened?" He asked Brian. "Did you lose a bet to the old man?"

"No, he wasn't feeling well when I got back, so I offered to give him a break."

"Nothing serious, I hope. Is he okay now?"

"I don't know. He was asleep the last time I looked in."

Dusty waited while the two men wolfed down the remains of their meal. Between mouthfuls, Kitch motioned him to a sample bag in the corner of the tent.

"Check those out."

Dusty picked up some rocks from the sack, giving each a cursory glance, then his interest quickened. The samples were granite, a new variety that had not been found in any of the areas they had examined. Spotted here and there in the fractured rock, like raisins in a pudding, were shiny specks of copper minerals.

"Where did you find these?" He asked impatiently.

"I thought those would catch your eye," Kitch replied through a mouthful of food. " It's the best stuff we've seen so far. Even my serious old partner here was impressed. Let's go over to your tent, and I'll show you on the map where we found them. That is even more interesting."

In Dusty's tent, he and Kitch were alone. Reuben had wandered off to bed.

"Reuben and I were flagging along the south boundary of that last block of claims. Somehow we got screwed up on our chaining direction on one of the lines, and we ended up about half a mile too far south. We had a little trouble figuring out where we were until we backtracked and found one of the corner posts. We had gone off the claims to about here." Kitch pointed on the map to an area just south of the claim boundary. "When we finally figured out where we were, we walked back there to get our gear and decided to stop for a break. Reuben brewed some tea while I wandered around pounding rocks. That's when I found these. Each one of the samples in the bag comes from a different outcrop scattered over an area of about ten acres. It all appears to be pretty well the same type of granite, although in some outcrops it is more shattered and fractured than in others. Most of the pieces are mineralized, and there is green copper stain all over the place."

Dusty went through the samples one by one methodically checking them under the microscope. He had expected mostly pyrite with a few flecks of the copper mineral, but it was all chalcopyrite with a few spots of bornite and some native copper and molybdenite. He motioned for Kitch to take a look.

"It must be pretty good," Kitch remarked. "This is the most excited I've seen you all summer."

"It is. It's damn good. It's the best looking stuff I've seen for some time. Tomorrow we will go and have a good look and do some systematic sampling. We'll take Brian and Arnold with us to cover a wider area. And, one other thing," he added hesitantly, "we keep this quiet until we have a good look at it. If this deposit is not on the claims we're mapping, it is probably open ground unless we find some other claims out there. What I don't need right now is this information getting out and starting a staking rush."

The next morning Curt was a bit puzzled by Dusty's actions. Usually they had a brief discussion of the day's work before he left for the bush, but this morning there was no meeting, and he was informed that he would be working alone, mapping an area along the western border. When he had gone, the crew gathered around the map in Dusty's tent and he gave them their duties for the day. He told them briefly about the new find, downplaying its potential but showed them the samples so they would know what to look for. He outlined the area on the map where they would be sampling and staking.

After the meeting, Brian and Kitch helped Dusty assemble the gear. Figuring the staking would probably be a two-day job, they packed enough supplies to spend one night, and two if necessary, in the bush. Lightweight sleeping robes and nylon tents, small stoves and extra food were added to their normal field gear. Cap remained in camp so that communications were adequately provided in case of emergency.

"Did you get paid by Wildwood?"

Dusty looked up sharply at Kitch. "Why do you ask?"

"You were concerned a few days back about Campbell coughing up some more dough."

"I hassled him for the next payment when I was in Vancouver. He's current with me, but as Suzanne predicted he appears to have quit paying other suppliers," Dusty replied, "but I'm still concerned."

"Have you any kind of a guarantee that you will get the rest?"

"No. I am required to hand over all the reports and maps when the Project is completed in order to get another payment, and they will need all that technical material for assessment requirements to keep the claims."

"Is that it?" Kitch asked. "What if they don't want to keep the ground? What if we don't find anything worthwhile on their claims? Those guys were pretty discouraged when they left the other day. They have probably already written this property off. I wouldn't get too excited about spending that last batch of cash."

"What are you getting at?"

"Two things. First, I got a letter yesterday from Suzanne. Before she left, she invited me to come and see her when the job was over, and I came back to Vancouver. Now, she tells me in the letter she may not be in Vancouver when I get there. That may be just her way of blowing me off, but the main message was that Campbell is planning to split and take the money with him. She thinks he has learned the cops are on his trail. He fired her, gave her two weeks pay and told her to leave right away. She feels he has somehow learned she blew the whistle on him. Secondly, it strikes me that if Campbell and his buddies heard of this new discovery, it would encourage them even more to drop the old claims, in which case they wouldn't have to pay you, and they would still have a property to keep their stock hot. It would probably convince Campbell to hang around a bit longer to pad his purse. I think these new claims are your only ace in the hole. Why not stake them in your name and then tell him what we found. Then let them know that you will transfer the ground over as soon as you get paid in full."

"That sounds like a good idea," Dusty replied, leaning back against the bulging packsack. "I was planning to stake them in my name anyway, but you're right, maybe I shouldn't be

in such a big hurry about transferring title to Wildwood."
"It sound like you have nothing to lose that way," Brian
added. "If they pay up, its great. Everyone gets what they
want. If they don't, you might just have yourself a mine."
Staking the claims took the better part of three days. Curt
was confused and suspicious. He questioned Cap about
their absence, but the old man assured him they were
prospecting a new area and would return soon. Other than
that, he professed to have no idea where they were. While
the rest of the crew ran the claim lines, Dusty prospected,
getting more excited with each new discovery. The area
around where Kitch and Reuben had found the first
samples was certainly the most promising but mainly
because it had the greater number of rock exposures.
Elsewhere, the ground was covered with soil and a moist
spongy layer of moss. At the few places that Dusty could
dig down through this blanket, he found copper in the
bedrock. Thirty claim units covered the richest ground and
a substantial surrounding area that Dusty wanted. Outside
these boundaries the ground surface sloped down in all
directions with a marked change in rock types. Dusty was
convinced that if he had missed any of the good areas, it
wouldn't be very much. Trying to stretch the rations into
three full days brought a hungry crew back to camp that
final evening.
But Cap was nowhere to be found.
On the table was a note.
*'If you get back before I return, I've gone fishing on the
north branch of the creek. I will be back in time to hustle up
dinner.'*
Dusty was concerned. He had observed the old man's
progressively weakening condition, and although Cap
refused to discuss it, he expected the worst. "He should
have been back by now. We better go look for him. Brian,
you and Arnold cook up some pasta while Kitch, Reuben
and I go find him."

Kitch walked along the left bank, while Dusty and Reuben went along the other side. Kitch found the old man along the shore, half submerged in the running water. He pulled him out of the water and stretched him out on the trail. Cap tried to get to his feet, but his legs wouldn't hold him and he fell forward. Dusty was on the other side and about fifty yards ahead. Before Kitch could holler for Dusty's help, the older man cautioned him to be quiet.

"What's the matter? Why don't you want me to get Dusty? I know about your condition, but he needs to be aware of it now. You're getting weaker each day. You can't go on like this."

Cap shook his head and attempted to speak, but his voice was barely a whisper. He tried again, without success, to stand. He was quiet for a few moments before he answered. "He doesn't need to know yet. I just get weak occasionally. It's no big deal. It comes and goes and will pass in a few minutes."

"I don't believe you. I have been noticing you losing weight and needing more sleep for the past month. I don't think you can keep going like this. There is no need to be a hero. Dusty needs to know about your condition, although I'm sure he has noticed your changes."

"Please don't tell Dusty. He'll send me out. I want to finish this job."

"Okay, what exactly is wrong? You never have told me."

"Cancer. It's spreading all through my body. The doctor gave me only a few months to live before I left to come out here and said this effort would probably kill me. I just want to finish this job before I go home to die."

"Jeez, if you knew that, why did you come out here in the first place?"

"What would you expect, that I would sit at home and have everyone feel sorry for me? That, I couldn't deal with. At least this gives me the will to hang in there."

"Okay, I'll keep my mouth shut for the time being, but let

me help you get through this. Brian and I can take over some of your tasks. Just be good to yourself and not try to do too much."

Kitch helped the old man to his feet, as Dusty and Reuben appeared on the scene. They supported the him as they trudged back to camp. Cap had made up a convincing explanation for his accident by the time Dusty joined them. He became progressively stronger on the trip back and was able to cover the last section without help.

THIRD CAMP

Dusty had originally planned one more camp move to finish the job. The last claim block stretched along the creek about three miles to the south. The news of Campbell's actions as reported in Suzanne's letter made him reconsider. Camp moves cost money and time, and he was becoming less and less confident of being reimbursed even for the expenses he had already incurred. From here on, this would have to be a shoestring operation for him to break even. On the other hand, he would be putting the boys into a three to four mile walk every morning just to get to work and then the same thing back to camp in the evening. That morning at breakfast he threw the problem out to the crew. Unfortunately for Dusty's peace of mind, they weren't much help. With the exception of Arnold, who wasn't too wild about the prospects of the long daily walks, the men were willing to do it either way, whatever Dusty decided. In the long run he opted for a partial move, taking only the bare essentials that would be required for the remaining two or three weeks that would be needed to finish the job. He continued to notice Cap taking longer than usual to prepare for his part of the move.

The day was spent sorting gear, one pile for the new camp and the rest to go to Smithers to be stored for eventual shipment back to Calgary. Lou Roman flew in by mid-afternoon with the big chopper. Three trips had men and equipment landed in the new location.

"It'll take two trips to get the rest of that stuff back to town. I'll take one load tonight and pick the rest up tomorrow," Roman shouted as he climbed into the aircraft. Kitch had stayed at the old campsite to help Lou put on the load. By the time they had the helicopter packed to capacity and nearly finished drinking a half a bottle of whiskey that Cap had mistakenly stored in the wrong pile, it was early evening.

"I guess I'd better get out of here while I'm still sober enough to fly, or I won't have enough daylight to find my way home," Lou remarked as he lashed the ropes tight. "Do you want a lift to the new camp?"

"Are you kidding?" Kitch remarked. "Where would you put me? I'd sooner watch you try and lift all that crap off the ground than be part of it. Besides, it's a warm night. I think I'll walk."

After Lou had launched the big bird into the air, Kitch settled back against a tree to finish off the bottle. He had debated whether to go into the village for the evening, but then he remembered that Della had gone berry picking with her mother for a few days. Anyway, it had been a long hard day and Kitch was beat. He sat and contemplated whether to tell Dusty of Cap's condition. He had promised the old man he would keep quiet about it, but he felt it was plainly obvious to everyone that Cap was seriously sick.

When he awoke it was dark. He had left his watch with his personal gear to go to the new camp, so he couldn't be sure of the time. Seeing the moon low on the east horizon, Kitch figured it must be on the evening side of midnight but not by much. His legs and back were stiff from lying on the cold ground, but he felt good enough to make the hike, and he didn't figure on having any trouble finding his way to the new camp, as he knew its location was on the banks of this same creek. All he had to do was follow the path south for an hour and a half and he would be there. The path was not nearly as clearly visible as the one north to the village, but with the moon tracking upward in the cloudless sky he had enough light to follow it. All he had to do was stay beside the water.

The going was easy and he had covered over half the distance when a nearby sound brought him to a sudden stop. He had been miles away in his mind, thinking of Glennda and Julie and a life that now seemed so foreign and long ago, but something had registered on his subconscious, a noise he didn't recognize, out of harmony with the night. Kitch froze and listened, but all he could hear was his own shallow breathing and the muted sounds of the water. Then, there was something, a splashing from down the creek. He moved ahead slowly, placing each foot silently on the ground until he heard the noise again directly below him. He moved to the edge of the trail and peered over the embankment. The drop to the creek was about fifteen feet along a steep bank overgrown with thick clumps of alder. Kitch tried to see through the foliage, but it was too dense. All he could make out were two silhouettes along the bank at the edge of the water on the opposite shore. To his right was a fallen tree extending from the path to the water's edge. Kitch climbed slowly up the tangled mass of roots to get a better view. He was now able to see over the alder patch. Two forms were crouched by the creek splashing quietly in the water.

"It looks like they are either setting traps or night lines," Kitch thought. "It's probably those two that Brian and I ran into the other night. I'll get out of here quickly. I'm not in the mood to take on the two of them tonight." As he crouched and moved downward, his foot caught in a root, pitching him forward down the bank into the alders. He felt a sharp pain along the side of his head as he landed, just before he passed out.

It was the sun's pink rays fanning the horizon that brought Kitch back to consciousness . He was lying in the middle of the alder patch. His clothes were torn, his arms and legs scratched and bleeding, and his head throbbed unmercifully. He eased himself down to the water's edge and submerged his head beneath the chill, swiftly flowing stream. It helped a bit, but the pain would not let up, and he could feel the sticky mass of congealed blood on the side of his head.

"It must be after six," he thought. "There won't be anyone from camp looking for me for at least a couple of hours. It would be interesting to know who I saw down here last night. They sure didn't make any attempt to help me out, but maybe I should be grateful they didn't stick a knife in me."

Kitch stumbled back up to the trail. Checking himself over as best he could, he found nothing missing or broken. With the exception of his head, there were no areas of serious pain. He reached for a cigarette, but his pack was missing. He searched the area in vain, backtracking down the slope to the creek and all around the area from where he had fallen and landed. "Great bunch of fellows," he thought. "They roll me for my cigarettes and leave me there. It's a good thing my watch and wallet are at the new camp. I think I'd like to settle the score with those two before I leave. Right now I need some food and sleep."

Brian was helping Cap prepare breakfast in the cooktent when Kitch arrived.

"Didn't expect you so early," Cap remarked. "There was no sign of you when we all crawled off last night. When did you come in?"

"Just got here," Kitch responded. "Brian, would you have a

245

look at the side of my head. I had a little accident last night and it's pretty sore."

Brian looked over the injured area and gave a low whistle. "What happened? It looks like a mountain fell on you. We'd better get it fixed up. Where did you stash the medical supplies, Cap?"

"I think they are over on the other side of the clearing under the big tarp," the old man replied.

Kitch followed Brian over to the pile of supplies and described the previous night's events.

"Are you sure it was those same two?" Brian asked when he had finished.

"I'm not sure, but it makes sense. Any of the other people from around here would probably have helped me. Those are the only two I've met or heard about that would walk away from that kind of a scene. Have you any other ideas?"

"No, but I'm going in to see Lisa tonight. Maybe, I can get some answers. At least I can find out if they are still around," Brian replied as he started to tape some gauze on Kitch's head.

"Just leave the wound open. I'll let the air heal it, and besides, I don't want a bunch of explaining to do."

The rest of the crew were at breakfast, and Dusty was outlining the day's work when Brian and Kitch returned.

"Cap says you banged your head. Are you okay?" Dusty directed the question at Kitch as they entered.

"Nothing serious. I just got off the path from the last camp and took a tumble down the creek bank on the way here last night," Kitch shrugged. "I'm as good as new after Doctor Tolman fixed me up."

With the exceptions of Reuben and Kitch, the crew was organized to set up camp. Dusty wanted his two prospector line cutters over the ground first. He knew they could cover the area quickly, and he needed to know as soon as possible if there was anything worthwhile on this last group of claims. Yesterday, Lou Roman's employers had insisted that Dusty assume responsibility for all future payments before they would schedule any more chopper flights.

As Suzanne had reported, Wildwood had not paid their last bill.

Kitch had originally planned to go with Brian to the village, at least he'd figured on it until about mid-afternoon when the previous night's events and the day's prospecting began to take its toll. The others had set up their tents and beds, but Kitch just crawled into his bedroll, bush clothes and all and slept until Cap's call the next morning.

He awoke to Brian's urgings. Sunlight was streaming into the tent and already the deerflys were buzzing out their symphony along the ridgepole. Kitch looked over to see Reuben's bed empty.

Brian noticed the glance and remarked. "I waited for Reuben to go to breakfast before I came over. Lisa and I went down to where you had your accident, and we found this under that old tree." Brian reached inside his jacket and pulled out an almost full pack of cigarettes.

"That's the pack I lost. I looked all over for them. I thought those fellows had robbed me before they took off."

"I can see how you missed them," Brian replied. "Lisa caught the glint of the setting sun off the silver wrapper. Most of the pack was buried under leaves. Also, we wandered a ways up and down the creek bank and found some footprints that were definitely not human. They were in poor shape, but Lisa is convinced they were wild men prints. She got pretty excited, and I couldn't convince her otherwise. She is going to try and talk Old Sam into going down and have a look at them today. I don't know what they were, as they were indistinct. They could have been made by bears. I just don't know."

"Well," Kitch sighed. "That's interesting, but from what I can remember, they were definitely not bears."

"And something else," Brian went on. "Those fellows, who we encountered the other night took off two days ago."

THE SEARCH

Sunday was another bright cloudless day. Although he hated to miss the good weather and pile up costs for time off, Dusty could sense the crew getting irritable and on each other's nerves after ten straight working days. Even Brian's steady diet of Curt was beginning to take its toll on his otherwise cheerful disposition. They were close to finishing the job, but a few more days were necessary to tie up the loose ends. It was late afternoon and Dusty had settled down at the table in the cooktent with a hot cup of coffee to finish off his weekly report when Arnold entered. "How was the fishing?"
"Not so good before I left," Arnold answered. "It must have gotten better. Cap is still up there."
He said he'd be back soon to make a meal. I was hoping he'd bake that cherry pie he's been promising."
But mealtime came and Cap had not returned. The crew put together a makeshift dinner from the previous day's leftovers and were in better spirits after the day's rest. Even Curt joined in the conversation around the table. No one had given Cap's absence too much thought until Brian

remarked that the fishing had to be exceptionally good for the old man to miss making the evening meal. "It is odd," Dusty thought, and with the lengthening shadows he began to feel concern.

"Let's keep a plate of food hot. He's still got an hour before dark."

"I don't know, Dusty," Kitch said slowly. "He hasn't been well. He confided in me the other night, but asked me to keep it to myself. He is terminally sick with cancer. He didn't want you to know, as he was afraid you would send him home. He wants to finish the job."

"You should have told me. We could have worked something out."

Dusty walked out of the tent unable to shake the uneasy feeling, especially with this new information. He strolled down the south trail for a ways, lit his pipe and settled down to watch the sunset. A wind had picked up from the west, rustling the branches and making their shadows jump along the trail. Fall was in the air, and Dusty had noticed a tinge of color in the leaves the last few days. As the sun slipped down behind the cloud bank on the horizon the wind became steadier, setting the woods alive with noises. "I must be getting spooked," Dusty thought. His mind had been far off, ignoring the passage of time. He was surprised at the darkness. He stood and turned to go back, just to see Kitch coming down the trail from camp.

"Cap isn't back yet. Have you seen him?"

Dusty shook his head.

"I'm really worried about him. He has to be in trouble, or he would have been back long ago. I don't think we should wait."

"Neither do I. We'd better get some lights and hike down to the big pool."

"I brought them."

Following the trail with the gas lamps was fairly easy and, they reached the pool in less than half an hour. They had hoped to meet Cap on the way, but there was no sign of him.

The pool was actually a small shallow lake that had been backed up by the beavers. The animals had built their dam across a narrow section of the creek at the end of a gently sloping plateau. With plenty of bottom feed, it had been the source of dozens of brook trout and a few two-pound rainbows that Brian and Cap had caught over the past few days. The surrounding bush was thick with willow, alder, and patches of devil's club.

As the trail became fainter their journey was slowed, punctuated every few minutes by calls for their missing friend and curses at the attacking vegetation. Most of the sound was lost in the thrashing of the wind-blown branches.

"Let's take the path to the upper end of the pond where it narrows below the scarp, cross over and come down the other side. He might have fallen down in the bushes and can't get up." They walked around the pond continuing their calling, but there was no answer.

"Look, over there." Kitch pointed to a glint of metal on the shore. Cap's tackle box lay open on a rock overlooking the water. Carefully they searched the surrounding area, but there were no other signs.

"It's funny he'd take off and leave his gear, " Kitch remarked. "Maybe he hooked into a fish and had to work his way along the shore to bring him in and is hurt somewhere."

"It is strange. All we can do in this light is methodically work our way along this shoreline and hope we find him. I'll go down this way and you backtrack. We'll meet back here in half an hour." Forty minutes later they had returned to the tackle box with nothing to show for their efforts.

"There is another overgrown trail back to camp from the top end of the pool," Kitch observed. "He might have gone back that way and is sitting in camp right now while we are

out here stomping around in the dark."
"I guess that is all we can do tonight," Dusty replied. "If he doesn't show up by morning, we'll get everybody out looking. Let's head back."
When they got back to camp they found that Cap still had not returned.
The next morning was wet and cold. The wind had strengthened, blowing rain and a few flakes of snow, which melted as soon as they landed. Dusty had spent a restless night and was wide-awake at the first light of dawn. Quickly he pulled on his clothes and hurried over to the cooktent. There was no activity and the stove was cold. Brian came in and said, "Give me a few minutes, and I'll have some hot coffee ready, just as soon as I get the old Coleman pressured up."
"Cap didn't come in during the night."
"I know," Dusty replied. "I checked his tent when I got up."
"Let's get a big early breakfast going and pack lunches for everybody with lots of hot coffee in the thermoses. Can you look after it? You're going to have to double as cook until Cap returns. We're going out to look for him as soon as we can. I'll go around and get everybody up. I hope there is nothing to worry about, but I just don't know."
"Dusty, I'd like to go with you. That old man means a lot to me."
"I'm sorry. I know how you feel, but I need you in camp in case he comes in. I can depend on you to take care of things here. We'll have radio contact and keep you posted as to what's going on."
"You're right, someone has to stay here, and with this bad ankle of mine, I would just slow you down out there."
By six-thirty the leaden sky was visible in the faint light and stretched to all limits of the horizon. They had decided to search their way back to the pond and divide into two groups, one for each trail. Dusty and Curt took the lower main trail that ran along the creek, while Kitch, Reuben,

and Arnold searched the fainter back trail. They agreed to meet at the upper end of the pond. The rain had slackened, but enough had fallen to dash Dusty's hopes of picking up any footprints near the tackle box.

As Dusty and Curt searched methodically along the creek trail the rain began to pick up again. Curt had been silent for most of the way.

"Let's stop here for a minute and get out of the wet," Dusty said as they walked under a thick canopy of firs that was keeping most of the water from reaching the ground.

"Did they ever shoot that old injured grizzly bear?"

"No, I don't think so," Dusty was surprised and irritated by the question.

"Have you ever seen one?"

"Not up close," Dusty replied. "I've seen a few from a safe distance."

"From my readings, I understand they will run if confronted by man unless they are cornered."

The statement came out almost as a question and Dusty could see that Curt was desperately trying to hide his concern.

"Maybe that is true for browns and blacks, but I wouldn't count on it for grizzlies. And, any kind of injured bear is a very real danger."

"I've read that if you climb a tree you are safe from grizzlies."

"You know, it would be interesting to know how many people have believed in that old fable through the course of history and ended up dead or injured. Grizzlies can climb, although it takes a lot of effort to get their bulk up a tree. I guess it depends on how bad the bear wants you."

"The other recommendation was to wear a bunch of bells on your clothing," Curt went on," so that they make noise as you hike. That is supposed to scare the grizzlies off when they hear you coming."

By now Dusty was getting a certain satisfaction in making

no attempt to allay his companion's concern, He thought for a minute, smiled, then replied, "I guess that explains how you can tell from the droppings on the trail whether it was a black or a grizzly. Droppings from a black or brown have a lot of berries and vegetable matter, while that from a grizzly is much the same, except occasionally it has these small bells mixed in."

He could see immediately the intended humor was lost on this serious young man.

They moved out of the shelter and back into the rain, which had eased off into a steady drizzle and continued their search to the lower end of the pool. A heavy mist blanketed the surface of the water limiting visibility to a few feet.

"I'm going to have a look around where we found the tackle box," Dusty decided. "You stay on this side and work your way along the bank. We'll meet with the others at the upper end."

As Dusty had expected, any signs that Cap might have left had been long washed away. Even their footsteps from the night before were no longer visible. Dusty spent a few minutes scuffing around in the bush, but there was nothing that he could identify as unusual or out of place. Picking up the tackle box, he headed for the upper end of the pond.

The wind had finally died down, but the constant irritating drizzle continued. Curt had beaten him to the meeting spot and sat huddled in his poncho beneath an overhanging rock, looking completely miserable. Dusty was just about to settle in beside him when Kitch came charging through the bushes.

"We found where he's been," he gasped. "It's back up the trail. Looks like there has been a struggle of some kind."

The spot was only a hundred yards back from the scarp. Reuben and Arnold were searching the bush when the three arrived.

"Right here." Reuben pointed to a faint track beside the trail. "I don't know what it is, but it's big. Looks like a claw mark."

Kitch picked up a broken fishing rod.

"We found this right beside it on the trail. We must have walked right over it when we came back to camp last night."

"Hey! You guys! Come over here." Arnold's voice came from some low bushes off the trail. "There's some cloth caught on the brambles over here. It's from Cap's shirt, the one he had on yesterday."

There was no path to the bramble patch, but forcing their way through the undergrowth, they could see areas where the bushes had been bent and broken off. A half a dozen shreds of the blue cloth clung to the thorny stalks, and in the soft ground beneath was another smudged depression. "It's not much of a track," Kitch observed, "but it's too big for Cap's shoes."

A few feet beyond was a second print, more clear than the first, and beyond that, Reuben found Cap's glasses lying unbroken in the mud.

No one spoke. The truth of the scene was evident. Kitch bent over the second track and cursed.

"It's that damn bear, the same one that chased me out of the river. Look at the depression that trails off from this track. He's still dragging that back leg. I don't want to think about what has happened. We've got to keep moving and follow these tracks if there's any chance of helping him. Have you got a gun, Dusty?"

"The Magnum is in my pack. I'm going to radio Brian and have him get Lou out here as soon as the weather lifts. Let's see if we can follow this trail. My guess is the bear has his den somewhere up in the high country, at least that seems to be the general direction these tracks are heading."

HIGH COUNTRY CAVE

The trail along the banks of the pond was tough to follow and ended where it joined the creek at its upper end. By the time Dusty had completed his call to camp and given instructions to Brian, Reuben had found more tracks upstream on the opposite shore. As they followed the erratic course westward, they found blood-spattered leaves and bits of clothing, which attested to their companion's plight. There was little discussion as each of the searchers had a good idea of what had happened. It was early afternoon by the time the group had reached the base of the talus slope, which marked the western limit of the plateau. With no soft ground, the trail was quickly lost on the rock-strewn grade that angled up to the steep ridge, which marked the edge of the main western mountain range. The morning drizzle had not let up and continued on into the afternoon. Everyone was soaked through, and their efforts to keep the rain out were futile. They ate their soggy sandwiches in silence as Dusty probed the scarp with his field glasses for any signs of movement or caves.

255

The talus slope was made up mostly of large slabs of shale. The source of this rock stretched upward for a couple of hundred feet beyond the top of the slope. This softer zone was recessed under the overlying bands of hard massive limestone.

"Chances are whatever grabbed Cap headed for that limestone scarp. If we hope to find any kind of a den or cave," Dusty said, "it has to be up there."

Focusing his glasses along the rock wall, he could see where erosion had etched a pattern of pits and holes on the face. Half a dozen of these appeared to have entrances large enough for a cave. He pointed them out to the rest of the crew.

"We'll have to climb up to the limestone wall and then split up and work our way along the scarp, checking out these openings for some kind of signs of life or recent use. It's going to be tough going up on these wet rocks, so be very careful, and it could possibly be dangerous when we get up there. I don't want anyone going in a cave, especially alone. Just check around the entrances for recent signs of activity, and if you find one that looks like it's being used, get the rest of us over there as soon as possible."

As Dusty had cautioned, the ascent was rough and slippery. The weary group slowly threaded its way up the incline. The talus was loose and foot pressure was often enough to send the flat fragments skittering down the slope. It was only through methodical placing each foot in front of the other that they were able to make any headway. They fanned out to try and pick up some sort of trail, without success. Finally, they agreed to follow Dusty in single file, placing their feet carefully in the traces of his steps.

Halfway up to the rock wall, Arnold suddenly pitched forward with a cry of pain. He had carelessly stepped in a narrow crevice and the fall had sprained his ankle. The pain was intense, and almost immediately his foot began to swell, as he furiously tugged at the laces to get his boot off to relieve the pressure

"Don't take it off," Kitch yelled, "or you'll never get it back on."

Dusty looked closely at the injured foot, and asked. "Can you walk on it?"

Reuben helped the boy to his feet, and he gingerly tried a few steps, wincing each time the injured foot touched the ground.

"I don't know. It sure hurts, but I'll keep going even if I have to crawl."

"You'll have to try and get up to higher ground at the base of the scarp, where we can find some cover for you until the helicopter comes in, unless you want to settle in here for a while."

"No. I can make it if you would stop every once in a while to let me catch up." The boy's mind had quickly pictured hours alone on the wet rocky slope in an area populated with bears and whatever else that lived there.

"Come on. I'll help you," Kitch said, "if someone will take his pack." He looked straight at Curt as he said the words, but Curt turned and resumed his climb.

"Grab that stick for a cane and put your other arm around my shoulder."

Reuben picked up the pack and tied it to his own.

They had gone only a few feet when Dusty could see that the boy's movement was limited, and their progress was going to be slowed considerably. He was concerned about reaching the scarp while they still had sufficient daylight to explore for any dens.

"I think Curt and I had better go ahead," Dusty decided. "You three head straight up the slope to the center of the basin. We'll go out to either side and work our ways back to meet you there. It looks like we are going to have to find a spot to spend the night out here. I don't think we can cover that entire area before dark."

Dusty and Curt took off in opposite directions to search

along the north and south ends of the limestone bluff. They moved quickly, and within an hour had reached their destinations.

It took most of the afternoon for the remaining three to climb to the small bench at the top of the talus. By this time, Kitch and Reuben were practically carrying Arnold over the rock pile and were exhausted. At this elevation above eight thousand feet, only a few scrubby birches struggled for existence on the barren slope, and the air was thin enough to make breathing difficult. Although sparse, the remnants of the thicker vegetation below had successfully prevented the discovery of a large cave entrance until the three were only a few feet below it. The opening was also hidden by the fact it faced along the ridge. A level area extended out for about ten feet in front, and this was dotted with small piles of broken and bleached animal bones. A strong musky odor drifted from the entrance.

"Do you think... the bear's... in there?" Arnold's voice betrayed his fear.

"I don't know," Kitch replied as he helped him into a sitting position on the ground. "Something has definitely been around here recently and may still be in there. We better wait until Dusty gets here before we do any exploring. Let's move away from the mouth in case there's something in there that wants to come out. It is the same odor I smelled when that bear attacked us on the way back from the fire. I do not want to meet that creature again. "

For the next hour Kitch listened near the entrance for any noises from within, while Reuben searched the area for fresh sign. All three jumped when the snap of a branch announced Curt's approach. A few minutes later Dusty appeared.

"This is the most promising one I've seen," he announced. "All the rest of the caves along this scarp are too small or obviously unused. Did you have a look inside?"

"No. You and Curt have the only flashlights."

"I had better have a look before it gets too dark. I don't know what we are going to find, if anything, but it could be dangerous. I understand anyone not wanting to go in, in fact, I'd rather all of you stay out here, and there is no criticism against you if you want to return to camp. None of you were hired to put your lives at risk here. Arnold, I definitely want you to stay out here."

"I'm not going in there either," Curt replied. "There's nothing in my contract about going into a bear's den."

"I figured that," Kitch replied disgustedly.

"Look. There's a good chance there's a man-killing grizzly in there. If so, and he dragged Cap in, there's very little chance the old man is still alive, and I'm not prepared to risk my life to find out."

"But, what if he is alive?" Kitch returned. "Don't you give a damn?"

"Not enough to take a chance on getting myself killed. It's stupid. You have no idea what to expect."

Dusty led the small procession of himself, Kitch and Reuben into the cave entrance. With the lights searching every crack and crevice along the tunnel they moved slowly ahead through the gloom. Kitch carried the Magnum, following the beams carefully, looking for any sign of movement. A few yards beyond the entrance, the tunnel opened to a large passageway, where strong animal smells immediately bombarded their nostrils. As they came slowly to a bend, Reuben moved up behind Kitch with the other light. They could see the tunnel ahead growing wider and opening into a larger chamber.

Reuben stopped and grabbed Kitch's arm. "Look! There!" He was pointing at the ground in front of Kitch. "That is another one of those big man tracks we saw in the bush." The print was well formed in the soft, damp limestone sand, much clearer than any they had seen before. Rectangular in shape, it was almost a foot and a half long.

The toes were well defined but without claw impressions. "Christ!" Kitch exclaimed. "That ain't no damn bear track." Dusty examined the print closely and then walked ahead a few paces looking for more, but all he could find were indistinct depressions, which were totally without form. "I sure wish I knew what is going on in here. It's tough to picture the kind of creature that could make that track."

"Dusty, I can't go any farther in here." Reuben's voice was low and apologetic. "You know I'm not afraid of the bear, but this is something I don't know about. It is a sign telling us not to go on. I don't want to see or know about the thing that made this track."

"I understand," Dusty replied. "You go back and tell the others what we've found so far and wait for me outside. I have to go ahead and find out if Cap is in here. I've got a strong feeling that he is and is either dead or badly hurt. If I'm not back out in an hour, I want you to radio Brian and have him get some help in here as fast as possible."

"What about me?" Kitch asked. "You're not planning on going in there alone, are you?"

"Look, I'm not holding you to stay with me. Maybe Curt is right. You fellows didn't agree to anything like this when you took the job, and I don't want to be responsible for something happening to anyone else."

"I'm staying. That's also my choice, and my curiosity is too strong to walk away without seeing it through."

They waited until Reuben had reached the cave entrance before continuing their journey. The chamber narrowed to a passageway barely wide enough for the two of them, with turns every few steps. They made their way slowly around the corners, unable to anticipate the sight that might greet their eyes at any moment. They could feel the tunnel taking them downward as it began to widen out again. Water was now dripping from the ceiling and along the walls, forming a small stream, which meandered along the tunnel floor. The air was becoming stale and difficult to breathe, and the musky smell grew stronger with each step as they moved along in silence. Suddenly, after coming around a particularly sharp bend they found themselves at the entrance to a large room. A high-arched ceiling with its huge stalactites gave the chamber a cathedral-like atmosphere. A variety of colored lime secretions formed murals along the walls and the floor was covered with a white carpet of limestone sand.

FINDING CAP

"Look Dusty! Over there!"
"My God!"
They rushed over to the almost unrecognizable remains of
their friend.
"It's Cap. That's his jacket, and the ring, and.... " Kitch had
to turn away. He stumbled over to lean against the wall as
the bile in his stomach forced its way to the surface. He
tried unsuccessfully to control the flood of tears.
"Don't make a sound and keep perfectly still." Dusty was
beside him with a hand on his shoulder.
"Turn slowly and look beyond Cap, over against the wall.
It's the bear. Looks like he's sleeping."
Kitch struggled to get control. He turned to see the large
gray bundle stretched out on the cave floor.
"Won't the light wake him up?"
"I don't know. It hasn't yet. I want to try and get close
enough to finish him with one shot. I'll move over there as
quiet as I can and maybe, if you keep the light away from

his eyes I can get a good shot before he wakes up. But, if there's any sign of movement, I'll let him have it from wherever I am and hope for the best."

"Wait! What's going to happen inside this cave if you shoot that gun? The whole damn thing is liable to come down on top of us."

"I know. It's a chance I've got to take. Maybe you should get out in case something does happen."

"Not now. I've stayed with it so far. There's no way in hell I'm leaving."

"Okay, but try and stay out from under one of those big icicles up there."

Slowly Dusty inched his way toward the bear, carefully placing each foot in front of the other until he was within twenty feet of the animal. He stood there playing the other light over the bear's huge frame.

"Christ, he's taking a long time," Kitch thought. "Why doesn't he shoot? Now he's lowered the gun. What the hell is he doing?"

Finally Kitch could contain himself no longer.

"Why don't you shoot him?" The loud whisper echoed off the walls.

Dusty turned and motioned him to come over. Up close the bear looked even larger than he had anticipated.

"I think he's dead," Dusty said as he pointed at the creature. "Watch him close. There's no breathing movement, nothing, not even any twitches."

Kitch peered intently at the bear, not blinking for fear he would miss a movement.

"You're right. His chest should be going in and out if he's alive, but there's no movement at all. But, I'm not sure enough about it to walk over and kick him in the nose to find out."

"Well, maybe we can do the next best thing. Take that big rock over there and heave it at his head. I'll keep the gun on him and if there's any sign of life I'll shoot."

Kitch's careful aim caught the animal behind the ear. There was no reaction as the rock bounced against the cave wall. Two more throws brought the same result. Only then did they venture close enough to touch the dead body.

"He's stiff," Dusty observed. "He's probably been dead for quite a while. This whole thing is getting stranger all the time. What could have killed him?"

"Look here, under his head, at all the blood. It's from a big tear along the side of his neck. It feels like his neck is broken. That big rock icicle sticking up from the floor could have done it."

The neck was broken. In spite of the body stiffening they were able to flop the head back and forth. The most startling discovery was the blood-encrusted footprint beside the body. It was the same print they had seen in the tunnel, and there were more this time. They traced the tracks with their flashlights across the floor to another passage on the backside of the room.

"It looks like that tunnel goes deeper into the mountain." They followed the tracks to the opening. This passage was larger than the one they had used and apparently much straighter, for they could see along a stretch of at least a hundred feet in the flashlight beam. Standing at the opening, Dusty lit a match, which was immediately blown out.

"There's quite a breeze coming down this tunnel. It must open to the outside somewhere up ahead."

"Even the smell is gone," Kitch observed. "I hope you're not planning on going down there to have a look."

"I'd like to, but I think we had better get outside. The hour is just about up, and they'll be wondering what happened to us."

"What about Cap?"

"We can't do anything for him now. I'm going to let the Mounties sort it out from here."

It was dark when they returned to the ledge. The rain had

stopped while they were in the cave, and the sky was beginning to clear. A new moon lit up the chilled night air. Reuben had wrapped his big warm parka around Arnold, and both were huddled close to a sputtering fire. Curt had packed his lightweight sleeping bag and was curled up in it on the other side. He awoke immediately as Dusty and Kitch emerged from the cave.

Dusty described briefly and simply most of what they had found. Arnold was the first to speak.

"Reuben and I talked about it while you were gone. It's kind of what we expected. Do you think Cap really suffered a lot before he died?"

"I think he probably did. Let's hope none of us ever find out. I'd better call Brian and let him know what happened."

"Reuben called him after he came out. He said he will be waiting to hear from you."

They sat around the fire as Dusty radioed camp. They heard Brian's voice break as he relayed the message that Lou Roman would be coming in at dawn with the Jet Ranger to pick them up. Brian was instructed to pass the rest of the information on to the RCMP.

"Have you fellows had anything to eat?" Dusty asked as he packed the radio away.

"No, we decided to wait for you. Besides, there isn't much left. Only, he made sure he was well supplied," Arnold said, nodding toward Curt. "He had his stew and peaches before he went to bed."

Supper for the remaining four consisted of the rest of the soggy sandwiches and two packages of dry soup, well watered and heated in the coffee pot.

The night on the mountain was cold. In spite of the discomfort, the arrival of the helicopter a few minutes after the sun broke the horizon found everyone except Dusty asleep. Lou Roman had to do considerable maneuvering to land the big chopper on the ledge, a feat, which the presence of a wind would have made impossible. An

RCMP corporal stepped from the aircraft.

"I'm Jerry Treboski," he announced as they exchanged greetings. "Lou told me a little bit about what happened up here, but I'd like to hear the whole story and have a look in the cave. We are having another helicopter come in to take the body out. He has to fly up from Prince George but should be here in a couple of hours."

Dusty described the events of the past two days as the Corporal hurriedly made notes. As Dusty and Kitch proceeded to show him the cave, Arnold came over to accompany them.

"I would like to see the bear," he announced.

Dusty thought of trying to dissuade him but said nothing. As they entered the cave chamber the Corporal was visibly shaken at the scene. "I guess I didn't expect it to be this messy. It kind of took me for a minute." He proceeded to methodically examine the room and the bodies while questioning Dusty on a number of points. As they talked, Kitch conducted his own explorations in the area of the second tunnel.

"Where's Arnold?"

Both men looked up as Kitch called from the far side of the cave. Quickly they searched the room with their lights.

"Maybe he went back out," Dusty replied. "Would you go out and make sure?"

Ten minutes later Kitch returned to the chamber.

"He's out there, but he's acting real queer, just sitting on a rock huddled up in Reuben's coat, swaying back and forth. He won't say a word. I tried to talk to him and ask him what was wrong, but he just looked at me and wouldn't say anything."

"I shouldn't have let him come in," Dusty replied. "The sight of Cap's body must have been too much. Maybe I can talk to him."

The Corporal had resumed his examination but now stood, closed his notebook and looked at the bear.

"I just don't understand how the bear died."
Kitch opened his mouth to answer, but a look at Dusty
stopped him before he could utter a word.
"It is almost like something else was in here," continued the
Corporal, "but there is no sign of anything. The only
explanation that I can see is that the animal somehow fell
against that rock icicle, cut an artery and dragged himself
over here and bled to death. Anyway, I guess I have all the
information I am going to get here. I had better head for
town and file a report. We will make the arrangements for
notifying his family. It would help if someone in your crew
would stay here and direct the men from the other chopper
when it arrives."
"I'll stay and meet them," Dusty replied.
Arnold was still huddled on the ledge as Kitch had
described. Dusty went over to the boy, squatted down and
began talking softly to him. There was no reaction. Lou
came over to them.
"He hasn't said a word since he came out of the cave. I tried
to get him to take some sandwiches and coffee, but he
wouldn't eat. He just sits there."
"I'd like you to take him back to camp, and as many of the
others you can find room for. Tell Brian that I'll try and
hitch a ride back when they take the body out."
With the Corporal, Lou, Curt and Arnold in the aircraft
there was room for only one more. Kitch, however,
volunteered to remain, and Reuben took the extra seat.
After the takeoff the two men settled down to the rest of the
food Brian had sent in.
"How about explaining a few things to me."
"I figured that's why you decided to stay," Dusty replied.
"It's a bit strange, don't you think? We went in that cave
yesterday and saw those footprints all over the place. This
morning we go in and there isn't one. I looked all over the
damn cave and all I could see was yours, mine and the
bear's. And your story to Treboski, it was exact in every

detail except there was no mention of any footprints. and no, we had no idea what happened to the bear. I'd just like to know why."

"I got thinking last night about this whole thing. Until yesterday when we saw that first track in the cave, I had just about discounted all these stories about Sasquatch, or Wild Men, or whatever you want to call them. I had come up with all kinds of logical explanations for the stories, but I cannot explain away those tracks. So, if we consider the possibility that this creature does exist, what do we know about him? I admit we don't know much, but the first impression that comes to me is that it has not tried to harm any of us. And, if we really stretch our imagination, we could say it was responsible for looking after Arnold when he fell off Jumping Rock and that it could have been trying to save Cap but got to the cave too late."

"You're beginning to sound like Gabriel. He would totally believe that. But, okay, maybe some of it is possible, but look at it another way. Maybe, in the cave, it was the creature that killed Cap and the bear came in late and then the two fought."

"I don't think so. It was bear tracks that we followed up here from the trail by the pond. We didn't see a creature track until we got to the cave."

"That makes sense, but why did you destroy the tracks in the cave. You did do it, didn't you?"

"Yes. I went in early this morning while you were all asleep and scratched up the ground until they were all obliterated. I knew that if we showed the tracks to the police and told them our ideas on the subject, it would go in their report and somehow the news media would get a hold of it. You know what would happen then. We'd have every nut, publicity-seeker, and trigger-happy hunter in the country up here chasing after it. If it is at all friendly, it doesn't deserve that kind of a fate."

"What about the rest? Aren't you worried about them

talking? All the cops need is an idea that you weren't leveling with them and they'll be all over you."

"I thought about that. Hopefully, it won't be a problem. You and I and Reuben are the only ones to see the tracks in the cave, and you saw how Reuben reacted. He would just as soon forget the whole thing. Curt thinks it is all some kind of hoax, and who do you think is going to take Arnold seriously without collaboration from the others. Anyway, I'm going to tell them what I've told you when we get back."

"You know, Dusty, I'd like to see one of those creatures. I'm beginning to understand Gabriel more and appreciate his obsession."

"I guess I would too, at least it would help sort all this out. I must be getting old. It's getting harder to change my concepts of the world without concrete proof."

It was noon before the other helicopter arrived. Dusty and Kitch helped the men hurry through the unpleasant task of collecting and packaging Caps remains. There was ample room in the aircraft to take everyone off the ledge.

GOING HOME

Kitch and Brian stayed the night in the village. When Kitch returned to camp the next morning, the first thing he noticed was the missing tent. As he entered his own tent Reuben was shaking his sleeping bag, getting it ready to hang on the line to air out.

"Where's Arnold? I see the tent's down."

"Gone home."

"How come? What happened?"

"Couldn't take no more, just wanted to go home."

"I saw you come in," Dusty announced as he entered the tent. "Didn't Brian come back with you?"

"No, he and Lisa are trying to sort things out. He wants her to go back with him and get married. He asked her last night. I don't know. She wasn't surprised. I guess she kind of expected it. Della and I tried to talk to them, but they were in their own little world. I think you need to talk to him. He definitely hasn't thought this through."

"I'm not surprised either. He is too intense about

everything. I'll sort it out when he gets back."

"What happened to Arnold?"

"By the time I got here yesterday he was all packed and ready to go out. He said he wanted to go home and asked if I'd radio for Lou to come back and get him. He was all ready to pay for the chopper. He just didn't want to travel in the same aircraft as the body."

"He didn't talk to nobody coming to camp," added Reuben. "When we got here he went into the tent, lay on the bunk and wouldn't talk until I brought him in some soup and sat down with him and put my arm around him. He cried for a long time and then started packing his gear."

"While we were waiting for the chopper," Dusty continued, "he told me he was never coming into the bush again. He is quitting geology to play his music, which is what he has always wanted to do. He was through listening to his father's and his uncle's advice. He left all his field clothes and asked me to give them to whoever in the village could use them, and then, the funny thing, just as he was getting into the helicopter he handed me those expensive boots of his, and said, "Dusty, would you give these to the most disgusting looking bum you can find and take a picture of him with the boots on and send it to me. It's a present for Uncle Mervin to show him how much I appreciate everything he has done for me.""

Brian made it back just after lunch. He grabbed a sandwich and sat down with Dusty.

"Do you want to talk?"

"Yeah. I guess Kitch told you about our all-nighter. I asked Lisa to come back home with me and get married. Essentially, she refused. She told me she wanted to wait. She wants me to go back, take this new job and see if I still feel the same in a year. When I asked her if this was just her way of breaking up, she said she wanted to be with me, but she also wanted us to have time to be sure. She thinks we haven't known each other long enough and need to be apart for a while."

"Well, I'm glad she has more sense than you do. You do need to wait. You've just managed to get out of this other potential marriage mess. You need time to find out what you want. You may think it doesn't matter to you now, but if you get into the corporate world, having a native girl for a wife will not help your chances for advancement."

"You're right, it doesn't matter, and I don't think it will, but I see your point. Actually, I want to walk your road and go freelance. I'll stick with the oil company for a couple of years to take their training courses, build up a list of contacts, then go on my own."

"I hear you and wish you the best of luck, but listen to Lisa and wait the year."

That night the whole thing finally hit Dusty. For the past forty-eight hours he had been going on nerve. Now it was coming home and taking its toll. All his life he had been an optimistic person, believing that even the worst situations and problems would work out somehow for the best in the long run. Most of the times this had been true. He could examine his misfortunes of the past and see where some good had subsequently come of them. Since he was a kid, all those years after burying his dad and being mostly on his own, through school and then university, had always been a struggle. A mother, who had essentially abandoned him, had left him to his own resources, but he had believed that it was worthwhile. He had to, or he never would have stayed with it. After graduation, working on a company team until he couldn't stand it any longer and then on his own, this confidence had never left him. But now, after today he felt that none of it would ever work out right again.

The light was still on in the cooktent when he looked out. "Maybe a coffee and someone to talk with would help," he thought. "I've got to get out of my head."

Reuben was still awake. He looked up at Dusty with red-rimmed eyes. "At least this old man can let it out," Dusty thought.

They sat without talking. Only the sounds of the creek and Brian's snoring in the far tent broke the silence. Dusty could sense the old man seeing behind his own mask of calm. Reuben reached down for the bottle and filled Dusty's coffee cup with whiskey.

"I never run out on a job in my life, but I got to leave here. I don't ever want to see another bush camp again. The whole damn thing doesn't make any sense. We come out here, spend the summer scratching around in the dirt so that Cap can end his life, and some hustler in the big city can get richer."

"Reuben, Cap was dying. He told Kitch a while ago that he had terminal cancer and only had a few months to live. Even so, he should have been able to go home and die in peace."

"That's what it is," Dusty thought, "the total lack of meaning in this whole thing." His work, which had been his life was meaningless. Years ago he had decided how he wanted his life to be and had worked steadily toward the goal. Now he was living his dream and doing the kind of work he liked. Often he had boasted to friends that, sure he wasn't making the big bucks, but how many nine to fivers really enjoyed what they spent most of their working life doing. But, he'd never really thought about it past that level. Even after Elena had been killed, he had avoided any tendency to consider the end point of his efforts or evaluate them on anything but an immediate and personal level. He had lived for the moment, trusting that the path he was on was right for him and that each succeeding moment would take its rightful place in the sequence. Tonight, he felt it was all a sham. Maybe time would distance him from this tragic loss, and his confidence would return, but he had this nagging fear that somehow everything had changed. Dusty hoped he could return to his old way of thinking. It was certainly less painful than this.

"When can I leave?"

Reuben's words broke into his thoughts.

"Tomorrow," Dusty replied. "I'm going to Vancouver to see Cap's wife. I don't know what I'm going to say or do, but I have to do it now."

"Are you going to finish this job?"

"I don't know. I would like to wrap it up quick, but I don't see how I can. Everything that has happened is telling me to shut the whole thing down and pull out, but I guess it's like you said about quitting a job. I need some time to think it through."

By morning he had decided. First light was showing through by the time his tormented mind had given up to sleep. He awoke with the clarity that had escaped him the night before. He would go to Vancouver. He would take Curt out, although he knew he risked a lawsuit for terminating his contract. Reuben could go home and Kitch and Brian could stay and look after camp.

Lou landed before noon with the mail and a few supplies. The chopper was loaded and ready to go within the hour. Twenty minutes out, Kitch's voice crackled over the helicopter radio.

"Dusty, I got another letter from Suzanne. She says Campbell has left the country. He got wind of being investigated and was gone the day before the cops showed up at his office. He managed to clean out all the money and burn the Company records before he left.

During the short time Dusty was in Vancouver, winter laid its claim on the northern land. Heavy frosts and two snowfalls had marked the passage of the days. In what seemed an instant, summer greens had given way to the yellows and browns of autumn. The frosts had shocked the leaves from the trees, and the earth and sky gave witness to creatures preparing to sleep or fly south. Dusty observed the changes as they landed. Each year it amazed him how quickly the land could shed its summer garments.

Brian had heard the chop of the blades break the morning stillness and was waiting by the pad.

"We ran out of fuel oil."

"I brought some with me," Dusty replied. "What have you been using for heat?"

"Martin came down to camp and made a wood stove from an old drum."

Further questions gave Dusty the information that Kitch and Brian had spent most of the time in the village with the girls.

"Are you ready to go home?" Dusty asked.

"I don't want to, but I'm supposed to report down in Houston nest week. Lisa and I said our goodbyes," Brian replied.

Dusty had Lou Roman wait until Brian packed his few possessions. When he reappeared from his tent, Dusty had his cheque ready. They walked to the waiting aircraft and shook hands.

"Good luck working with the suits."

"Yeah, It'll be a change" Brian replied. "If you're still working these jobs in a couple of years, give me a call no matter where it is. I'd enjoy working for you again. And maybe I can talk my future wife into doing the cooking."

"I'll call you," Dusty promised.

Kitch strolled into camp the next morning as Dusty was fixing breakfast.

"We are going to pack it up and go home," Dusty announced as he sat down to eat.

"I thought we would. I heard all the news about Campbell over the radio. Coupled with what Suzanne wrote me, he must have really shaken the local money-grabbers to make the newscast."

"He did a pretty good job of it, took a few of the brokers to the cleaners as well as his shareholders."

275

"What happened anyway? The news on the radio was pretty sketchy."

"They are still piecing it together, but evidently he's been selling Wildwood stock all summer. Then he sold a bunch of stock he didn't own. They call it selling short."

"I've heard of it."

"Then he cashed in all the funds in the Company and took the whole bundle of money to Brazil. He's got bills all over. Wildwood owes so much money that it's going into receivership."

"So, you don't get your final payment."

"That's a reasonable assessment of the situation."

"How much are you on the hook for."

"About thirty thousand," Dusty replied, "plus some chopper bills I signed for."

"That's rough. Have you still got those claims we staked in your name?"

"Yes. I went to see the lawyers looking after the Company mess. The lady that is trying to sort it out is a good mining lawyer. I've known her for a couple of years and found her to be honest, so I took a chance and explained the whole deal about the claims and the money they owe me. She says that since Wildwood broke their contract with me by not paying, the Company has no claim on any ground I staked. She figured I should hold them for a few months in case the other Directors came up with my money somehow, but after that I'd be free to dispose of them any way I like."

"That sounds okay," Kitch replied. "At least something worked out right. Maybe you'll end up ahead after all."

"If it works out that way, we will all benefit. I'm going to keep a half interest in the claims and divide the other half among the crew."

"You can leave me out," Kitch replied. "Sign my share over to the others, and the rest of my pay, you can keep it. I've got enough money to keep me going for a year."

"That's crazy, you will need it when you get back to the

city."

"I'm not going back," Kitch replied quietly. "I'm staying here."

Dusty paused. "I don't understand."

"It's kinda hard to explain. Cap's death really got to me, not so much when it happened, like the others, but since. You and Cap and Brian were my friends. Only since Cap's death have I realized it, that I actually felt inside a strong bond with other human beings. That kind of stuff has never been with me before. All my life my so-called friendships have been based on what I could get out of them. You guys could see this and it didn't matter. You didn't try to judge me, you were just my friends."

"I understand that. What we have been through the last few days makes you examine yourself, your life, and your values. I think, with the exception of Curt, we were all deeply affected by Cap's death. What I don't understand is why you want to stay here."

"What is there for me to go back to? My wife has a new husband; my little girl has a new dad. All that's left is a bunch of losers I knew from prison or the parties. Does it make any sense to go back to the city and go on unemployment, or welfare, or hustle a straight job that will drive me back to the old life? I can't go back to that scene. The friends I have, with the exception of you and Brian, live here. I spent most of the time you were away at the village with Della. Gabriel just came back from the hospital and we spent a lot of hours talking. When I think about him risking his life to save me, it blows my mind. I don't know if I could do that for someone. Hopefully I will never have to find out. Gabriel wants to hunt the Wild Man. He doesn't want to harm him, he just wants to see him, and to finally know once and for all that this creature really exists. I know his obsession doesn't make sense, at least to most people, but that doesn't matter, it's important to him. I told him about the cave and what we found, and he was ready to go, crutches and all. We're going in the spring, Gabriel and I, to look for the creature. I feel I owe him this. Our talks and the things he taught me have helped me get my head clear. It's time to repay some debts."

ABOUT THE AUTHOR

My name is Guy Allen. I have operated most of my life as a freelance explorationist in the mineral and oil and gas industries of North America, as well as bouts of teaching at the high school and junior college levels. I used to call myself a Consultant until I realized that this term, in many cases was synonymous with Unemployed.

My formal education consists of an Honours BSc from the University of Western Ontario, as well as graduate geology and education courses from the University of Calgary. I have been qualified as a Professional Engineer in British Columbia, and as a Professional Geologist for Alberta. I hold high school teaching certificates for British Columbia, Alberta and Washington state.
I have both Canadian and U.S. citizenship and with my wife, Geri, I spend time equally in these two countries.

My mineral exploration activities have taken me to British Columbia, Alberta, Saskatchewan, the

Yukon and Northwest Territories, the Western U.S. and the counties of Devon and Cornwall in England. In the oil and gas industry, I have worked as a prospect and wellsite geologist in Alberta and Sakatchewan. I have also been employed as a company and stock analyst, a high school science teacher, and a junior college mathematics instructor. Finding work has never been a problem, but finding a mine, not so successful, although like many prospectors I have probably walked over a few that have made money for others.

The story line for Bush Camp was originally developed while working in the Dease Lake area of Northern B.C. in the 1970s. This book is the result of four rewrites over the intervening years.

I hope you enjoy my fiction novels. I welcome your comments and feedback at guyallen3303@gmail.com

My other novels in ebook and paperback:

TALISMAN: A historical novel set in the California gold rush of the 1800s

AMYOT: Mystery and murder in a wildcat oil-drilling project in Northern Saskatchewan.

SUN CITY: Arizona is the scene of a mining company cover-up for a drug-running cartel.

Visit my website: www.talismanpublications.com to review initial chapters of these books.

www.ingramcontent.com/pod-product-compliance
Lightning Source LLC
Chambersburg PA
CBHW071309170626
46809CB00001B/385